DISCARD
FCPL discards materials that are outdated
and in poor condition. In order to make
room for current, in-demand materials,
underused materials are offered for
public sale

People of the Forest

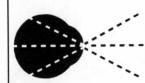

This Large Print Book carries the
Seal of Approval of N.A.V.H.

WILDERNESS

PEOPLE OF THE FOREST

DAVID THOMPSON

THORNDIKE PRESS

An imprint of Thomson Gale, a part of The Thomson Corporation

THOMSON
™
GALE

Detroit • New York • San Francisco • New Haven, Conn. • Waterville, Maine • London

THOMSON

_____ ™

GALE

Copyright © 2006 by David L. Robbins.

Thomson Gale is part of The Thomson Corporation.

Thomson and Star Logo and Thorndike are trademarks and Gale is a registered trademark used herein under license.

ALL RIGHTS RESERVED

Thorndike Press® Large Print Western.

The text of this Large Print edition is unabridged.

Other aspects of the book may vary from the original edition.

Set in 16 pt. Plantin.

LIBRARY OF CONGRESS CATALOGING-IN-PUBLICATION DATA

Thompson, David, 1950–
    People of the forest / by David Thompson.
        p. cm. — (Wilderness) (Thorndike Press large print western)
    ISBN-13: 978-0-7862-9601-9 (alk. paper)
    ISBN-10: 0-7862-9601-1 (alk. paper)
    1. Large type books. I. Title.
PS3570.H5969P46 2007
813'.54—dc22   2007008828

Published in 2007 by arrangement with Leisure Books,
a division of Dorchester Publishing Co., Inc.

Printed in the United States of America on permanent paper
10 9 8 7 6 5 4 3 2 1

Dedicated to Judy, Joshua and Shane.

PROLOGUE

Fear nipped at the girl like the fangs of a rabid wolf, but she did not give in to it. To do so, to plunge through the forest in panic, would mean her capture, and worse. *The white men must not get their hands on her.*

Tenikawaku would rather die than be defiled. Since childhood she had been taught that the most important quality people possessed was their dignity. She valued hers more than life.

Not all tribes shared the Nansusequa belief. The whites certainly did not. Teni had seen how many whites behaved, and had been appalled. They did not treat anyone with respect, even themselves. As for "Indians," as the whites called her people, they were considered inferior.

Teni's father, who had worked so hard at mastering the white tongue, once told her that some whites regarded Indians as little better than animals. Their own words.

Incredible words, since they implied the whites regarded animals as inferior, too, instead of as their brothers and sisters. So much about the whites was strange. So much about them mystified Teni.

But now was not the time for Teni to think about white and red beliefs. Not with four men after her. Four whites who reeked of the drink that intoxicated, and who had pursued her from New Albion with one thought in mind.

Teni trembled at the thought of the vile deed they intended to commit.

The men had made their lust plain when one of them, the one whose name was Byram Forge, had grabbed her as she walked past and tried to press his lips to hers. She had slapped him, as was her right. Because she was strong and had used all her strength, she had nearly knocked him down. Forge's lust was replaced by rage, and at a bellow from him, his three friends leaped to seize her.

But Tenikawaku of the Nansusequa was not so easily taken. She was as fleet as her sister the doe and as canny as her brother the fox, and she fled into the forest with every confidence she would elude them.

The Nansusequa took pride in their woodcraft. Males and females alike were taught from birth the woodland ways that had ensured the survival of her people for untold summers. It was why the surrounding tribes referred to them as the Old Ones. But that is not what the Nansusequa called themselves. Among themselves, they always had been and always would be the People of the Forest.

The forest was their home. It sustained all their needs, and asked in return only that they treat it with the respect and dignity with which it treated them. To the Nansusequa, the forest was not a mere collection of trees and rocks and creatures. It was the source of all, part of the living presence of That Which Was In All Things.

The snap of a twig brought Teni out of herself. She was being careless. She must concentrate on the whites and only on the whites. The sound warned her they were close, much closer than she thought. She stopped and crouched, straining her senses, seeking them.

The forest was as still and silent as the cave of bones. Teni looked and listened, but saw no one, heard nothing. It troubled her greatly, for she had not suspected the whites possessed such stealth. She reminded herself that for all their bizarre beliefs, the whites were not to be taken lightly.

How well Teni remembered the first time she had encountered a white man. She had seen but six summers, yet the memory was as vivid and fresh as if it had happened only yesterday. Word came to her village of a camp of strange ones on the bank of the Serpent River. The strange ones came to trade, it was said. They offered marvelous articles in exchange for furs.

Many of her people had gone to visit the strange ones. Hand in hand with her mother and father, Teni was among them. The whites scared her; they were so different. Where the Nansusequa tended to be slender and sinewy, the whites were big and blocky. Where the Nansusequa tended to be quiet in manner, the whites were loud. They were like bears that ate the berry that caused creatures to lose their sense of self and blunder noisily about.

That had been ten summers ago, and Teni's outlook toward whites had not changed. Were it not for their trade goods, she would have nothing to do with them. She loved the jewelry most of all, the necklaces and bracelets that flashed in the sun and dazzled her when she admired her reflection in the stream or the mirror her mother had obtained for a mink fur.

Teni clenched her fists, upset with herself.

She was doing it again. She must stop withdrawing into herself and concentrate on Byram Forge and his friends.

About to move on, Teni started to rise, then froze. Not a stone's throw away a dark silhouette appeared against the backdrop of greenery. It was the figure of a crouched man. He was searching for her, but had not seen her thanks to her green buckskin dress, which made her seem part of the forest. The Nansusequa, men and women alike, always wore green buckskins, one of many practices that set them apart from other tribes.

The white man's face swung in her direction. Teni saw that it was Byram Forge himself, saw his rough features and the hairy growth on his chin. Forge wore buckskins too, but they were not green like hers. His moccasins were shorter than hers, and fringed. In his knobby hand he clutched a rifle, and a brace of pistols and a big knife adorned his waist.

Teni had a knife of her own. She had been taught to use the bow and the lance, but women did not carry them everywhere, as the men did. The women relied more on their feet and their heads to get them out of trouble, as she was doing now.

Forge's head swiveled this way and that. He sensed her. But so long as Teni did not move, he should not be able to spot her. Hardly had the thought crossed her mind when Forge looked right at her. His cruel mouth split in a triumphant grin.

Byram Forge shouted something.

Teni whirled and fled. To her right and left the undergrowth crackled under the headlong passage of hurtling forms. The whites were converging. Keeping low, Teni ran as she had never run before, threading through the trees with flawless skill. In long, graceful bounds, she vaulted obstacles in her path.

From behind her came the crash of brush and the pant of heavy breathing. Teni risked a glance and beheld three of the four, Forge foremost among them. They grinned in anticipation of what they would do when they caught her.

Where was the fourth one? Teni wondered. She assumed he had fallen behind. She was confident the others would give up the chase eventually, too, once they realized they had no chance of catching her.

Teni plunged into a thick stand of saplings and burst out the other side. A willow stood ahead. She raced under its overspreading boughs, and almost immediately a form sprang from behind the bole. She tried to veer aside, but iron arms banded about her waist and she was lifted off her feet and shaken as a bobcat might shake a mouse. Teni kicked and thrashed, but the man held fast while bawling excitedly at the top of his lungs.

Fear spiked Teni as Byram Forge and the other three came flying out of the saplings. Smirking, they slowed, and Forge pointed at her and said something that made the others laugh.

Teni's blood ran cold. She would bury her knife in her belly before she would let them have their way. But that was a last resort. She was Nansusequa, and the Nansusequa did not let their dignity be violated without a fight.

Forge came up and relieved Teni of her knife. Tossing it in the grass, he cupped her chin and looked her up and down, eating her with his eyes. He talked at length, and although Teni did not understand the language, she understood his meaning well enough. When he licked his thick lips, she repressed a shudder.

The other white men gazed at her with undisguised lust.

Forge let go of her chin and stepped back. He made a comment that produced more mirth. The whites were enjoying themselves. They anticipated enjoying themselves even more.

Teni had stopped struggling. Not because she had given up, but the better to gird herself. She hung her head, as if in despair, and when Byram Forge took his eyes off her, she galvanized into motion. She whipped her right foot forward and planted it where it would hurt Forge the most. Simultaneously, she arced her head back into the face of the man holding her. She heard the crunch of cartilage and felt the moist spurt of warm blood. The man howled and let her go to press his hands to his face.

Teni bolted. There were too many to battle. Better that she get away while she could. But she had only taken a few strides when her legs locked together and she crashed to the earth. Twisting, she discovered one of the whites had tackled her. He uttered a string of harsh gutturals, cursing her, no doubt. He would have been wiser to restrain her arms as he had her legs.

Teni balled her fists and punched him. She hit his eyes, his cheeks, his nose. He yelped for help, but before anyone else could reach them, Teni bucked and kicked and broke free. In a twinkling she was up and streaking off into the forest.

A hand snatched at her dress. Fingers

caught her sleeve. It did not stop her, but it slowed her enough that heartbeats later Byram Forge rammed into her with the impact of a falling tree. Down Teni went, the breath whooshing from her lungs. Her vision swam. Desperately, she sucked in air and clawed for purchase so she could rise.

It was too late.

Blinking, Teni looked up and blanched. The four men had her surrounded. They stood there, hands on hips, regarding her with harsher looks than before. The face of the man whose nose she had broken was smeared with blood.

Byram Forge spoke. This time no one laughed. Instead, the man with the busted nose and another one seized her arms. None too gently, she was hauled to her feet.

Teni did not resist. She met Byram Forge's glare evenly, betraying no trace of the anxiety that gnawed at her like a muskrat gnawing at tender shoots. She wished she spoke their language so she could tell them what she thought of them.

Standing sideways so his hip was to her, instead of the part of him she had kicked, Byram Forge gripped her jaw much harder than the first time, and violently shook her head, as if of a mind to rip her jaw off. Snarling, he slowly drew back a hand so she could see what was coming. Then he slapped her.

The blow stung, but Teni had felt worse. She stoically held her head high in mute defiance.

It made Forge madder. Seizing her long raven hair, he fiercely shook her head from side to side.

Teni could have sworn he was tearing her hair out by the roots. Excruciating pain flooded through her. Gritting her teeth, she bore it without a cry or a whimper. That was another trait of the Nansusequa. From childhood they were taught to never, ever show weakness to an enemy.

Byram Forge stepped back. His face was flushed. He drew his big knife and held the blade so it gleamed brightly in the sunlight that filtered through the willow's boughs. He reached for her hair again, but instead of grabbing a handful, he plucked a single hair and held it so she could see as he sliced the hair in half with a deft flick. He was showing Teni how sharp the knife was. Smirking, he lightly jabbed the sharp tip into her shoulder. The tip pierced her dress, and with a twist of his wrist, he opened a slit as long as her little finger.

Teni could guess what was next. Byram Forge intended to cut the dress from her body. The violation was not to be borne. She would not permit it, even to the point of dying, if need be.

Since Teni was not struggling, the pair holding her had relaxed their grips enough to permit her to do what she did next. Namely, she shifted toward one and then the other, and stamped the heel of her foot onto their toes. One yelped and the other sprang back, enabling her to wrench loose and try, yet again, to escape.

Teni fairly flew. She did not look back. She did not need to. She could hear the breathing of the fastest of them.

It was Byram Forge. An elk in rut, he would not be denied.

Teni was fleet, but it was a long way to her village. Her hope was to outlast them. The Nansusequa were known for their stamina. During the celebration her people held each summer at the time of the ripening of the raspberries, she always placed in the top five in the foot races.

On Teni ran, as tireless as a panther. She noticed that Byram Forge's heavy breaths were not as loud. A swift glance showed her that he was beginning to tire and had lost ground. The others were even farther back. Soon she would outdistance them.

Teni debated whether or not to inform

her parents. Her father might want to confront the whites of New Albion. Angry words might lead to blows, and blows to reprisals. She made up her mind to keep silent. No real harm had been done. She would just make it a point to never venture alone to the settlement.

Deep in thought, Teni rounded a maple. Too late, she spotted an exposed root. Her foot snagged, sending pain clear up her leg, and before she could even think to right herself, she sprawled on her belly. Her elbows absorbed most of the fall, racking her arms with agony. Barely able to move her hands, she sought to rise before Forge reached her. She failed.

It was akin to having a tree fall on her. Teni bit her lip to keep from shrieking. He deliberately gouged his knee into her spine. His hand clamped in her hair and her head was jerked back so hard, it was a wonder her neck did not snap. He snarled at her in the white tongue and cuffed her.

Dazed and helpless, Forge flipped Teni onto her back. The knee that had gouged her spine now dug into her stomach. Forge bent low. His breath, which reeked of ale and onions, filled her nostrils. He was saying incomprehensible things.

A wave of nausea afflicted Teni. She was

vaguely aware the other three had come up and circled her.

Byram Forge put a hand to her bosom. Leering, he squeezed, hard, and then laughed when she weakly sought to push him off. He was still laughing when a lance transfixed him from front to back. The tip caught him below the heart and sheared completely through his body.

Teni recognized the type of lance. No two tribes fashioned their weapons exactly the same.

This lance was Nansusequa.

Forge gaped at the smooth hardwood haft. He blinked, then coughed. Blood spurted from his nose. He looked up, past Teni. He opened his mouth to say something, but all that came out was more blood. Gurgling and twitching, he oozed off of her like mud.

The three remaining whites were glued in shock. The spell was broken when a lithe figure flashed past Teni and attacked the whites like a wolverine gone amok. A knife darted and danced. Ironically, it was a knife obtained in trade with the whites. The person wielding the knife was as dear to Teni as her own heart.

"Dega!"

Degamawaku was Teni's brother. Older by two summers, Dega had always looked out for his sister when she was little. He was still looking out for her, only now he had done the unthinkable. He had given in to raw rage.

"Dega! No!" Teni cried, but her plea fell on ears rendered deaf by the roar of boiling blood.

Degamawaku of the Nansusequa had been out hunting when he'd heard harsh sounds. Curious, he had investigated. He had come on the source of the voices just as Byram Forge had slammed into his sister's back. Shock had washed over Degamawaku, a great wave of shock that caused the world to spin and delayed his reaction. Then Byram Forge put his hand on Teni, and deep within Degamawaku rage boiled such as he had never known and never imagined a human being could feel.

Dega's right arm had moved of its own accord. His lance had left his hand before his head realized what his hand had done. Drawing his knife, Dega was on the other three in a rush of blazing wrath. He slashed and stabbed and cut, moving so swiftly that their efforts to defend themselves seemed the efforts of two-legged turtles. Two were down, bleeding profusely, when a hand fell on Dega's arm. He whirled, thinking it was the last white, and went to plunge his bloody blade into the white's chest.

"Brother! You must stop!"

Dega's eyes met Teni's. It jarred him. The full import of what he had just done hit him with the force of a physical blow.

The crash of a thicket alerted them that the fourth man was fleeing. Dega started after him, but his sister would not relinquish her hold.

"No! Let him go," Teni urged. "There has been enough killing."

Dega almost went after the white man anyway. "What they did —" he blurted, but did not finish. The deed the whites had been about to do was too hideous to be spoken of.

"It is over," Teni said soothingly. Worry filled her, both for him and for her people, over the consequences of his anger.

Degamawaku of the Nansusequa gazed at the blood-smeared forms on the ground. "What have I done?" he breathed.

Teni did not bother checking Byram Forge for a pulse. There was no need. But she did kneel next to the other two, and in turn took their wrists and pressed a finger to their veins. One was dead. The other had a weak heartbeat. He would not last long.

The white man's eyes opened. He swallowed a few times, then mewed and blubbered.

Teni shook her head to signify she did not understand. Only a few of the People of the Forest spoke the white tongue with any fluency. Most, like herself, knew only a few white words, mainly having to do with the barter of furs for the marvelous assortment of white trade goods.

Dega stood with his knife at his side, scarlet dripping from the blade and spattering his moccasins and the ground.

The white man wailed at the sky. He clutched Teni's wrist and squeezed with phenomenal strength, pleading to her with tears in his eyes.

Teni tried to pry his fingers off but couldn't. His dirty nails dug into her, breaking her skin.

A strident cry tore from the white man's throat. In the extremity of his impending fate, he lunged at Teni's neck, seeking to wrap his hands around her throat.

There was a blur of steel. The white man arched his back, gasped, and collapsed, staring blankly at the knife buried in his chest and at Dega's hand on the hilt.

Another groan sounded, but not from the white man. His days of making sounds of any kind were over. The groan came from

Teni. "Three of them, my brother. Three lives our people must answer for."

"They deserved to die for what they were going to do to you," Dega replied.

"They were living creatures. They had in them That Which Is In All Things," Teni said. The People of the Forest had a name for the mystery of mysteries, but it was seldom spoken out loud. To do so would reap calamity.

"Did they?" Dega questioned. "Do any of them?" He was skeptical. The whites reminded him of nothing so much as locusts. At first there had only been a few. Then more came, and even more, until the land between Nansusequa territory and the great salt sea far to the east was crawling with them. And still more whites were arriving all the time.

The growth of New Albion was added proof of the influx. It had started as a trading post, but the population swelled summer by summer until now nearly a hundred wooden lodges flanked the Serpent River, which the whites had renamed the Albion River.

"They are people like us," Teni said.

"Not like us," Dega retorted. "Never like us." He began wiping his knife blade on the shirt of one of the dead men. When he was

23

done he slid it into the sheath wedged under his green breechclout. The breechclout and knee-high green moccasins were all he wore. In the winter Nansusequa men preferred buckskins, but in the heat of summer breechclouts were favored.

Brother and sister showed their blood ties in their similar builds and facial features. Both were slender, but then, all the People of the Forest were prone to leanness and long limbs. Both had black hair, slicked with bear fat, that hung past their shoulders. In addition, Dega had a short clasp, made from porcupine quills, that splayed his hair at the back in a fan effect. Their eyes were dark brown. High foreheads, prominent cheekbones, and oval chins completed the image.

By any standard, red or white, Tenikawaku was a beauty, her brother strikingly handsome. Not that either gave much thought to such matters. Among the People of the Forest, a person's worth was not measured by how attractive he or she was, but by character, maturity, and wisdom.

"We must tell Father and Mother," Teni urged. She could not keep it to herself now, not with three dead whites.

"I should go after the one who got away," Dega said.

"What for?"

"Maybe I can catch him before he reaches New Albion." Dega did not say the rest of it.

"And do what? Kill him?" Teni gestured at the sprawled forms. "Has there not been enough blood spilled?"

"If I silence him he cannot tell the other whites," Dega noted. "They will not know who did this."

"You would have us keep our part in it a secret?"

"Either that or risk war."

"Surely it would not come to that?" Teni said. "We have traded with the whites for many summers. We are their friends."

"Are we?"

"You have never truly trusted them, brother. Not from the very beginning. Why is that?"

"Their eyes always say one thing and their mouths another." Dega nudged the body of Byram Forge. "I sometimes wonder if any of the whites are truly our friends. Even Reverend Stilljoy." He sighed. "But I will not go after the last one if you do not want me to."

"Thank you," Teni said, and clasped his hand. "Now come. We must not delay any longer."

They headed west, loping at a pace that

would eat the distance rapidly.

"I hope you are right, sister," Degamawaku said. "If you are not, more blood
will stain the earth." He added ominously,
"A lot more."

PARADISE LOST

CHAPTER ONE

It was rare for Evelyn King to get to sleep in. Her mother insisted she be up at the crack of dawn to begin her chores. So when Evelyn opened her green eyes and saw by the sunlight streaming in her window that the sun had been up an hour or more, she was sure she must be dreaming. But no, for when she rolled on her back and languidly stretched, she heard voices coming from the front room of their cabin. Her bedroom door was closed, and she could not tell what her parents were talking about.

Evelyn opened her mouth to call out to her mother and ask why she had been allowed the extra sleep, then changed her mind. If her mother had seen fit to grace her with this rare treat, why spoil it? Grinning, Evelyn pulled the quilt over her head and closed her eyes. Another hour would be deliciously wonderful. The only other days she was allowed to stay in bed were her birthday and January first. It was a King tradition to celebrate the new year by loafing the entire day. Needless to say, it was Evelyn's favorite tradition.

A pleasant drowsiness came over her. She felt herself drift on the incoming tide of slumber. Another few moments and she would float away. Then came a knock on her door.

"I knew it was too good to be true," Evelyn muttered. Louder, she hollered, "It's open, Ma." She heard the latch and a light tread on the plank floor. "How come you let me sleep in so late?"

The voice that answered was not her mother's.

"Is that your excuse? You've always been lazy as sin, brat. When you were little, I was always cleaning up after you."

Evelyn poked her head out from under the quilt and glared. "What in blazes are *you* doing here?" she demanded of her sibling. "You have a place of your own now. Or have you forgotten?"

Zachary King grinned. He was her senior by nine years, and he had a wife. He looked every inch the Indian half of his ancestry except for his piercing blue eyes. As was his custom, his muscular frame was clothed in beaded buckskins. A walking armory, he had a Hawken rifle in the crook of an elbow, a pair of flintlocks under his leather belt, a tomahawk on his right hip and a Bowie on his left. "I had to come see for myself once I heard."

"Heard what?" Evelyn asked, sleepily rubbing her eyes.

Zach did not answer right away. He walked to her window and gazed out over the lake. "Lou told me about it. She came over early to borrow syrup for breakfast."

Evelyn's brow puckered. Lou was short for Louisa, her brother's wife. "What are you babbling about?"

His back to her, Zach said, "I'm surprised you didn't say anything to me." He deliberately sounded hurt. Teasing his sister had always been great fun, and this latest development would give him ammunition for months to come.

"About what?" Irritated, Evelyn sat up.

Zach turned. He tried to adopt a serious expression but his mouth kept quirking. "What will you two do? Build a cabin of your own? Let's see. I live on the north side of the lake, Shakespeare lives on the south side, Ma and Pa live here on the west. That leaves the east for you and your beloved."

Evelyn practically exploded. "Beloved!" At last she thought she knew what he was prattling about. "I don't love Chases Rabbits or Niwot. Not in the way you mean, anyhow."

Much to Evelyn's considerable consternation, she had acquired suitors. A young Crow named Chases Rabbits and a young Ute named Niwot were vying for her affection, despite making it plain she had no interest whatsoever in acquiring a husband. For eight months now, the pair had visited the valley every chance they got, pressing their suits. Sometimes they both showed up at the same time, which created no end of embarrassment for her. An uneasy truce existed between the Crows and the Utes, and so far Chases Rabbits and Niwot had honored it, but Evelyn fretted that one day one or the other would pounce on his rival, precipitating all-out war.

At the moment, though, Evelyn's immediate headache was her brother. "Unless you have something important to say, scat. I want to get dressed."

"Wear your best dress in honor of the occasion," Zach suggested.

"What occasion, dang you?"

"It isn't every day a girl is asked for her hand in marriage."

Evelyn forgot herself and sprang out of bed in her nightshirt. She went to poke Zach in the chest and demand that he explain when she heard a new voice out in the front room. "Is that who I think it is?"

Zach nodded, then sputtered, fighting down his glee. "Niwot. He has six horses tied out front, along with a pile of furs. You should be flattered. That's quite a lot to offer for a runt like you."

"Dear God!"

No longer able to contain himself, Zach cackled uproariously.

"It's not *that* hilarious." Evelyn had dreaded this. She could only put her suitors off for so long. Eventually, impatience had been bound to drive one or the other to do what Niwot was about to do, propose. Among his people, when a man wanted to take a woman for his wife, he left a horse outside his intended's lodge. If the woman accepted the horse, she in effect agreed to become his wife. If she left the horse untended, she had no interest.

"Ah, but it is," Zach teased. "You were the one who was always going to live east of the Mississippi, remember? You wanted nothing to do with the wilderness. Nothing to do with Indians, or Indian ways."

"I never said that," Evelyn snapped. While it was true that for the longest time she was more partial to her father's people than her mother's, she did not dislike the Shoshones.

She merely disliked living as they lived.

"You didn't have to," Zach said. "It was as plain as the big nose on your face." He dodged a hastily thrown fist and backpedaled to the door. "I'd best leave you to get dressed. Your suitor is probably eager for a glimpse of your beauty." Zach snickered.

Evelyn would gladly have beaned him with a rock, were one handy, but he skipped out the door, chortling merrily. She slammed the door after him, then strode to her closet to decide what to wear. Usually she dressed as white women did, in dresses bought in St. Louis or ones she had made herself, patterned after the latest fashions. Today, she tried something different. She donned a buckskin dress, the plainest she owned, and let her hair hang limp instead of doing anything fancy with it. She figured she'd show Niwot she was as ordinary as dishwater, and not the beauty he claimed.

The instant Evelyn stepped from her bedroom, she realized she had blundered. Niwot was by the table, chatting with her mother and father. A stocky, swarthy youth, attired in his best buckskins, his dark eyes lit up like twin candles at the sight of her. In thickly accented English, he exclaimed, "Pretty dress! You never wear."

"It's just some old thing I threw on."

"It give hope," Niwot said.

Puzzled by his meaning, Evelyn was given a temporary reprieve by her mother.

"If you don't mind, Niwot," Winona King said kindly, "my husband and I would like a few words alone with our daughter." Her English, unlike Niwot's, was flawless, a result of years of hard study and use, as well as her knack for learning languages.

Winona was a full-blooded Shoshone. She had met Nate King shortly after he came to the mountains to hunt beaver, and ever since, the two had been inseparable. She liked to say there were two things the Great Mystery had bestowed on her that she valued more than anything else: life itself and Nate.

Though in her forties, Winona looked younger. A beaded buckskin dress, most of the beads blue, added a splash of color. She had an air of perpetual calmness about her, but it was deceptive. When aroused, she made a fierce adversary.

"Alone?" Niwot repeated. "Oh. Yes. Me wait outside." Smiling adoringly at Evelyn, he strolled out.

"Me wait outside, too," Zach playfully mimicked. At the door, Zach paused to glance at Evelyn and indulge in a long sigh. "There's nothing quite as grand as two children in love, is there?" With that parting volley, he was gone.

"I could strangle him," Evelyn complained, crossing to the table.

The other person in the room stirred. Nate King was a mountain of a man with a deep, rumbling voice. He was dressed exactly like his son. He had green eyes and a black beard that he kept neatly trimmed, as his wife liked it. His was an imposing presence, and when he spoke, others listened. "This is serious, daughter."

"It's true, then?" Evelyn said, looking from mother to father and back again. "Niwot isn't leaving me any wiggle room?"

"I am afraid not," Winona answered. "He arrived late last night. I was first up, and when I looked out the window, there he was with all his horses and furs. I woke your father."

Nate continued the account. "We have been trying to convince him he is rushing things, but he won't listen. He has already courted you longer than most Utes court their intendeds."

"What am I to do?" Evelyn asked. She did not want to hurt Niwot's feelings, but she simply and truly did not love him. Not *that* way. Her parents were aware of her sentiments.

"Be honest with him," Winona said. She was a firm believer in always being honest. In her estimation, truth was the bedrock of love. "Tell him you are sorry but you cannot be his wife."

"But what if it makes him mad?" Evelyn worried. "We don't need trouble with the Utes."

The relationship between the King family and the Ute tribe had been strained at times, to put it mildly. When Nate first came to the mountains, he had lived in a cabin built by his uncle. A cabin that happened to be in Ute territory. The Utes took exception, and for many years tried repeatedly to take his life. After Nate befriended an Ute chief and helped rid the Utes of the menace of a killer grizzly, the tribe regarded him more favorably. But he was still white, and that made a difference.

Now Nate raised a tin cup to his lips and took a sip of steaming hot coffee before commenting. "Your mother is right. Do what you have to. We are no longer in Ute territory, and I can't see them going on the warpath over a rejected suitor."

Vexed by the unwanted stress, Evelyn stamped a small foot and said bitterly, "Why did this have to happen to me?"

"It is life, daughter," Winona said. "Difficulties happen to everyone, whether we want them to or not."

Nate shrugged. "You are young. You are pretty. If we were back in civilization, you would have more beaus than you could shake a stick at."

"But I don't want any!" Evelyn declared. "I'm not hankering for a husband. I might never get married, in fact." She noticed her mother's smile, and asked, "What is so amusing?"

"I felt the same way at your age," Winona replied. "Most girls do. We think we will never meet a man who can claim our heart. We imagine we will live our lives alone, and think we prefer it that way. But we will and we won't and we don't."

Evelyn moved to the window. Zach and Niwot were standing by a hill of furs, talking. Judging by her brother's expression, he was having a marvelous time. "I suppose I should go out there."

Winona rose and came over. "We have tried every argument we can think of, but Niwot is in love with you, and love will not be denied."

"It will in my case," Evelyn said flatly. From behind her came her father's rumbling tones.

"Go easy on him, girl. He might not look

it, but he has butterflies in his stomach. It takes a heap of nerves to ask a girl to wed. Believe me. I know."

Winona glanced over her shoulder. "It was that hard for you with me?" She did seem to recall he had been a bundle of nerves.

"You have no idea," Nate assured her. "For a man, asking for a woman's hand is one of the hardest things he ever has to do."

Evelyn's interest was piqued. "Why should that be? Didn't you tell me once that when two people are in love, it's like —" she strived to recall his exact words, "— how did you put it? Like having their two hearts entwined?"

"That's how it is," Nate confirmed, "but it doesn't make the asking easier."

"You have an eloquent way of phrasing things, husband," Winona said in her impeccable English.

Nate shrugged again. "Blame the books."

Against a wall stood a large bookcase. The books that crammed the shelves were Nate's most valued possessions. He had always been a reader, even as a boy. Many an hour he had whiled away absorbed in works of fiction, like those of his favorite writer, James Fenimore Cooper. He loved *The Last of the Mohicans,* and had read it several times. Among the many other works that adorned his shelves: *The Iliad* and *The Odyssey*, *Robinson Crusoe*, *Gulliver's Travels*, *Ivanhoe*, *Pride and Prejudice*, *The Sketch Book of Geoffrey Crayon.* He had works by Byron, Shelley, and Keats, although mainly for Winona's benefit; she adored poetry. Among the score of nonfiction volumes, perhaps the ones he cherished most were the writings of Thomas Paine. In particular was he fond of *The Rights of Man.*

Of Nate's two offspring, only Evelyn read with any frequency. Zach had no interest in books. He could never sit still long enough to read.

Leaning back in his chair, Nate folded his arms across his broad chest and remarked, "You might as well get it over with."

"I'm in no hurry," Evelyn said. Niwot wasn't the only one with butterflies. "I need to work out just what to say."

Winona shot Nate a glance, then placed a hand on her daughter's shoulder. "Take your time. Niwot is not going anywhere. And sometimes Ute women take two or three days to make up their minds."

"Why me?" Evelyn lamented again.

Nate hid a grin by raising his cup to his mouth. To the young, existence seemed to revolve around them. Their worries and woes were exaggerated out of all proportion. He had been that way once. But life tended to knock the stuffing out of self-importance, and to teach that in the greater scheme of things, human beings were dust motes caught up in circumstances over which they had scant control.

"Would you care for breakfast?" Winona asked. She was concerned over Evelyn's emotional state. What her daughter had to do would not be easy, and although Evelyn liked to act as if nothing ever bothered her, deep down she was as fragile as her Shoshone name of Blue Flower implied.

"I don't have much of an appetite," Evelyn said. Normally she liked a big breakfast, but not today. She looked down at herself. "What did Niwot mean by my dress gives him hope?"

It was Nate who answered. "You hardly ever wear buckskins, daughter. He must figure it's your way of showing him that you prefer Indian ways over white ways, and there is a chance you will say yes."

"Oh, Lord." Evelyn was aghast at her mistake. "I didn't think of that." She turned toward her room. "I'll go change."

"That's not necessary," Winona said. "It's not the dress that matters. It's *you.* Go do what you must. To keep him on a tether would be cruel."

"I suppose," Evelyn agreed, but without relish.

The front door opened and in sauntered Zach. "Yes, sir," he declared. "Niwot will make a fine brother-in-law."

"Go climb the tallest tree you can find, clear to the top, and jump off head first," Evelyn retorted.

Zach ignored her barb. "I reckon Louisa and me will be able to come visit you two or three times a year."

"What?" Evelyn said.

"At the Ute village," Zach said. "Niwot just told me he has no intention of living in our valley. As soon as you agree to be his woman, he's throwing you over a horse and carting you home." He paused for effect. "Personally, I admire a man so forceful with his woman. If I tried to tell Lou what to do, she would take a rolling pin to my noggin."

"It might do you some good to have your brains rattled," Evelyn said. She did not let on how disturbed she was by Niwot's plans for their presumed future together. He took it for granted that his wishes were her wishes.

"Speaking of home," Winona said to Zach, "shouldn't you be at yours instead of here teasing your sister?"

"Is that a hint, Ma?" Zach asked.

"I have a rolling pin, too," Winona said, "and you are never too old for a swat."

"That would be a first." Zach's parents had never once struck him in all the years he was growing up. The Shoshones frowned on punishing children by beating them. To the Shoshones, the notion of taking a child out to the woodshed, as the whites liked to say, was unspeakably cruel. Winona had insisted on raising Zach and Evelyn in the Shoshone manner, and their father had agreed.

Just then Nate rose. "I will walk you out, son."

"You too, Pa? A man can't have any fun anymore."

"Not at your sister's expense, no," Winona scolded. "This is a serious matter. It must be handled delicately."

Zach turned to Evelyn. "I can talk to him for you if you want, sis," he offered. "Man to man, as they say. Maybe it would be easier on him coming from me."

Flabbergasted, Evelyn had to remind herself that every now and then her brother did something so incredibly sweet, she would swear he was an imposter. "Thank you," she said, "but it's mine to do."

"Suit yourself." Zach reached for the latch and grinned. "You know, it's too bad you don't have five or six suitors. You could marry them all and have more horses and furs than you could shake a stick at."

"I would like to shake one at you and hit you with it," Evelyn told him, smiling. But the smile was a sham. She did not feel lighthearted. She felt as if a knife had been thrust into her gut and was being twisted back and forth.

Nate and Zach went out. Through the window Evelyn saw them stop and talk to Niwot. "Why couldn't he pick an Ute girl?" she said under her breath.

Winona heard her. "He is in love with you, daughter. The color of your skin is unimportant to him."

"Are you trying to make me feel worse?" Evelyn asked.

"There is no reason you should," Winona said. "Never once, by word or deed, have you so much as hinted to Niwot that you considered him more than a friend. He sees love where none exists."

"I should have discouraged him long before this," Evelyn said. Although Niwot wore his affection for her on the sleeve of his buckskins, she had never imagined he would take so drastic a step without encouragement on her part.

"We are not soothsayers," Winona noted.

44

"We cannot predict the future." The closest she had ever come was when she met Nate. Somehow, call it intuition or instinct or wishful thinking, she had known Nate was the one for her.

"Common sense should have told me," Evelyn said. If she had been smart, she would have told Niwot months ago to stop coming around. But she had been loath to hurt his feelings.

"Our hearts do not always want to do what our heads tell us is best," Winona remarked.

"Ain't that the truth." Evelyn never ceased to be amazed at how well her mother understood her sometimes. Granted, they were mother and daughter, but Winona was Shoshone born and bred, while Evelyn was a product of both the white and the red worlds. And until recently she had much preferred the former. Until she learned that the white world was not the paradise she thought. Until she discovered that just like the red world, with its dark underbelly of counting coup and occasional torture, the white world had a dark underbelly, too, a shadow realm in which humans made slaves of one another, or sold their bodies for money, or worshiped at the altar of greed.

"Isn't," Winona corrected her. "Isn't that

45

the truth."

"Isn't," Evelyn said absently.

Nate and Zach were moving off along the lakeshore. Zach beamed at Niwot and wriggled his fingers in parting.

"Here goes nothing," Evelyn declared, and went out. She blinked in the bright glare of the morning sun and licked her suddenly dry lips. Her stomach was doing somersaults.

"Blue Flower!" Niwot happily exclaimed, using her Shoshone name. "You make answer?"

Evelyn hesitated. His sincerity could not be denied. When they first met, Niwot did not speak a word of the white man's tongue. Months of hard effort had resulted in his broken English, an accomplishment of which he was justly proud. And all to please her, so they could talk without having to use sign language.

"Blue Flower?" Niwot said.

Evelyn looked at the horses. They were fine animals. The furs were exceptional. Long hours of tedious work had gone into their skinning and curing. "You flatter me, Niwot."

"That good?"

"Very good, yes," Evelyn said, and was crushed when he brightened like a lamp that

46

had been turned all the way up.

"It make you happy?"

"They would make any girl happy," Evelyn hedged.

"Then why you have sad eyes?" Niwot asked.

Evelyn decided to quit beating around the bush. He deserved that much. After all, he had always treated her with the utmost respect, and never once overstepped himself. "I hurt for you, Niwot. Because I like you, I truly do. As a friend, as a good friend. But not, I am sorry to say, as someone who could be the father of my children." It was strange, her saying those words. She never, ever had given any thought to having a family of her own.

"Oh." The young Ute was crestfallen.

"Please don't be upset," Evelyn said. "We can still be friends, can't we? It's not as if I never want to see you again."

Niwot managed a wan smile. "You so pretty, Blue Flower." He had more to say, but he was prevented from doing so by an arrow that streaked out of nowhere and sheared through his throat.

CHAPTER TWO

Green was the color of their world. Green grass, the green leaves of the oaks and maples, the willows and elms, the beech and other trees. The green of the dense thickets and brush, the green of moss, the green of sweet clover. Green, green, everywhere, befitting the thick woodland and rolling lowland the Nansusequa had roamed since time out of mind.

The People of the Forest, they called themselves, and no name could be more fitting. The forest was their home. The forest was their mother. The forest was their father. The forest nurtured and protected them, and in return, the Nansusequa nurtured and protected the forest. They lived as part of the land without defiling the land. Every plant, every animal was precious, part of That Which Was In All Things, including the Nansusequa. It was why they always wore green. Why they dyed everything they wore green. Never any other hue but green. Green shirts, green pants, green breech-clouts, green dresses, green blouses, green skirts. It was said that in ancient times they even dyed their skin green.

It was surprising, perhaps, that neighboring tribes did not call them the Green People. But it was not the green that most impressed their neighbors. It was the fact that the Nansusequa had existed longer than any tribe known. Their beginning was lost in the mists of antiquity. They had always been, the stories had it, and thus were they called the Old Ones.

While many of their neighbors lived in wigwams, the dwellings of the Nansusequa were communal. Built to withstand the fiercest of storms and the coldest of winters, the Great Lodges, as the Nansusequa called them, were, not surprisingly, painted green inside and out. Thick timbers, treated so they arched, supported the roof and braced the sides, which were constructed of tightly interwoven boughs and covered with bark. A central aisle ran down the center of each Great Lodge. Partitions separated the living areas of each family.

The largest was known as the Council Lodge. Long enough and wide enough for the entire tribe to gather, it was decorated with their sacred totems, including the most sacred of all, the green hickory circle that represented That Which Was In All Things, or the Manitoa. The name was so sacred that the Nansusequa rarely spoke it aloud. To do so, it was believed, invoked powerful forces beyond the ken of human understanding.

The leadership of the People of the Forest was hereditary, passed down generation to generation. The current leader, Hunumanima, was deeply respected for his wisdom and compassion. Gray at the temples, his face seamed by the wrinkles of his advanced years, he now stood on the platform that overlooked the Council Lodge and raised his thin arms to silence the murmur of voices. At once, the Nansusequa fell silent.

His body nearly lost inside the green robe he wore, Hunumanima stepped to the edge of the platform and gravely intoned, "You have heard the words of Wakumassee. You know what his son Degamawaku has done. Now we must decide what to do."

Closest to the platform stood the elders, resplendent in their striking green garments and headdresses. It was one of the elders who spoke the thought uppermost in all their minds. "There will be trouble with the whites. They will want revenge."

More murmuring broke out and was again stilled by Hunumanima. "The whites are not without reason. I will talk to our friend, the one they call Stilljoy, and seek his advice."

One of the elders made two fists and held them knuckles-to-knuckles, a sign of disagreement. "Stilljoy is no friend of the Nansusequa. He visits us not to learn our ways, but to impose his ways on us. He wants us to believe as he believes, and drink of the blood of the man he calls his God."

A barely perceptible shudder rippled through the room. The idea of spilling human blood was abhorrent to the Nansusequa. Although they would fight to defend their territory, they were not, by nature, a warlike people. To them, the spilling of blood was something to be avoided, not embraced. Which made Degamawaku's bloodletting all the more unacceptable.

Hunumanima responded to the dissent. "Yet Stilljoy does spend time among us, which is more than most whites do, and he listens, and treats us kindly. Talking to him can do no harm and might do much good."

"I am uneasy around him," said the dissenter. "He treats us as children."

The faces of many mirrored their agreement. Hunumanima stood in thought a bit, then said gently, "There is much about the whites we do not understand. Their ways are so strange, they do not seem normal to us."

Another elder spoke. "It is said they take all the land for their own. It is said they have wiped out many tribes, or driven the tribes west, to get the land."

"Are we to believe stories told by those who offer no proof?" Hunumanima asked. "The whites have not tried to take our land, have they?"

The same elder answered. "It is said they seek an excuse to take ours. Degamawaku has given them that excuse."

"I do not think the whites will go on the warpath against us. The furs we trade are too valuable." Hunumanima turned to the abashed family that stood in a row between the elders and the rest of the Nansusequa. "But it could be they will want a life for a life."

The family of five betrayed no emotion. In the middle stood the father, Wakumassee. Among the People of the Forest he was noted for his great love of peace; he was the tribe's peacemaker. Broader of chest than most, he had a high forehead and a noble bearing.

On Wakumassee's right stood Tihikanima,

his wife. She was noted for two things. First was her beauty, for her features were the epitome of all the physical traits the People of the Forest admired: fine, high eyebrows; a slender, small nose; upturned lips; and wide, doe-like eyes. The second thing for which Tihikanima was noted was for being the daughter of their leader, Hunumanima.

On her right stood their youngest child, Mikikawaku, a sprite of a girl who had seen barely twelve summers. She was too young to be noted for anything other than being a dutiful daughter.

On Wakumassee's left was Degamawaku. He stared straight ahead, refusing to acknowledge the many glances bestowed on him. Some of those glances were kindly, but most betrayed worry, and more than a few showed resentment.

On his left was Teni. She burned with the desire to speak in her brother's defense, but she could not unless called on by their leader or an elder.

Hunumanima beckoned for Dega to approach the platform. "You are sure the three whites were dead? There can be no mistake?"

"None," Dega confirmed.

"This day you have planted a seed that could grow into hatred," Hunumanima said sorrowfully. "The whites will resent what you have done. They will blame all of us for your actions." He stopped and looked at Dega expectantly.

"I will not say I am sorry, if that is what you want. I did what I had to in order to save my sister." Dega refused to feel shame for doing what was right. Had he to do it over again, he would do exactly the same.

"But was it necessary to slay them?" Hunumanima asked. "Could you have struck them down without killing them?"

In his fury at the violation of his sister, the idea had never entered Dega's head.

"I did not hear your answer."

"They had guns," Dega said, which, in itself, was not justification. But everyone there shared a disquieting unease about the alien weapons that crashed like thunder and spat fire and smoke — and small pieces of metal — to lethal effect.

"Many whites carry guns, as we carry lances," Hunumanima noted. He switched his attention to Tenikawaku. "Have you anything to say in this matter?"

Grateful for the opportunity, Teni said, "Only to repeat what I have already told everyone. The whites meant to have their way with me. Had my brother not come along, they might have killed me." She added, "Or I would be dead by my own hand."

"My heart is happy that you were spared," Hunumanima said. "But my heart is also heavy with misgiving. We must prevent the spilling of more blood. The best way to do that is to talk with the whites and explain our side of things. I will arrange a meeting with Reverend Stilljoy. You and your brother will accompany me."

Wakumassee started, mute appeal on his face.

"You wish to speak too?" their leader asked.

"Yes, Hunumanima." Wakumassee had a deep, resonant voice that carried to every corner of the Council Lodge. "Whites often behave rashly. They also have short tempers. The sight of my son and daughter may be too much for them, and they may kill Degamawaku and Tenikawaku without giving them a chance to explain."

"His words are wise," an elder observed.

"I will send a messenger to Reverend Stilljoy," Hunumanima proposed. "I will ask him to come alone to the clearing by the black tree. I will take Degamawaku and Tenikawaku with me to give their account. We will ask his advice. Does this meet with your approval?" Hunumanima gazed along the rank of elders, then at Wakumassee. "I hear no objections."

The messenger was sent to New Albion. The young man entrusted with the task was the fastest of the People of the Forest. By nightfall the runner returned with word that Reverend Stilljoy had agreed.

The meeting was to take place at midday. The black tree had once been a giant maple, a magnificent patriarch of the woodland, which had had the misfortune to be struck by lightning. The bolt set the tree on fire and much of it was burned before rain from the same storm extinguished the flames.

The clearing was in the shape of a half-moon. Dense vegetation bordered it. Located barely ten arrows' flights from the village, it was reached by a narrow trail.

Hunumanima was in the lead, his long green robe flowing about him. Behind him came not just Degamawaku and Tenikawaku, but the entire family.

Wakumassee had insisted on coming. He loved his children dearly and was greatly troubled by his son's plight. The talk of a life for a life had prompted him to go to Hunumanima, with Tihi at his side, and request that the whole family be permitted to go along.

"Stilljoy only expects me and your two

oldest," Hunumanima had reminded him.

"Reverend Stilljoy will not object," Wakumassee had predicted. "He and I have had many talks. He calls me his good friend."

Hunumanima was aware of that. "You also speak the white tongue well."

"There is much I have not yet learned," Wakumassee had said modestly.

"You know more of their language than I do," Hunumanima had said. "Faugh! How strange their tongue is. In our language one word means one thing, but in theirs, one word may mean many things. And that sound they make with their tongues pressed to the back of their teeth, or the one where they puff like a teased snake. Their tongue is different from any we know."

"Everything about the whites is different," Wakumassee had said.

Tihikanima had done something she rarely did when her husband and father were talking. She interrupted. "So it is all right, then, for us to accompany you?"

"You may come," Hunumanima had said. "But you may not bring weapons. I gave Stilljoy my pledge we would not be armed."

Now, winding along the trail, Wakumassee looked forward to talking to the reverend. If anyone could help them, Stilljoy was the one. Like him, Stilljoy was a man of peace.

"I will be happy when we have worked things out with the whites," Tihi commented, so softly that only Wakumassee heard.

"As will I, wife."

Twisting, Tihikanima glanced at their son. Dega seemed to be more calm than any of them. "We will not let the whites harm you," she assured him.

"I will accept what comes, Mother." Degamawaku was a product of Nansusequa customs, and those customs dictated people must take responsibility for their acts even when the consequences were not pleasant.

Tenikawaku, hiking behind him and holding little Miki's hand, had a different opinion. "You must not give up your life."

"The decision is not mine," Dega said. "It is Hunumanima's. I will do what he thinks is best for our people."

Wakumassee overheard and was torn. On the one hand he was proud of his son's maturity and devotion to their people, and on the other, the thought of the whites demanding a life for a life terrified him. He must accept Hunumanima's final decision, whatever it was, but he did not know if he could hand over his son to be killed.

Dega, despite what he had just said, was unsure if he would meekly submit to white justice. Losing his temper was a lapse, yes. More specifically, it was the degree to which he had lost it, since the Nansusequa prided themselves on their self-control. But did that merit his death?

Dega cast the question from his mind. He was weary of thinking about it. He focused on the forest he loved so much, listening for the warble of songbirds and the chatter of scampering squirrels. He heard the rustle of the breeze, nothing more, and realized how uncommonly still the forest had become. In his surprise, he slowed, and Teni nearly bumped into him.

"Are you all right, brother?"

"Yes," Dega said. But a vague unease had settled over him. He knew the workings of the forest as he knew the workings of his own body, and when the woods were this quiet, it was a bad omen.

"We are almost there," Hunumanima announced.

Only by a supreme force of will did Dega compose himself so that when they entered the clearing, his face was as inscrutable as the air. It was well he did. Things were not as they should be.

In the center of the clearing waited Reverend Stilljoy. A stiff, stern-visaged man with a hook nose and a cleft chin, he was dressed in a black coat, black vest, black pants and black boots. His only concession to color was his white shirt. As always, he held what whites called a book, one that was as dear to Reverend Stilljoy as life itself. On seeing them emerge from the woods, Stilljoy smiled. But Dega noted that the smile did not touch his eyes.

The reverend was not alone. Three other whites were with him but stood well back, next to their horses. Their clothes and hats were homespun. One was a burly slab with bushy brows. Another had a sandy mane and beard. The third was clean shaven.

That the reverend had broken the agreement and brought others was troubling enough. Even more troubling were the rifles and pistols the white men carried.

Dega came to a stop and glanced at his father, who had done the same. But not Hunumanima. Their leader crossed to Stilljoy and extended a hand in greeting, white-man fashion.

"Friend," Hunumanima said in English.

Stilljoy's smile seemed carved in place. "Hunu!" he said amiably. "It is good to see you again."

One of the men by the horses, the burly one, made a sound that resembled a duck being strangled.

If Hunu heard, he made no sign of it. Motioning at the ground, he said, "After you, friend."

"Thank you, Hunu." Reverend Stilljoy sank down cross-legged, the large book in his lap.

Dega thought it odd that Stilljoy did not glance at him or his family. The other whites were staring, though, particularly at him.

"Not alone," Hunu said to Stilljoy.

The severe white man in black jabbed a thin finger. "You brought some extras, too, I see." He looked up and blinked. "Waku? Is that you? I'm sorry. I didn't realize it was you. What brings you here? Are you serving as interpreter?"

Waku boldly stepped forward. "I not come speak tongue." He motioned. "I come for son, Degamawaku."

"What does — ?" Reverend Stilljoy began, and stopped. "Oh." He cast a furtive glance at the three whites by the horses. "So he is yours, is he? I don't believe I was ever introduced. Tihi, I recall. These others must be your daughters."

"Yes," Waku said, and translated for the benefit of his family. Then, to Hunu in the Nansusequa tongue, "May I?"

"You may."

Waku adopted the cross-legged posture.

"We need help, friend Stilljoy. We come say why whites die." He immediately repeated what he had said in his own tongue for his family's benefit.

Reverend Stilljoy grew grim. "I must say, it was quite a shock. I was under the impression your people are a peace-loving tribe."

"We much like peace," Waku assured him.

"Much," Hunumanima echoed.

"Then why did your son murder three white men for no reason other than the color of their skin?"

The accusation shocked Waku and Hunu. Waku was the first to find his voice. "That not true, friend Stilljoy. Son not hates whites." Again he translated so his family could follow their conversation.

Over by the horses, the burly man with the bushy eyebrows unleashed a string of harsh invective, ending with, "I knew it! I told you they would deny it, the stinking heathens!"

Reverend Stilljoy shifted to glance at the other in disapproval. "What did I tell you, Arthur, about speaking out of turn? We must keep them here, remember, and not have them walk off in a huff." He smiled thinly at Hunu and Waku. "Please forgive him. His son was one of those murdered."

"What mean murder?" Hunu asked.

"Murder is when someone kills someone else wrongly," Reverend Stilljoy explained. He bobbed his chin at Dega. "As Waku's son did when he murdered Byram Forge, Gulliver Hundicott and Robert Wayne."

Waku translated, then said, "My son not do wrong, friend Stilljoy. My son help sister."

"I don't understand," the reverend said. "Helped her how?"

"The dead men chase her," Waku related, with a gesture at Teni. "They catch her. They try —" Waku could not bring himself to say it.

"Are you saying Byram Forge and the others had unscrupulous designs?" Reverend Stilljoy was incredulous.

"If that mean they want harm her, yes," Waku said, seeking the right words from his limited store of English. "They very bad. They try touch her."

Arthur Forge was the same shade as a beet. "That's a damned lie!" he roared, coming toward them. "Let me at them! I'll end this nonsense."

Again Stilljoy glanced sharply at him. "Must I keep reminding you? I sympathize with your loss. But you agreed to let me handle this, remember?"

"You're too damned nice to these savages," Arthur Forge grumbled, "and that's a fact. But go ahead. With what's at stake, I can afford to be patient."

Dega listened to his father's translation without truly comprehending. It did not help that his father was unsure of the meaning of some of the words, and had to guess.

Tihikanima was studying the faces of the whites. On her visits to New Albion to trade, she had found that their expressions often said as much as their words, and she was troubled by the expressions she saw on the whites here. There was hatred on the faces of the three near the horses, and flashes of regret from her husband's friend, Reverend Stilljoy. She edged closer, hoping to catch her husband's attention.

Waku was speaking. "Please. Listen to son. Decide which true."

"Very well," Reverend Stilljoy said, folding his hands on top of the book. "Proceed, Dega, if you please."

Dega did not like having his familiar name used by a white. Only Nansusequa were entitled to do that.

"Tell him, my son," Waku directed. "Do not leave anything out. I will say what you say, in his tongue."

Dega related the event exactly as it had happened. His father then asked his sister

64

to do the same.

The whole while, Reverend Stilljoy listened attentively, his features offering no clue as to whether he believed them or not. With the other whites, it was easier to tell; their scowls and muttering showed they did not believe a word.

Teni finished and stepped back.

Reverend Stilljoy sat as if carved from wood for so long, the patience of the waiting Nansusequa was strained. Finally Hunu coughed.

"What say you, friend?"

A heavy sigh fluttered from Stilljoy's thin lips. "There is so much to say I do not know where to begin. Perhaps with an apology. I am sorry, truly sorry, for all of your sakes. But what must be, must be."

"Pardon?" Waku said.

"It is your word against that of the man who escaped," Reverend Stilljoy said.

"Dega, Teni speak true."

"So you say. But Stanley Bendis tells a different story. He says that he and his friends were minding their own business when your son attacked them without any provocation."

"You not believe?" Hunu asked.

"Were it up to me, I might be inclined to accept your version," Reverend Stilljoy said.

"But it is not up to me."

"Who then?" Waku pressed him.

"The leading men of New Albion have agreed on what must be done. All I can do is pray for your souls."

"Pardon?" Waku said again. He was troubled at how the other three whites were fingering their rifles.

"Do you know what an object lesson is?" Reverend Stilljoy asked.

"No," Waku admitted.

"It is when you punish someone so others will not make the same mistake." Stilljoy bit his lower lip. "I regret I must inform you that it has been decided to make an object lesson of the Nansusequa."

Waku grew alarmed. "What this mean?"

"Even as we speak, your village is being surrounded. Before this day is done, the Nansusequa will be no more."

CHAPTER THREE

Shock seized Evelyn King. She saw Niwot stagger, saw him clutch at the hardwood shaft that had transfixed his neck, saw his shock and bewilderment. Blood gushed from his mouth as, with awful gurgling and choking sounds, he sank into oblivion.

Evelyn screamed. She emptied her lungs in a shriek of sheer mortal horror. It did not occur to her that she might be the bowman's next target until a glittering shaft whizzed past her neck, missing by inches only because she had inadvertently taken a step to one side. Evelyn spun toward the woods to the west of the cabin, her shriek dying. Another shaft came streaking out of the foliage. This one she evaded by throwing herself to the ground.

That there was more than one attacker became evident when three arrows flashed toward her at once. The arrows were in midflight when Evelyn heaved erect and bolted for the door. In her haste she tripped. Down she went, hard. She glanced up. The shafts were descending toward her. Scrambling to the right, she sought to avoid them. One thudded into the earth next to her arm, another overshot her. The third was going to strike. Frantic, Evelyn flung her legs wide and the arrow sliced into her buckskin dress between her knees, missing her legs but pinning her dress to the ground. In her relief, she lay there grinning idiotically. It was a mistake.

More arrows came arcing out of the woods.

Then a rifle banged, and her father and brother were there. Zach lowered his Hawken and snatched at a pistol while Nate bent and ripped the arrow from Evelyn's dress with a powerful wrench of his broad shoulders.

Nate had thought for sure his daughter was hit. When he heard her scream, his breath had caught in his throat. The next instant, instinct took over and he hurled himself to her aid. Now, holding on to the arrow, he scooped Evelyn into his other arm and spun toward the cabin and safety.

Zach fired his pistol. He could not see the attackers. They were too well hidden. He was firing to cause them to hug their cover and give his father the precious seconds Nate needed to get Evelyn inside.

Just as Nate reached the doorway, Winona rushed out. She had her own rifle, and, seeing her son shoot into the trees, she did the same. Nate went on past.

At a gesture from Zach, Winona backed into the cabin and immediately began to reload.

A moment later Zach was inside and he slammed the door shut. Running to the window, he sought some sign of the hostiles. His gaze happened to alight on Niwot. "Damn," he said aloud, and set to reloading his weapons.

Nate sat Evelyn and the arrow on the table, and placed his big hands on her shoulders. "Are you all right?"

"I'm fine, Pa," Evelyn said hollowly, struggling to come to grips with Niwot's death and the attempt to slay her. It had all happened so fast.

"Stay put," Nate directed, and darted to where his Hawken was propped against the wall near the door. From a peg on the wall he took his ammo pouch and powder horn and slung them across his chest.

"Who do you think it is?" Winona asked while sliding the ramrod from its housing. "The Blackfeet, maybe? Or the Bloods?"

They had clashed with both tribes on several occasions.

"There hasn't been any sign of a war party anywhere near our valley since we got here," Nate said. He joined his son in peering out. "Anything?"

"Not a lick of movement," Zach said. "I wonder how many there are."

"At least three," Evelyn informed him.

Winona finished reloading and noticed the arrow. Picking it up, she examined it closely as she crossed to the window. "I have never seen one like this, husband. Have you?"

Nate had forgotten about it. He studied the shaft, his brow knitting in perplexity. No two tribes fashioned arrows exactly alike. Some used ash. Some used white elm. Some used hickory or mulberry. Some tribes cut grooves on their arrows; others did not. The markings, too, were always different. The upshot was that a savvy frontiersman could tell which tribe had made a given arrow simply by looking at it. Nate was familiar with the arrows used by every tribe in the northern Rockies and plains, but he had never seen an arrow like this one. He said as much.

"A new tribe?" Winona said. "From where?"

Nate had a hunch. Their new valley was

situated deep in the mountains where no white man had ever gone before. Few Indians, either. To the west, over the next range, lay thousands of square miles of unexplored country, virgin wilderness like that which existed when the first human set foot on the North American continent. He had been to the top of the range and found a pass through to the next valley. Twice he had spied tendrils of smoke in the far distance, signifying a possible village. But he had not gone to investigate. Now he wished he had.

"Whoever they are, they made a mistake tangling with us," Zach growled. "If they had harmed sis, I'd kill every last one."

Evelyn was moved by the emotion in his voice. At moments like this she realized he truly did care for her. "What about the others?" she asked.

Zach turned. "Other Indians?"

"No, stupid. Your wife, and Shakespeare and Blue Water Woman? Won't they have heard the shots and come running?"

Worry bit into Zach. That was exactly what they would do. His wife would be an easy target for the lurkers in the trees. "I'm going out," he announced, and made for the door.

"Hold on," Nate said, taking hold of his

arm. "They might be waiting for us to show ourselves."

"I don't care," Zach said. "Lou will be here any moment." The mere thought of her being harmed was enough to turn his blood to ice. Louisa was everything to him. He loved her so deeply, sometimes it hurt. He would lie in bed at night, watching her sleep, in awe of her beauty, and amazed by the fact that she had chosen him out of all the men there were.

Nate saw his son's face darken. "Don't be rash." He was all too aware of the rages to which Zach was prone in the savage heat of a fight. Zach would go berserk and wouldn't stop until all his foes were dead. "We'll hear her. Then we will run out together to warn her."

"I can't wait, Pa," Zach insisted, shrugging loose. "The war party might be attacking my cabin."

"We haven't heard any shots," Nate said, but he was wasting his breath. His son was already opening the door.

"Go with him," Winona said.

Nate did not need more urging. He glued himself to his son's heels, moving to one side and crouching once they were out. Wedging the Hawken to his shoulder, he waited for more arrows to rain down. But none did.

Zach gazed to the north. A horse and rider were flying toward them. Louisa was riding bareback, her lithe form bent low. She was prudently watching the trees. "That's my gal," he said proudly.

The doorway framed Winona. "What are they waiting for? Why don't they do something?"

"Strange, we haven't heard a peep out of them," Nate said, probing every shadow and nook. Warriors had a habit of whooping and yelling when they attacked, but not these.

"Maybe we scared them off," Winona ventured.

"With a few measly shots?" Nate was skeptical. But if it *were* a tribe from the far valley, it could be they had never seen a gun. Many tribes were terrified of firearms at first.

In a flurry of hoofbeats and a cloud of dust, Louisa King arrived. She vaulted from her roan while it was still in motion and sprang to her husband's side. "I heard the shots and came as quick as I could."

Hardly had she spoken when more hooves drummed, and around the cabin from the south came Nate's best friend and mentor, Shakespeare McNair, and McNair's Flathead wife, Blue Water Woman. Both bristled with rifles and pistols and knives and tomahawks. Shakespeare glanced about, bellowing, "How now, Horatio? What is the meaning of this unseemly uproar?"

Nate could always count on McNair to talk like no other man alive. It came from McNair's fondness for the Bard of Avon. Some might call it an obsession. Decades ago, McNair had come across *The Collected Works of William Shakespeare* and lost himself in its excellence. McNair had read the volume so many times, he could quote William S., as McNair called him, by the hour. It accounted for McNair's nickname, which he gladly adopted.

"Well? Answer me," Shakespeare said, swinging down. "Or have you so much ear wax for brains that you can't speak?"

"Be nice, husband," Blue Water Woman scolded. She was remarkable for her finely chiseled features, and for her ability to match wits with her husband. "Is everyone all right?" she asked, handing her reins to Shakespeare.

"So far," Winona said.

Shakespeare was staring at the reins. A big bruiser of a man, his shoulder-length hair, mustache and beard were as white as the snow that crowned several of the encircling peaks. "What's this, then? Am I the stable boy?"

"Pay no attention to him," Blue Water Woman said dryly. "He's in one of his moods."

"She puts her tongue a little in her heart, and chides with thinking," Shakespeare quoted. Then, to Nate, "I hope you know you interrupted my morning nap."

"What?"

"I take one in the afternoon, too. At my age naps are like chocolate. You can never have enough."

Temporarily distracted by their arrival, Nate sobered and motioned at the arrows that dotted the ground. "We have company."

"A friendly bunch, I see." Shakespeare let the reins drop. Facing the wall of vegetation across the cleared space, he cupped a hand to his mouth. "Thou art a boil, a plague-sore! I find you cowardly and vile!"

"What good did that do?" Blue Water Woman asked.

"It showed them who can yell the loudest." Shakespeare leveled his Hawken and started toward the trees. "Come, Horatio. Let's greet them properly. The rest of you, inside."

No one argued. As the first white man in the Rockies, Shakespeare's experience was vast, his judgment rarely wrong.

"I wish I could get my wife to listen to me like she listens to you," Nate commented while catching up.

"Wives always think other men are smarter than their husbands. It gives them an excuse to act superior. Now hush, pup."

Nate strained his senses but heard nothing, saw no one. He had a fair idea of where the bowmen had been, and warily advanced on the spot. The woods were unnaturally still. Half expecting to be greeted with a war whoop and cold steel, he slipped soundlessly into the undergrowth.

Shakespeare slowed so he could watch Nate's back. To him, Nate was the son he'd never had, and as dear to him as life itself. Not that he would ever admit it to Nate. Some emotions ran too deep for words.

Shakespeare had been joshing about the nap. He had been behind his cabin on the shore of the lake their homesteads bordered, fishing, when the shots rumbled across the valley and echoed off the timbered slopes high above. It had been the work of mere minutes to saddle the horses, and by the time he was done, Blue Water Woman had rushed out armed to the teeth. *A good woman, that gal,* he reflected.

The stillness of the forest bothered Shakespeare not one whit. He suspected the Indians were gone. A short search proved him right.

— The ground was hard packed and rocky. Nate roved about, seeking tracks anyway. He found a partial heel print and the indistinct outline of an entire foot in some dust. Neither showed much detail, which was too bad. Just as no two tribes made their arrows exactly alike, neither did they craft identical footwear. A clear footprint might tell Nate whom he was up against.

"You're wasting your time, Horatio. They're long gone."

"We don't know that for sure," Nate said.

"Yes, we do." Shakespeare pointed.

Half a mile up, on the very mountain crowned by the pass into the next valley, was a meadow. Crossing it, strung out in single file, were three dusky figures.

"It's them!" Nate exclaimed.

"I didn't think it was wood imps."

"What are we waiting for? Let's go after them! On horseback we can catch them before they reach the pass."

"Maybe. Maybe not," Shakespeare replied. "The question is, do you really want to?"

"Huh?"

"Your way with words astounds me sometimes," Shakespeare quipped. Placing the stock of his rifle on the ground, he leaned on the barrel. "Follow me on this, son. Say we go after them. Say we do overtake them. What then?"

"I pay them back for what they've done," Nate said.

"Ah. By paying them back, you mean kill them. What do you think will happen when they don't show up at their village? I'll tell you. Warriors will be sent to find them. We could find ourselves up to our necks in hostiles. Is that what you want?"

"No," Nate grudgingly admitted. "But we have to do something. They killed Niwot."

"I saw," Shakespeare said. "A shame, that. I didn't know the lad well, but he was always polite, and anyone with good manners is worth his weight in chipmunks."

"I can never tell when you're serious."

"Watch my nose. It twitches when I'm not." Shakespeare thoughtfully regarded the distant figures, then said, "This is bad. We can't post a guard at the pass every minute from now until eternity."

"What do you suggest? That we pay their village a visit and smoke the pipe of peace?"

"For all we know, they kill strangers on sight." Shakespeare shook his head. "No, we're better off avoiding them."

Nate was mildly exasperated by the notion that they do nothing. "But they know where we are now. They'll be back."

"Not if we slam the door in their face."

"I've lost your trail," Nate admitted. Which was not unusual, given the quirky mental meanderings to which his friend was prone.

"So far as we know, the only way into our valley from the other side of that range is through the pass, correct? So what if we close the pass? They can't spill our blood if they can't get to us."

Nate thought of the defile with its high walls of solid stone. "And how exactly do we go about achieving this marvel? Will you sneeze and bring it crashing down?"

"Sarcasm ill becomes you." Shakespeare sniffed. "But as it so happens, I have a keg of black powder I can spare. Place it right, and our new neighbors will have to dig through tons of rock to come a-calling."

Scratching his chin, Nate nodded. The idea had merit. They could set out tomorrow at first light. It would take most of a day to climb to the pass. Add a few hours to set the charge where it would cause the most damage, and by tomorrow night his family and friends would be safe. Or as safe as life in the wild ever was. He complimented McNair.

"When you have lived as long as I have, Horatio, you learn a few things," Shakespeare said. "First and foremost, marry a female with brains and some of it is bound to rub off. Second, it's wiser to avoid a battle than take part in one. Spilling blood is fine and dandy except when some of the blood might be yours."

"You make it sound as if you are ancient," Nate said.

"I am, son, I am," Shakespeare replied. "We are all the sullen presage of our own decay. And of late I have more aches in my joints and bones than I have joints and bones."

"We all grow old."

"Spoken like someone in the prime of his life who has no notion of what old age is about."

"You'll be around a good long while yet," Nate predicted, but secretly he was troubled. His friend did appear somewhat peaked. To lose McNair would be the greatest hurt since the death of his mother.

"As a fortune-teller you would make a good bartender," Shakespeare joshed. "But I like grasping at straws as much as the next jasper. Let's hope you're right. And let's head back."

Zach and Lou had moved Niwot's body

close to the south wall. Winona was draping a blanket over it while Evelyn looked on.

"Reckon she'll take this hard?" Shakespeare whispered with a bob of his white beard at Nate's youngest.

"Not as hard as I would take it if she had been killed," Nate said. "Or any of you, for that matter." It was his deepest fear.

Zach and Lou came over, rifles ready. "Anything, Pa?"

"They've flown the coop," Nate said. "We saw them making for the pass." He related McNair's plan to ensure the mystery Indians did not return.

"I'll go with you," Zach offered.

"One of us men should stay here, just in case."

Winona walked around the corner. "Why don't all of you come inside? I'll put coffee on and we can talk this over."

"I'll get Evelyn," Nate said, and went to walk past Winona. Her hand on his chest stopped him.

"She needs to be alone, husband. I heard you say Niwot's killers are gone, so she should be safe. But stay near the window, just in case."

Nate not only stayed near it, he opened it so he could hear better. From the side of the cabin came a soft sob that plucked at his heartstrings. No parent liked to see his children suffer. He was gazing at the towering peaks to the west when McNair appeared at his elbow. "What's on the other side?"

Following his gaze, Shakespeare said. "Mountains and valleys and valleys and mountains."

"In all your wandering you never set foot in this neck of the country?"

"Hell, Nate, the Rockies stretch from Mexico to Canada and from the prairie to the Great Salt Lake. There's more I haven't seen than I have. It would take ten lifetimes to cover every acre."

Nate would not let it rest. "You must have heard stories. Didn't a few trappers try their luck hereabouts in the early days?"

"Most of the trapping done was north and east of here," Shakespeare said. "But yes, I've heard stories."

"Tell me."

"What for? You can't tell what's true and what isn't. Remember Jim Bridger and that whopper he liked to spout about the time he went to California and came across petrified birds warbling petrified songs in petrified trees?"

"Tell me anyway," Nate persisted.

"There's usually a kernel of truth to every

tall tale."

Shakespeare sighed. "The Utes say the country yonder is bad medicine. They won't go anywhere near it. The same with the Paiutes, who live to the southwest. To the northwest are the Diggers, who some say are Shoshones even though they don't have anything in common with Winona's people." He paused. "Due west is taboo for them, too."

Sudden insight filled Nate. "That's why we found this valley empty." He had wondered about that. Rich with game, thick with timber on the slopes and grass on the valley floor, and with a crystal lake fed in part by runoff from a glacier, the valley had everything anyone could ask for. Yet there had been no trace whatsoever of previous inhabitants. "It's too close to the part of the mountains all those tribes regard as bad medicine."

Shakespeare gave a light cough. "Actually, Horatio, it's *part* of the bad medicine. The Utes say there is a fish in the lake big enough to swallow canoes. The Paiutes call this the Valley of the Hairy Men. The Diggers believe the red-haired cannibals used to live here."

Nate had heard of the cannibals. A surprising number of tribes had legends about them. It was claimed that back when the world was young, the red-haired cannibals preyed on the unwary, killing countless people, until they were wiped out in a great war. Some tribes believed a few pockets of cannibals still remained, deep in the mountains where no one ever went. Nate had scoffed when he initially heard the story. Just as he had scoffed at stories about lake monsters and thunderbirds and the deadly dwarves and the tree men. Since then he had learned not to dismiss the accounts out of hand.

"I thought you knew all this," Shakespeare said.

"I don't care if the valley is supposed to be bad medicine," Nate replied. "It's our home now. We will do whatever it takes to keep it."

"You can count on me," Shakespeare assured him. "I'm too old to move again. This is where I stay until I'm planted six feet under."

Nate looked at him. "There you go again with that old-age talk. I notice you have all your teeth yet, and men half your age would be happy to be half as spry."

"Beggar that I am, I am even poor in thanks, but I thank you," Shakespeare quoted. "I just never knew you were color blind."

Nate started to laugh but caught himself. From around the corner wafted gentle sobs. Evelyn was still shedding her grief.

Shakespeare heard her, too, and said softly, "Oh, lady, weep no more, lest I give cause to be suspected of more tenderness than doth become a man."

"Losing a friend is hard."

"That's not the half of it," Shakespeare said. "The important thing now is to not lose anyone else."

CHAPTER FOUR

Wakumassee of the Nansusequa had been set adrift on the incoming tide of chaos. The idea that the whites intended to wipe out his people was so preposterous, he imagined it must be some strange joke on the part of Reverend Constantine Stilljoy. "But we be friends!" he exclaimed.

"What does that have to do with anything?" Stilljoy sniffed. "Your son killed white men. Your people must pay. It is as simple as that."

"*All* my people?" Waku was horrified beyond measure. He could understand if the whites demanded Dega must die. A life for a life was fair; three hundred lives for three was not.

"What is wrong, Father?" Dega asked. "Why are you so upset?" His father had stopped translating and looked ill.

Hunumanima, the leader of the Nansusequa, had been slower to grasp the reverend's meaning. But now he rose to his full height, rare anger contorting his features. "You no kill my people!"

"I am afraid you have no say in the matter," Reverend Stilljoy said stiffly.

"But you friend!" Waku reiterated. "You call us children."

Stilljoy indulged in a wry smile. "You poor, deluded savage. When I referred to you as my children, I used the term spiritually. In God's eyes all of us are His children. But some of us are closer to Him than others."

"I not understand," Waku said. "You say you not like us? Your God not like us?"

"My God is your God, whether you know it or not," Reverend Stilljoy explained. "But I have been baptized. You and your people have not. My sins have been forgiven. You and your people have a host of sins to account for. Surely you can see the difference?"

"No," Waku admitted.

"How can I make it simple?" Reverend Stilljoy asked himself. "I know. Think of it this way. Have you ever had to take a rod to one of your children?"

"A rod?" Waku repeated.

"Beat them, either with a switch or your hand," Reverend Stilljoy said. "My father took a switch to me once a week whether I needed a beating or not."

"He hurt you?"

"Only to keep me on the straight and narrow. Sometimes we are too weak to resist temptation by ourselves and must be helped along."

Waku's temples were beginning to pound. "I still not understand." He doubted he ever would.

"Your people had a chance to walk the straight and narrow and chose not to. Their punishment is perdition." Stilljoy parted his coat and removed an engraved silver watch from a vest pocket. He opened the casing to check the time. "It should commence any minute now."

"Father," Dega said. "Tell us what the white man is saying."

In the turmoil of the moment, Waku had been remiss. He made up for it now, and no sooner did he finish than his world was forever altered by three things that took place in a span of heartbeats.

"I go!" Hunumanima announced to Stilljoy, and turned to depart, saying in the Nansusequa tongue, "Our people need us. We must leave."

Thunder pealed, even though there were only a few clouds in the sky, and at the blast

Hunu was violently propelled forward, his arms flung out. Simultaneously, the front of his chest exploded in a shower of blood, bone and gore. Tottering, he looked down at the hole in his sternum. "May Manitoa receive me," he said, and pitched to the ground.

Arthur Forge and the other two white men ran up. Thin tendrils of smoke curled from the end of Forge's rifle. He drew a pistol. All three trained weapons on Wakumassee and his family.

"You better go, Reverend," Forge said. "We'll finish it."

"In a moment. There is no rush."

Waku stared in dismay at Hunu's still form. A scarlet pool was spreading under the body. He had seen men killed before, but never like this, never so coldly, so callously. He wanted to roar in rage. But the self-control for which the People of the Forest prided themselves, and which he had so diligently practiced since he was old enough to embrace the ideal, demanded that he contain himself.

Tihikanima took a halting step toward her father but stopped when one of the white men pointed a rifle at her and growled in his incomprehensible tongue. The three whites were aglow with blood lust. It would not take much to provoke them.

Teni had a hand to her throat. She was transfixed with indecision. Every instinct warned her to flee, to grab Miki and get out of there, but the white men would slay them just as they had slain Hunumanima.

Only Degamawaku showed no apparent concern. Inwardly, he was girding himself for what he must do. All he needed was the right moment.

Reverend Stilljoy was staring at Hunu. "I regret that. I truly do. But what must be, must be."

It was as if a veil lifted from Waku's eyes. He saw Stilljoy as the reverend truly was and not as Waku had imagined him to be. "You not our friend. You enemy."

"Not true," Reverend Stilljoy said resentfully. "I am beyond those distinctions. I am my brother's keeper. I do what is best for the good of all."

Waku pointed at Hunu. "That good? Kill my people good?"

"You haven't been listening. Yes, much good will derive from it. The other tribes will know not to oppose us. Your land, some of the best in the entire region, will be opened for settlement."

"You not right in head," Waku said.

Reverend Stilljoy smiled that maddening

smile of his. "Quite the contrary. I will go among the other tribes preaching salvation. I will use the Nansusequa as an example of the fate that befalls those who refuse to embrace the one true faith."

Waku had it then, and was appalled. Not at the white man in the black coat, but at himself for being so blind and gullible.

"That is another reason I agreed not to oppose this cleansing," Reverend Stilljoy was saying. "I realized your people would never accept our religion. You are too entrenched in your heathen ways." He shrugged. "Since you are bound for hell anyway, it might as well be now as later."

Suddenly, from the distance, there came the boom and pop of many guns.

"Ah. That would be our militia. They were to surround your village and at a given command, shoot every warrior in sight with their first volley. Then they will deal with the few men who are left." Stilljoy added offhandedly, "And the women and children, of course."

An invisible hand had gripped Waku's chest and slowly squeezed. He had never cried in his life but now tears misted his eyes.

"Enough of this jabber," Arthur Forge said. "Out of the way, Reverend. I have a son to avenge."

"Very well." Stilljoy stood. "But wait until I am out of sight."

Dega's moment had come. He was wearing a green buckskin shirt and leggings, the shirt hanging loose below his waist. While Stilljoy talked, Dega had eased his hand up under the shirt and molded his palm to the hilt of his knife. Stilljoy was between him and the one called Forge. He sprung forward and shoved Stilljoy against Forge, then turned and slashed his knife across the jugular of one of the other white men before he could even raise his gun. Dega quickly plunged the blade deep into the ribs of the third gunman, moving so fast his opponent was frozen in fear. Both were killing strokes.

The Nansusequa were a peace-loving people but they were realists. On occasion they were compelled to defend their territory, and to that end they practiced the arts of war under the tutelage of warriors who had proven their merit in battle.

Reverend Stilljoy squawked and clutched at Arthur Forge to keep from falling. "I beg your pardon. The silly youth pushed me."

Stilljoy had not seen what happened to the other two, but Forge had. "Out of my way, you damned simpleton!" he bellowed, and shoved Stilljoy far harder than Dega had. Forge leveled his rifle at Dega's chest, but Stilljoy's flailing arm struck the barrel, swatting it aside just as the rifle went off. The lead that was to end Dega's life plowed a furrow in the earth instead.

Dega pounced. But as he struck, Arthur Forge shoved Reverend Stilljoy toward him. Dega's knife sheared into the reverend's scrawny back high on the left side. Stilljoy stiffened, then collapsed, falling to his hands and knees.

Arthur Forge whirled and ran.

Racing around Stilljoy, Dega gave chase. He had only gone a few steps when Forge reached the horses and without slowing or breaking stride swung up onto a brown horse and slapped his legs against its side. In a twinkling the animal had borne him out of the clearing and into the forest, which promptly swallowed them.

Dega came to a stop. He could not catch them on foot. The other horses were still there, but he had never ridden and would not know how to go about it. A loud gasp and a groan drew him back to Stilljoy.

Blood dribbled from the reverend's slack mouth. He looked up. "What have you done, you wretched heathen?"

"What did he say?" Dega asked his father, but Waku was listening to the distant crackle of rifles and pistols and did not answer.

"A pox on you and your kind!" Reverend Stilljoy wheezed. "I call on the Lord to smite you for your sins!"

Dega debated silencing him but elected not to. His little sister was trembling with shock at the violent deaths.

"I am a light in the wilderness, and you have snuffed out my wick," Reverend Stilljoy declared. "Countless souls will not be redeemed because of you. May you burn in perdition for all eternity."

"I wish he would stop talking," Teni said. She had never liked the sound of the reverend's voice. It always made her skin itch.

Stilljoy raised his pale face to the heavens. "Hear me, oh Lord! Hear your humble servant! May angels bear me to your bosom that I may bask in your glory and righteousness for all time."

"He babbles," Teni said.

"He calls on his God." Dega hefted his knife but still did not use it. "On That Which Is In All Things."

"They are not the same," their mother said. Tihi used to think that perhaps they were. Stilljoy, on his visits to their village, had claimed that his God Almighty was the white name for Manitoa. But now she saw that was not true. To believe in Manitoa was to have a reverence for all living things. You could not have one without the other. The whites clearly did not.

Stilljoy's head drooped and his thin frame swayed. "May all of you rot and fester in torment," he said weakly. "I cannot forgive your foul offense." He raised a hand to the sky. "Into Your hands I commend my spirit." With that, he died.

The crack of rifles and pistols to the west had become more sporadic. Mingled with the shots were screams and shrieks and wails.

Dega did not waste another moment. He turned to his father, saying, "Our people need us." The stricken look on his father's face held him until one of the horses whinnied. Dega looked at them. A man on horseback could go a lot faster than a man on foot. Maybe he had been wrong in not trying to go after Arthur Forge. But he could use one now even more. *Dare I try?* he asked himself.

Sheathing his knife, Dega ran to the animals and gripped the saddle of a dusky horse as he had seen Forge grip his saddle. He swung up and sat waiting for the horse to do something, to bite or rear or buck. But all it did was stand there, unmoving. Dega remembered how Forge had gripped the long strips of leather, the reins, he believed they were called, and he did the same. The horse did not move, so Dega slapped his legs as Forge had done. He nearly went tumbling when the animal lunged into motion. Bending, Dega grabbed its mane and clamped his legs tight.

The horse was heading north. Dega needed to go west. But he did not know how to turn the thing. He tried jerking on the mane but that had no effect. He pulled on the reins, and to his consternation the horse came to a stop.

Dega experimented. Since the reins were secured to the animal's head, he reasoned that they must have something to do with determining the direction the horse took. He pulled to the left and the horse turned. He pulled to the right and the horse turned again. When he pulled the reins toward him, the horse stopped.

"This is not so hard," Dega told himself, and slapped his legs. The horse galloped westward. Pleased with himself, Dega straightened. Too late, he saw the low limb in his path. It caught him across the chest. Pain nearly caused him to cry out as he was knocked off and tumbled head over heels.

Dega lay on his stomach, a ringing in his ears, his ribs a welter of torment. Rising on his elbows, he gingerly pressed a hand to his chest. Nothing appeared to be broken. Even better, the horse had gone only a short way and stopped, and now was looking back at him as if confused.

"Be patient with me, brother," Dega said.

The animal was well trained. It did not act up as Dega slowly approached and patted its neck.

"Thank you, brother. I am new to riding. Help me to learn, and I will treat you well." Taking the reins, Dega mounted. This time when he flicked the reins he did not hold on to the mane. He did not need to. His confidence climbing, he brought the horse to a gallop. He found that if he let the animal do as it pleased, it avoided trees and thickets and other obstacles without him having to do much of anything except keep it pointed in the direction he wanted it to go.

The thunder of the guns had faded. Dega was surprised he had not heard the war whoops of Nansusequa warriors as they rallied to defend the village. Surely the whites had not slain them all.

The horse was bearing him so swiftly that Dega would soon find out. He was congratulating himself on his cleverness when it occurred to him that the animal's pounding hoofs were making a lot of noise, noise the whites were bound to hear. Since stealth was called for, Dega pulled on the reins.

Just then a figure hurtled out of the trees toward him.

Back at the clearing, Wakumassee of the Nansusequa could not tear his gaze from the body of the man who had meant so much to him. Hunumanima had been more than the father of his wife. Hunu had been his best friend. They were much alike, the two of them. Both had been devoted to peace.

Their voices, more than any others, had urged the People of the Forest to live in harmony with the whites. There were dissenters, a few elders and others who said the whites could not be trusted. Always, it was Waku and Hunu who persuaded the dissenters to smother their animosity and reach out to the whites in friendship. To set an example, Waku and Hunu had even gone so far as learning to speak the white tongue.

The two of them had done all that on behalf of the whites, and now Hunu was dead, their people under attack.

"What have I done?" Waku asked aloud.

"Husband?" Tihikanima grasped his arm. "We must hurry to our village. Why do you

98

stand here like this?"

"Hunu," Waku said simply.

"He was my father and I loved him dearly," Tihi said. "But now we must think of the rest of our people. Do you not hear the screams?"

Only then did Waku become aware of the new sounds mixed with the shots. "Come." He made for the trail, settling into a jog. His wife ran on his left, and his daughters trailed them. They ran smoothly, with the practiced ease of long-distance runners.

Tihi cocked her head. "How is it that the whites invaded our land without us being aware?" she wondered.

"They traveled at night," Waku guessed. His people invariably retired to the Great Lodges after the sun went down. Sentries were always posted, which Reverend Stilljoy had known, making it likely the whites had waited until dawn, when the village was astir, to sneak in close and wait for the command to kill.

"How many do you think there are?"

"I cannot say." Waku had never bothered to learn the population of New Albion. It had to be in the hundreds, and that just in the settlement. Add the farms and homesteads in the outlying areas and the total white population was likely two to three times that of the Nansusequa.

"Our people must go on the warpath," Tihi urged. "We must call a meeting of all the tribes and unite to drive the whites from our lands. The Shawnee, the Yuchi, the Chickasaw, the Muskogee — we must send runners to each."

Waku had never heard his wife talk like this, and said so.

"This is war," Tihi said simply.

"It is the Nansusequa way to seek peace with all," Waku said.

"You can still say that after what the whites have done?"

Waku had spoken out of habit. He had been a staunch advocate of living in harmony with all people for so long that to contemplate doing differently did not come easily.

Teni was listening to her parents with only half an ear. A great fear had seized her. Not for herself, or her family, but for her people, the People of the Forest, and the life she loved. Her parents did not seem to see the truth, but she did. Her mother talked of sending messengers to the Yuchis and others and driving the whites out, but her mother was blind to that which Teni had seen with her own eyes. They couldn't drive the whites off. The whites were too strong, too many.

Plus, the whites had two other advantages over the Nansusequa and the surrounding tribes: horses and guns. Horses enabled them to travel much more swiftly than the People of the Forest or their potential allies. Guns let the whites kill from a greater distance than lances and most bows, and had the added effect of cowing those unaccustomed to the noise and the smoke and the small balls of lead that were invisible until they tore through flesh and organs and left wounds far disproportionate to their size.

The tribes could never hope to withstand such might. Especially as Reverend Stilljoy had once told them that the whites possessed other, more formidable weapons, among them a great gun that fired lead balls as big as her head and containers of black sand, that, when lit, could destroy a Great Lodge.

Teni's fear writhed inside her like a living thing. Her people were not merely fighting to defend their village and their territory; they were fighting for their very survival against an enemy who so far had defeated every tribe that dared oppose it.

Teni realized her parents were pulling ahead. She went to run faster but had to stay at the same pace or little Miki would be left behind. They rounded a bend in the trail, and then another. Soon they would be near the village. She was surprised to see that her parents had stopped. Then shapes materialized out of the vegetation.

Degamawaku was leading the horse by the reins. Cradled in his arms was a small crumpled green form.

A gasp escaped Teni. She recognized her cousin Keti, who was two summers younger than Miki.

Keti's dress was splattered with red and her forehead, leaking blood, had collapsed inward. Her eyes were closed, and she quaked as if she were cold.

"A white man clubbed her," Dega said, kneeling and gently depositing the girl on the grass. "She told me she was the only one to escape. Then she passed out."

"That cannot be," Waku said softly.

Miki turned to Teni and buried her face in Teni's dress. "I cannot bear to look. I am so sorry."

The shooting and the screaming had ceased. A profound silence had fallen over the primeval forest.

Tihi knelt and carefully examined Keti. "She has been shot as well as clubbed," she said, indicating a hole low on the girl's side.

Keti moaned. Her eyelids fluttered open "Aunt Tihi?" she said so softly they barely heard her. "Is that you?"

"It is, child." Tihi lightly kissed the girl's cheek. "Be still. We will tend you."

"They killed them," Keti said. She had an oval face with large eyes that lent her the innocence of a fawn.

"Killed whom?"

"My mother. My father. My brothers. The whites killed them. They killed everyone."

Tihi gently squeezed the child's shoulder. "My sister is dead? Who else? How many are alive yet?"

Dega let the reins drop. They were too close to the village to use the horse. "I will go look," he volunteered. "Stay hidden in case the whites are searching for her." He spun to hasten away.

"I am going with you," Teni said. She had given care of Miki to her mother.

"It is not safe."

"I can be as quiet as you," Teni said. She had to see for herself. "They are my people, too."

Dega glanced at their parents. Tihi was hugging Miki and holding Keti's hand. Their father stared blankly into space, overcome by the calamity. "Very well."

As children, the pair had spent countless

days playing in the woods. It got so they moved as if joined at the hip. Now, Teni's movements duplicated Dega's. She made no more noise than he did. When he stopped, she stopped. When he eased onto his belly and crawled, she eased onto hers.

Coiling columns of smoke rose above the treetops while an acrid fog clung close to the ground.

Teni's nose tingled. She quickly pinched it to keep from sneezing. When the urge faded, she lowered her hand.

Dega thought he heard something. He glanced to the right and saw trees shrouded in smoke. He glanced to the left and froze.

Stalking in their direction was a stocky white man. He carried a rifle and had a big knife in a leather sheath on his left hip.

From his right hip dangled a fresh scalp.

CHAPTER FIVE

Dega felt his sister's fingers clamp on to his arm, felt her nails dig into his skin. He did not blame her. The scalp hanging from the white man's belt was a Nansusequa scalp. The whites were taking the hair of those they killed.

Dega had heard of the practice. Neither the People of the Forest nor their immediate neighbors took scalps, but he knew other tribes did. So, too, did the whites, he had heard, usually for bounty money. The thought jarred him. Could it be, he asked himself, that the whites would collect a bounty on his people? Did that have something to do with the attack? Was there more to it than simple revenge? It was worth later thought.

The white man had not seen them.

Dega pried at Teni's fingers, and she slowly removed her hand. He drew his knife and coiled. He counted on his sister not to move or make a sound. But she did. Teni gave vent to the chilling horror that struck her at sight of the scalp with a part sob, part mew.

Instantly, the white man swung toward them. An oath escaped him, and he jerked the rifle to his shoulder.

Dega was already in motion. Even as he bounded forward, he realized he could not reach the white man before the rifle went off. So he did the only thing he could; he threw his knife. Since the white man's arm was in front of his chest and the rifle blocked his throat, Dega threw the knife low. The keen blade sliced into the man's groin, startling him, and he raised his cheek from the rifle to glance down.

Another bound, and Dega slammed into the scalptaker's shoulder while simultaneously wrenching the rifle free. He nearly tripped over the white man's legs. Recovering, he swept the hardwood stock against the man's temple just as the man opened his mouth to scream or shout. There was a crunch and the white man folded.

Crouching, Dega glanced about them. Evidently the white man had been alone. Dega saw no others. Tugging his knife from the body, he wiped the blade clean on the dead man's shirt. He began to rise when an idea gave him pause. Quickly, he stripped off the powder horn and ammo pouch and slung them over his own chest.

"What are you doing?" Teni whispered. "You do not know what to do with any of those."

"I can learn." Dega thrust out the rifle. "Hold this for me."

Teni averted her gaze from the scalp. "You carry it." She did not care to touch anything that belonged to the awful man.

"I need my hands free in case we meet another one." Again Dega thrust the rifle at her and this time she gingerly took it.

Only a few shrieks were borne to Dega's ears as they crept on, first on elbows and knees and then on their bellies.

Teni was stricken with fear that they would stumble on more whites. She held the rifle close to her so it would not drag or snag, which made it harder for her to move silently.

A thicket loomed. Beyond it lay the village.

Dega motioned for Teni to stay where she was, but when he moved on, so did she. Exercising painstaking stealth, they edged forward. Mixed with the scent of smoke was the sickly sweet smell of blood.

Teni dreaded what they would see. She bit her lower lip to keep from crying out, and it proved well she did.

Dega's whole body seemed to go numb.

A gray pall hung thick above the Great Lodges. Of the five, four were ablaze. But it was not the flames that riveted brother and sister; it was the bodies. Bodies lay everywhere. Hundreds of bodies, the majority garbed in green. Bodies of warriors, bodies of women, bodies of children. Bodies strewn in postures of savage death. Bodies that had been shot. Bodies that had been clubbed. Bodies that had been stabbed. In places the blood had formed pools deep enough to wade in.

Among the fallen, whites roved with bloody knives, finishing off those not dead and lifting hair.

Teni's fear turned to horror. She stared at lifeless face after lifeless face. To her left lay one of her best friends. At another spot sprawled her aunt, forehead blown away. A youth of seventeen summers, of whom Teni had been especially fond, was on his back with two bullet holes in his chest, his face mutilated, his hair gone. Teni bit down hard on her lip to check a sob.

Some of the whites were standing around talking and smiling, pleased by the slaughter. Laughter rippled across the nightmare scene.

Dega had to resist an impulse to rise and fling himself among them in a killing rage. It would accomplish nothing other than to get him and his sister killed. There were more than a hundred whites. Some he recognized from New Albion. Others were from the outlying farms. They evinced no remorse, no regret.

Remembering Reverend Stilljoy's comments, Dega wondered if maybe the whites had wanted to wipe out the Nansusequa long before this, and had only been waiting for an excuse. An excuse he gave them by killing his sister's attackers.

Not all the whites were talking or taking hair. About twenty were at both ends of the only lodge still standing, the Council Lodge. Their rifles and pistols were trained on the openings.

A tall white in buckskins cupped a hand to his mouth and called out in the language of the Nansusequa.

Dega had seen this man before. His name was Hardegan, and he was well known among the tribes of the region. Hardegan lived deep in the woods with a woman of the Delaware and was more like an Indian than a white man. He knew the country well and often hired out as a guide and scout to those who did not. Now and then, when passing through Nansusequa territory, he stopped at their village and drank green tea with Hunumanima and the elders. The Nansusequa had considered Hardegan a friend. Yet again they had been mistaken.

"Come out with your arms above your heads!" the scout bellowed. He spoke their tongue fluently, as he did many others.

"You will kill us!" came the muffled reply.

Hardegan consulted with a portly white man with a pig face, another man whom Dega recognized. Luther was his name, and among the whites he was held in high regard because he had more land, and more money, than anyone else.

"We give you our word we will not harm you," Hardegan shouted into the lodge.

"You lie!"

Dega knew that voice. It was Mawama-neuk, an elder. The same elder who had opposed Hunu's plan to meet with Reverend Stilljoy.

In confirmation Hardegan shouted, "There can't be more than thirty of you left in there, Mawa. We will starve you out if we have to."

"At least we will die with dignity."

Hardegan was translating for the benefit

110

of Luther, who shook a pudgy fist and spat words at some length. When Luther was done, Hardegan turned to the Council Lodge. "The whites are not willing to wait for you to starve."

"Let them rush us then," Mawa said. "We are few but we will kill as many as we can before they kill us."

"The whites are not so foolish," Hardegan said. "They have a better idea." He paused. "If you do not surrender, they will burn the Council Lodge to the ground with you and all the others inside it."

There was no response.

"Mawa, we have shared tea," Hardegan said. "Believe me when I say you do not want to die this way. Think of the women in there with you. Think of the children."

"Yes, we have shared tea." Mawa's tone was bitter. "Yet you helped the whites. You brought them here. Thanks to you, they surrounded us and shot us from ambush. They are cowards, these whites of yours."

"They pay well," Hardegan said.

"How much was our blood worth to you?" Mawa asked.

"Five hundred dollars." Since there was no word in the Nansusequa tongue for the money the whites used, Hardegan had to say it in English. But Mawa understood.

111

Years of trading with the whites had taught the Nansusequa that money was the one thing whites valued more than any other. "Half to guide them, half to keep my mouth shut after."

"May the money be a curse on you and yours for as long as you draw breath," Mawa said.

"It won't work. I'm not superstitious." Hardegan had made it a point not to show himself in the opening. Now he leaned toward it, saying, "I promise your end will be quick and painless. A bullet to the brain beats being roasted alive."

"We are the People of the Forest," Mawa said. "We do not give up."

Luther listened to Hardegan's translation in mounting fury. He barked orders, and men ran to comply. Exactly what they were running after soon became apparent: torches. Other whites gathered at the two ends of the lodge to reinforce those already there.

Teni bent her lips to Dega's ear. "We must do something, brother," she anxiously whispered.

"No."

"They will be killed!" Teni could scarcely contain herself. Her every nerve tingled with the impulse to rise up and run to the aid of the Nansusequa in the Council Lodge.

Dega knew his sister as well as he knew himself. Accordingly, he clamped one hand over her mouth and the other around her wrist while hissing in her ear, "Lie still! The whites will see us if you do not calm yourself, and there are too many for us to fight." Teni tried to speak, and Dega gave her jaw a hard shake. "Listen to me! I like Mawa as much as you do. I would save him and the others if I could. But I cannot, and if we die, who is left? Father and Mother and Miki and Keti. That is all."

Tears filled Teni's eyes.

"I am sorry, sister," Dega whispered. "But for you and me to die for no purpose is pointless."

Most of the whites were drifting toward the Council Lodge to witness what would come next. A dozen torches were in evidence, but so far no one had applied them to the lodge walls or roof. They were awaiting the command.

Hardegan and Luther had their heads together. Finally the scout stepped close to the opening and shouted, "This is your last chance, Mawa. Come out now or be burned alive."

Mawa did not reply.

Luther nodded at the men with torches and they dashed in close and flung their brands. One of them strayed near an opening. As his arm rose to throw, a lance streaked out of the lodge. The point caught him high in the chest and pierced his torso from front to back. He screamed as he died.

Angry shouts erupted. A white man jerked his rifle and fired into the opening. Others followed his example. Still others fired at the walls.

Luther waved his stout arms and did a lot of shouting, and the whites stopped shooting. Relatively few set to reloading.

Later, much later, Dega would wonder if Mawa planned it that way. For no sooner did the firing cease than Mawa and a dozen warriors led a charge out of the Council Lodge. Behind them came the women, and behind the women, the children. Everyone who could bear weapons did: lances, knives, clubs, sticks, anything that was handy.

Teni whimpered and sought to stand, but her brother slammed her down again. He was right to do so but she resented him for it.

The charge caught the whites off guard. Mawa and the wedge of warriors slew right and left. They were making for the forest, but a hundred whites rushed to bar their way.

It was a magnificent, valiant, doomed effort.

Mawa and the remaining Nansusequa fought with a ferocity born of desperation, but there were simply too many whites. Many of the latter did not reload but plunged into the melee wielding their rifles like clubs or slashing with their broad-bladed knives. Curses and screams rose as thick as the dust.

The press of furiously battling figures became so intertwined, Dega could not tell friend from enemy. He glimpsed a Nansusequa here and there, fighting fiercely. Always, they were buried under an avalanche of rifle stocks and gleaming blades.

Teni was on the verge of tears. She closed her eyes to shut out the carnage, but she could still hear the shrieks and oaths and thuds. Jamming her fingers in her ears, she pressed her face to the grass and choked down great sobs, smothering them in her throat.

Dega anxiously scanned the vicinity, afraid the whites would hear her, but none was anywhere near the thicket. "Please," he whispered.

Teni slowly subsided and lay as limp as a

wet fur. She felt drained of emotion and vitality, and craved nothing so much as to curl into a ball and cry. But she dared not shed tears or risk being found out.

The bedlam was also subsiding. The din faded to random grunts and groans and a few last blows.

The Nansuseqa were down. Every warrior, every woman, every child had been slain. Multiple wounds testified to the ferocity of their struggle.

Luther, Dega noticed, had not taken part. He had stood well back and let the other whites do the fighting. The reason was not hard to fathom; cowardice was etched plainly on his piggish features.

One other person had not taken part: Hardegan, the scout. But it was not cowardice in his case. His features reflected deep sorrow and disgust.

Wounded whites were being tended. A handful spread out and walked toward the woods on the other side of the clearing. Another handful started moving to the north.

"We must go," Dega whispered, and started to slide back. But Teni did not move. "Did you hear me, sister?"

"I want to lie here a while. Go without me."

"It will mean your death. The whites are searching for any who escaped." Dega cupped her chin and raised her head, so she could see for herself. "Enough of this. Are you the same woman who fought to keep from being raped? Yet now you are ready to give up?"

"It is not the same, brother," Teni said.

"Why save yourself then, only to throw your life away now?" Dega countered. Both of their lives, for he would not leave without her.

Reluctantly, Teni let him pull her backward. She thought she was past the point of caring what happened to her, but she was wrong. Images of the massacre splashed across her mind, giving birth to a deep rage. The rage, in turn, lent strength to her limbs, so much so that as soon as Dega deemed it safe to stand and run, she raced like a doe back the way they had come.

"I hate whites," Teni declared.

Dega looked at her. "Not all whites are like Luther and those with him."

"Did any try to help us?" Teni snapped. "Where were all our white friends from New Albion? Why did no one warn us?" She did not give him a chance to reply. "The stories told by other tribes are true. Whites are never to be trusted. They speak with two tongues. They have only evil in their hearts."

— For reasons he could not explain, Dega felt compelled to say, "Remember the white man we traded furs to? He always treated us fairly. And his grandmother, the silver-haired woman, always had sweet cakes for us."

"They do not count," Teni said.

Dega was going to argue but a yell from their rear lent wings to their feet. He worried they had been spotted, but time passed without hint of pursuit. They approached the spot where they had left their parents and younger sister and little Keti, and Dega slowed. "Do you see them?"

Out of the undergrowth stepped Tihi and Miki. Mother and daughter had been weeping.

"Keti?" Dega asked.

"She succumbed to her wounds," Tihi said. "Your father is hiding her body so the whites do not find it."

"Father told us to wait here," Miki said. She sniffled and added, "I liked Keti. She always had a smile for me."

Dega looked about them. "Where is the horse?"

"It wandered off," Tihi said. "Why? Did you want it?" She had been doing her best to comfort Miki and had not given the animal any thought.

"It does not matter."

Tihi motioned toward their village. "What did you see? We heard more shooting and yells."

Dega hesitated. He was trying to think of a way to lessen the hurt, but his sister had no such compunctions.

"The People of the Forest are no more, Mother. We are the last of the Nansusequa."

"That cannot be."

"There may be others who survived," Dega said. It was the hope at which he clutched. The whites could not have killed them all. Surely not *all*.

Teni mouthed a short snort of derision. "Did you not see what I saw, brother? Did you not lie there and watch our people being slaughtered?"

Tihi looked from her daughter to her son in bewilderment. "You did not try to help them?"

"There was nothing we could do," Dega said. He believed that. He believed that as much as he had ever believed anything.

The undergrowth crackled, and Wakumassee appeared. He walked as one in his sleep, his face empty of emotion. "It is done."

"Father?" Dega said. To see him so devastated was profoundly disturbing. Their father had always been the fount of inner strength on which the rest of them depended.

"I heard what was said about our people." Waku spread his arms wide. "Would that I had not lived to see this day. The Old Ones are old no more. We have been severed from all that is. I no longer feel Manitoa within me."

"Do not say such things," Tihi said. Of her husband's many fine attributes, she had always admired his devotion to That Which Was In All Things foremost.

"It is the end," Waku declared. "Our ways have flown on the wind, and with them all that we were."

"Not so long as a Nansusequa breathes," Dega vowed.

Teni glanced toward the village. "We must keep moving, or the whites will do to us as they have done to everyone else."

"We must not let that happen," Dega said, and appealed to his father. "Which direction would you have us go?"

Waku did not seem to hear.

"Father?"

"All ways lead to ruin. Do you not see that, son? Do you not see that we are dead but have not yet been killed?"

Young Miki grasped Tihi's hand. "I do not want to die, Mother. What must we do to live?"

Dega had the answer. "We must leave. This land has been the land of the Nansusequa since before the memory of time. But no longer. We must find new country in which to live. Somewhere without whites."

"There is no such place," Teni said. "The whites control all the land from here to the Eastern Sea."

"They do not control all the land to the west," Dega reminded her.

Their mother gazed westward, her expression thoughtful. "They control much of it, though, as far as the Muddy River. The river the whites call the Mississippi." The word was strange on her tongue.

"I was not thinking of the land between here and there," Dega informed her. "I was thinking of the land beyond the Muddy River. I have heard there is a vast prairie, and beyond that, mountains that rise as high as the clouds."

"The Rocky Mountains." Tihi's trade with the whites had made her conversant with the wider world beyond their own. Or, rather, her husband had, for it was he who translated for her. The Nansusequa did not have a name for those far distant mountains.

They had not even heard of them until the coming of the whites.

"It is said a man could spend a lifetime wandering their peaks and valleys and still not see all there is of them."

"It is also said," Tihi remarked, "that the mountains are home to many tribes who would regard us as enemies."

"We have enemies here," Dega reminded her. "Enemies who will hunt us down and exterminate us as they did the rest of our people. We must flee. We must go far, and quickly."

Teni had an objection of her own. "We know nothing of these Rocky Mountains. The land, the animals, they will be new to us."

"So? How different can they be?" Dega rejoined. "And do not forget. There is one aspect to the mountains that should please you. It should please you greatly." It certainly pleased him.

"What is that, brother?" Teni asked skeptically.

"Few whites live in the Rocky Mountains, sister. Fewer whites than anywhere else."

That was all Teni had to hear. "I say we go."

Son and older daughter fixed their eyes on their mother.

Tihi did as she always had done; she appealed to her husband. "Waku? What do you say? We will abide by your decision."

Wakumassee took a moment before speaking. When he did, it was in a listless tone devoid of vitality. "All is gone. All is flown. The mountains are as good as anywhere and better than here."

Dega smiled. "Then it is settled. We will swing to the south to avoid our village and then push on west."

"How long will the journey take?" Tihi wanted to know.

"I cannot say, exactly," Dega answered. "But this I can promise you. By the time the leaves of the trees change colors and the north wind turns cold, we will have found a new home in the Rocky Mountains."

"And we will kill any whites who try to take it from us," Teni vowed.

CHAPTER SIX

"It's a nice day to blow up a pass," Shakespeare McNair commented.

Nate King agreed.

The golden disc was near its zenith. Above them stretched more of the heavily timbered slopes they had been climbing since daybreak, slopes thick with spruce, pines and firs. They were high enough that they came to a belt of aspens, the thin boles like pale ivory, the leaves shimmering in the slight breeze. Mountain daisies grew in abundance. On their ascent they had also seen columbines and violets.

Ravens beat heavy rhythms in the rarefied air. Jays squawked from treetops. Magpies were common near the lake, but not so common higher up. Nutcrackers occasionally uttered their harsh cries. Brightly colored warblers, chickadees and sparrows flitted in the brush. Now and again Nate would spy a bluebird or a tanager.

Deer were abundant, the bucks as unwary as the does. Twice Nate spotted elk as they vanished into the vegetation, their yellowish-brown rumps in contrast to the prevailing green. It always amazed him how silently they could move, given their size. Some stood five feet at the shoulders. The females weighed up to six hundred pounds, the larger males close to a thousand. Yet they glided through the woodland like gigantic ghosts.

The valley was also home to pockets of mountain buffalo. Most people east of the Mississippi River were unaware there were two kinds of buffalo: the common prairie variety, which numbered in the many millions; and their shaggier, rarer cousins, the mountain buffalo, which preferred dense woods to open grassland. Many of the latter had been killed off by the early trappers.

So had many of the beaver. The trapping years had taken a fearsome toll on the beaver population. Recently, the beaver were reestablishing themselves over much of their former range. Here in the new valley, they were plentiful along the streams that fed the pristine lake.

Squirrels, of course, were as common as pinecones. Chipmunks chattered loudly. Rabbits thrived, enough to fill the King and

McNair supper pots forever.

Now and then Nate came across a black bear sign. But never sign of a grizzly. There had been one, and only one, a huge silvertip that claimed the valley as its exclusive territory. Nate had not wanted to kill it. He had done all in his power to try to get along with it, only to be forced into a slay-or-be-eaten nightmare he would not soon forget.

All in all, the valley was a natural paradise. Virtually untouched by the outside world, it was a thriving example of how the Rockies had been, not only before the coming of the whites, but before the coming of the red race, as well.

"A piece of quartz for your thoughts," Shakespeare said.

Nate twisted in his saddle. McNair was astride his white mare, leading the pack horse. "The last of the big spenders," he quipped. "Are you sure you don't want to make it a lump of dirt?"

"My, my," Shakespeare said to the mare. "Isn't *someone* in a mood today? What happened, Horatio? Did you get up on the wrong side of your wife?"

Nate snickered, but could not sustain the levity. "I can't stop thinking about our visitors. The last thing I want is another feud.

It took me years to come to terms with the Utes."

Shakespeare shifted and jabbed a finger at the keg strapped to the pack animal. "As soon as we set that off, you can breathe easy."

"Provided there isn't another way into our valley that we don't know about," Nate said.

"Do you know what I like most about you, my prince?"

"The fact I put up with you?"

"Your marvelous outlook on life. If you're not fretting, you're not happy." Shakespeare made a show of breathing deeply of the mountain air. "You need to learn to relax, to take things in stride."

"Like the death of Niwot?"

Shakespeare's smile transformed into a scowl. "I declare. By thy favor, sweet welkin, I must sigh in thy face."

"If you ever talk normally, it will be a miracle," Nate shot back.

"His wits are not so blunt as, God help, I would desire they were," Shakespeare quoted to the mare.

"You do realize you are talking to your horse?"

"What of it? She is as intelligent as most men I have met, and has a better gift for conversation." Shakespeare chuckled. "I do so amuse myself at times."

"Next you will be talking to trees," Nate muttered.

"I heard that. And for your information, trees have a virtue to recommend them. They don't wake up surly and nitpick sweet innocents like King John and myself."

"John the innocent? Wasn't he the one who ordered a boy's eyes to be burned out? If you're an innocent, then innocence is dead."

Laughing uproariously, Shakespeare slapped his thigh. "You're learning, Horatio! You're learning! A few more years of my company and you will not be a half-wit by half."

"Thanks. I think."

An overhead screech drew Nate's gaze to an eagle sailing on outstretched pinions in search of prey. The bird was so high, it was a speck in the sky, yet its cry carried clearly in the thin air.

"Ever wanted to have wings?" Shakespeare asked out of the blue.

Nate snorted. "I'm perfectly content with arms."

"But you can't flap them and fly." Shakespeare tilted his head back to better admire the eagle. "I should think it would improve a person's perspective to view the world from up there."

"People would look like ants," Nate suggested.

"Exactly. The human race could do with some humbling. In our ignorance we are arrogant. We think the world is ours to do with as we please."

"It's not?"

"Oh, Horatio. Surely you jest? Whatever man touches, we taint. Look at conditions back in the States. We strip the land of trees. We kill off all the animals. We dump our waste in the water so it's not fit to drink. Why, in just the few short decades the white man has been in these mountains, we nearly wiped out the beaver and are close to wiping out the mountain buffalo."

"And you say I woke up in a bad mood?" Nate asked, but was ignored.

"Don't think I'm singling us out, either. The Indians say that once this land teemed with hairy elephants and other creatures long since butchered for the cooking pot. It is human nature to destroy, son. That is why so much blood is spilled. That's why you and I are on our way up to the pass to seal it."

"I admit our natures have a dark side," Nate conceded. "But we also have our good sides, as well. We care for one another. We can love. It's not all blood-spilling."

"You are the true innocent here," Shakespeare said. "But yes. We are not entirely worthless. I only wish more were like you and less like our visitors, who saw fit to kill a boy for no other reason than he was different from them."

"It could be they regard this valley as part of their territory, even if they don't come here often."

"Maybe we should stake out territory of our own, and serve warning to all and sundry."

"How do you mean?"

"This valley is our new home, correct? Well, let's make it ours and only ours. Remember how it was at your last homestead? People were dropping by every time you turned around."

"We were close to the main trail up into the central Rockies," Nate noted. "Folks could hardly miss spotting our cabin."

"Quibble all you want," Shakespeare said. "My point is that a lot of those people caused you trouble. It got so you might as well have hung out a sign that read 'Lost souls and cutthroats welcome.' "

Shakespeare's own cabin had seen its share of passing strangers. More than its share, in his estimation, which was part of he reason he had agreed to move to the new valley. The other part was that he cared for Nate King as the son he'd never had, and relished the idea of spending his waning years in Nate's company.

"You have a point," Nate admitted. The location of their last cabin had become too well known. It was regarded as a stopping point, the same as Bent's Fort. Then there had been the hostile tribes who knew where to find him, and were a constant threat to his loved ones. "All this is leading up to something."

"I thought I was already at the summit," Shakespeare bantered. "It's simply this: If you are bound and determined to make this valley ours and our alone —"

"This is your idea, but go on," Nate amended.

"— then we should take steps to safeguard our slice of heaven. How do we do that, you ask? By not letting anyone else settle here. Not white or red."

"You are serious?"

"Why not?"

"Claiming a homestead is one thing." Nate gestured at the broad valley floor that ran three miles from north to south. "But for us to lay claim to all this, why, it's unheard of."

"Sam Houston laid claim to all Texas and you didn't hear anyone complain. Well, except Santa Anna and the rest of Mexico."

"Have you brought a jug and not told me?"

"Bear with me. It will be easier than you think. We simply tell anyone else who shows up that they are to skedaddle."

"And of course they will do it, just like that," Nate said sarcastically, with a snap of his fingers.

"We can post signs if you want, telling folks to stay out or else."

"And everyone will honor them, of course." Nate glanced over his shoulder. "Weren't you counting ducks last week?"

Shakespeare looked up, and blinked. "What?"

"When I came by your cabin. You were counting how many ducks were on the lake. Remember?"

"What does that have to do with any-thing?"

"You were saying as how you had devel-oped a new fondness for the noble duck," Nate said. "Your exact words."

"Again, what does that prove?"

"And remember that time you were blow-ing soap bubbles with Evelyn, and you told her some of the bubbles would be blown clear to Norway?"

"If there is a point to your babble, it eludes me."

"No signs."

"That's your point?" Shakespeare asked, and when Nate nodded, he muttered, "You will make a wonderful nitpicking crone one day."

Nate laughed.

"Thou disease of a friend," Shakespeare quoted. "At what do you scoff? I still say we should claim the entire valley as ours."

"Are you addlepated? To all this? It's just not done."

"Who says?"

"A homestead, yes. Half the Rockies, no."

"Methinks you need spectacles," Shakespeare said. "This valley is but a dust mote. Besides, there's no government west of the Mississippi. No land offices. No procedures for filing claims. The land is ours to do with as we please, and if we please to have this valley as our manor and set ourselves up as squires, that is our privilege."

"We will be laughed to scorn," Nate predicted. While it was true the land was there for the taking, the general consensus among the few whites who had braved the frontier and built homesteads was that the land was there for everyone, white and red, and no man should take more than his fair amount.

"Who will do this cackling, Horatio?" Shakespeare demanded. "There are no other whites within a week's ride."

"It smacks of greed."

"Oh. I see. Your princely nature balks at taking the entire pie because you are content with a slice. Well, I have no such qualms. Leave the signs to me, and you can bask in the rewards of my hard work."

"No."

"All I ask is that you consider it. For me, if for no other reason. In case you haven't noticed, I'm not as spry as I used to be. I'm too old to keep moving."

"Not that silliness again," Nate grumbled.

"I heard that. But these white hairs of mine aren't a wig." Shakespeare encompassed the valley with a sweep of his arm. "I like it here, son. I like it a lot. So does Blue Water Woman. So I will be damned if I will sit idly by while other homesteaders move in and crowd us out."

"That won't happen for another two hundred years."

"Says the gent who left his last home after twenty years because he was feeling hemmed in."

Nate fell silent. The problem with arguing

with McNair was that nine times out of ten, McNair was right. It would be a shame to have to share the valley with others. If that sounded selfish, so be it. Nate did not want to move, either.

Frontiersmen liked open space. They liked their breathing room, as they referred to it, and the privacy the breathing room bestowed. Those elements, and an abundance of game, were essential.

It had never failed, though. The same pattern occurred again and again. It began along the eastern seaboard, when the first wave of hardy frontiersmen pushed west and built their homesteads at the fringe of civilization. Before long, settlers showed up, and settlements sprouted. Most of the game was killed off, and a man couldn't turn around without bumping into a neighbor. The frontiersmen were forced to move west yet again, to the new fringe of civilization, to find their breathing room. And so it went, decade after decade, an endless cycle that opened up new vistas for settlement at the expense of those who blazed the paths into the wilderness.

As conditions currently stood, the leading edge of the westward tide had been temporarily stemmed at the Mississippi. But the tide would not stay contained for long.

Signs of restlessness were everywhere. Tales of the Oregon Country had stirred many an emigrant, and California's allure grew year by year. It would not be long before the westward expansion resumed in earnest, before hordes of hopefuls poured across the Mississippi and made of the plains and the mountains the same bustling beehive they had made of the East.

Nate dreaded that day.

"So what do you say, fair prince? Are you with me?" Shakespeare asked. "Have we a pact, and should we sign it in blood?"

"I was with you until the blood part."

"Growing squeamish at your young age? Don't worry. I won't tell Winona. She likes her men manly."

"Remind me to pick up the next rock I see and bean you with it."

Chortling, Shakespeare happily exclaimed, "That's the spirit! Woe to the miscreants who try to take any part of our valley from us. We'll make them sorry they were born." And McNair let out a lusty whoop.

They conducted the rest of their climb in silence except for the creak of saddle leather and the plod of hooves. The sun dipped on its downward arc; the shadows lengthened.

Nate was constantly on the lookout for sign of the hostiles. He suspected they had left the valley, but he had learned the hard way never to take anything for granted. It was a surefire invite to an early grave, and he hankered to live a good many years yet.

Nate did not say anything to McNair, but secretly, he was having doubts about the wisdom of blowing up the pass. If there were another way over the range from the next valley, closing the pass would accomplish nothing other than to further anger the tribe that regarded them as intruders. He wished he had time to explore the rest of the range, but that could take years.

Deep in thought, Nate let his attention lapse. His mistake proved costly. He was skirting a talus slope when his bay nickered and pricked its ears. Glancing at the top of the slope, Nate was startled to behold three warriors, undoubtedly the same three who had slain Niwot. His shock did not last more than a few seconds. "Shakespeare!" he hollered, and brought up his Hawken.

The three warriors did not have weapons in their hands. They held rocks the size of watermelons. At Nate's outcry, they hurled the rocks down the slope. A senseless act, on the face of it, except that talus was notoriously unstable, and at the three smashing impacts, the loose layer of stones and dirt shifted and moved and flowed down the slope with ever increasing speed.

Straight at Nate and Shakespeare.

"Ride, Horatio! Ride!"

Nate needed no urging. A slap of his powerful legs brought the bay to a gallop, and he raced for the far edge of the talus. Should they fail to make it, tons of crushing weight would sweep over them and bury them. He thought of Winona, and slapped his legs harder.

Shakespeare's mare fairly flew. She was a sure-footed animal and swift over short spurts. He had every confidence she could bear him to safety, but his sorrel was much slower. He tugged on the lead rope to hurry it along, but he might as well be pulling on an anchor for all the good it did him. The pack horse could not go any faster.

The clatter and rumble of the talus rose to a roar as it gained momentum. Rocks leaped and bounced. The earth itself rippled like waves on the lake.

Nate hated talus. He had nearly lost his life to it several times. He always strived to avoid it, as he would the den of a grizzly. He would not have come as close as he had to this particular slope, except that the pass was just above it, and he had been eager to reach the pass before nightfall.

Nate shot a glance at the warriors only to find they had disappeared. The threat of an arrow catching him in the back or the side was very real. But it was the talus that demanded his immediate attention. If he lived, he would deal with the hostiles. One threat at a time. But *would* he survive it? The leading point of the slide was much too close.

Shakespeare was having similar thoughts. He gauged the distance to solid ground and the distance the talus had to cover before it crashed into him, and knew he would not make it. Not if he stayed with the pack animal. Glancing back, he said sadly, "I'm sorry!" and let go of the rope. A few jabs of Shakespeare's heels, and the mare proved her mettle by flying like the wind. Neck and neck, the two horses exerted their sinews to their fullest. She overtook Nate's bay.

The roar of the talus was like thunder in their ears as they swept into the trees. Instantly, they drew rein, and turned.

"No!" Nate said.

The sorrel was doomed. Head extended, nostrils distended, mane flying, it was putting forth all it had into reaching them, but was still ten yards away when the flood of cascading rocks and dirt slammed into it. Squealing in terror, the sorrel was smashed onto its side. It kicked and whinnied and struggled to stand, but the talus swept up and over, burying the horse alive. In a span of seconds the animals was lost to sight.

For another hundred yards the talus tumbled and flowed, seeming to shake the very earth. It came to a stop almost as abruptly as it had started. Stones rattled and bounced and spumes of dust rose. Then all was still.

Nate tore his gaze from a solitary hoof that jutted up out of the mound. Raising his Hawken, he scanned the top of the slope. "Where did they get to?"

Shakespeare was wondering the same thing. His joints might creak, but his eyes were as sharp as that eagle's they had seen, and try though he did, he saw no trace of the three warriors. "One of us has to try for the keg while the other keeps watch," he proposed.

"I'll go," Nate said without hesitation.

"Why you?" Shakespeare was more than willing to do it himself.

"As you keep pointing out, you're not as spry as you used to be. This is a job for a hare, not a tortoise."

"Damn my leaky mouth, anyhow," Shakespeare said. "You be careful, son. It might start sliding again. And there are the sinkholes."

Nate understood perfectly well. The talus had stopped, but it was still unstable. The loose rocks made footing treacherous enough, but there were also soft spots where a man could sink in over his head and suffocate within seconds. Dismounting, he hefted his Hawken.

"Better leave that here so your hands are free."

Nate heeded the advice. He leaned the Hawken against a fir, then warily moved into the open. He had seldom felt so exposed. At any moment glittering shafts might come flashing out of the sky to do to him as had been done to poor Niwot. But it was on the talus he must concentrate. Only the talus. He had to trust that McNair would watch out for him.

A wall of vegetation had brought the talus to a stop, resulting in a mound as high as Nate's cabin. Small noises came from under the mound, shiftings and scritchings where the talus was settling. Puffs of dust rose at various spots.

Nate made sure his pistols were tightly wedged under his wide leather belt and that his Bowie knife and tomahawk were snug before he took his first step onto the talus.

The sorrel's hoof was forty feet away. It looked to be a mile.

His mouth dry, Nate slowly advanced. He placed each foot with care and tested before applying his full weight. The expectation of a barbed shaft piercing his body caused the skin on his back to crawl. He moved his right leg. He moved his left. The talus stayed firm underfoot.

Shakespeare could not stop glancing at Nate even though he knew he should keep his eyes on the timber. He was not so old that he no longer became scared, and he was scared to death for Nate. In the wilderness, the difference between living and dying was often measured in a whisker's-width of reflex. No one lived forever. That he had lasted as long as he had was more the result of luck than anything else.

A flicker of movement stiffened Shakespeare in his saddle. He took a quick bead on the spot but did not see the hostiles. It could be, he reasoned, that the warriors were circling to flank them from several directions at once. In that case, he could not possibly protect Nate. His palms grew slick with sweat but he did not take his hands off the Hawken to wipe them. A moment's lapse was all the warriors needed. "How is it coming?" he hollered without looking.

"I'm almost there!" By almost, Nate meant fifteen feet to go. Each step left a shallow depression. Nervously licking his lips, he eased his leg forward.

From out of nowhere came an arrow. The buzz of its flight was the only warning Nate had. He glanced up, saw it, and sprang to the right. The arrow cleaved the space he had occupied, struck a rock, and went skittering. Nate twisted to yell to Shakespeare, and suddenly the talus gave way under him.

CHAPTER SEVEN

Talus was not like quicksand. Sinking into quicksand was like sinking into wet mud. A person caught in quicksand could still move, to a degree, although the more the person moved, the faster he sank. With talus, it was more like falling into a hole in the ground, and then having the hole cave in.

Nate King felt the talus give way under him and tried to stop his plunge by casting the Hawken aside and throwing out his arms. But it happened so quickly, he was in the hole up to his elbows before he could throw his arms out. Worse, he was wedged fast. He told himself he should be grateful he was not completely buried.

Then another arrow thunked into the talus not a yard away, and Nate realized what an inviting target he made.

Shakespeare had glimpsed the arrow's flight out of the corner of his eye, and spun.

His shock at Nate's predicament slowed his reaction a trifle. The shot he snapped off at the furtive figure who had loosed the arow was a shade late. The figure ducked behind a tree as Shakespeare squeezed the trigger.

Shakespeare would have to take his eyes off Nate to reload, but he didn't want to do that. Instead he jerked a heavy flintlock from under his belt, and hollered, "Can you free yourself?"

Nate was striving mightily to do just that. Wriggling furiously, he twisted back and forth in an effort to enlarge the hole enough for him to slide his arms out. But the talus had him so tightly wedged, he could barely move.

"Can you get free?" Shakespeare yelled a second time, worried. By now all three warriors had to be aware Nate was helpless.

"Give me a bit!" Nate replied. He did not want McNair to rush out to help and take an arrow on his account.

"Hold on!" Shakespeare broke from cover.

"I can manage! Stay where you are!"

"Bite your tongue!" For twenty years Shakespeare had looked after the younger man, helping him out of one scrape after another. He would be damned if he would stop now.

A whizzing sound made Nate look up. His

breath caught in his throat. Not one, not two, but three arrows were near the apex of their arcs and about to rain down. He redoubled his struggles, but he was lucky if he could move half an inch, if that.

"Look out!" Shakespeare bawled.

Nate hunched his broad shoulders and tucked his chin to his chest. The next instant the arrows struck — *chak, chak, chak* — two missing him by inches and the third clipping a whang on his shoulder.

Shakespeare spotted one of the bowmen and fired. He was sure he missed. Shoving the spent flintlock under his belt, he drew the second. Heedless of the danger, he crossed the talus and sank onto a knee next to Nate.

"Go back."

"Not without you." Shakespeare hooked a hand under Nate's right arm and pulled. Nothing happened. "Have you been overdoing it with the pies again?"

Watching the vegetation, Nate responded, "They'll get us. They'll get both of us. Go back before it's too late, damn you."

"It's not only the joints that bother coons my age," Shakespeare said. "We don't hear so well, either." Wedging the flintlock under his belt, he slid behind Nate and slipped both hands under Nate's arms. "On the count of three, I'll lift. You pretend you are a fish on a hook."

"You are the most contrary cuss alive! Do you know that?" Nate growled to mask his true feelings. He could not bear the thought of anything happening to McNair.

"That's the trouble with sprouts like you," Shakespeare said. "Always jabbering when you should be wriggling." He firmed his hold. "Ready? One. Two —"

"More arrows!"

Shakespeare had seen them. Two shafts let fly simultaneously, the third a few heartbeats later. "Three!" he bellowed, and strained upward.

Nate wrenched madly from side to side. But instead of dislodging enough of the dirt and stones to free himself, he only succeeded in wedging himself tighter. "Down!" he roared. He expected McNair to throw himself out of harm's way.

Shakespeare bent over, using his body as a shield.

"No!" Nate cried.

The arrows reached them. One broke in half on hitting a rock. Another sank into the talus to its feathers.

"Again!" Shakespeare bellowed, and pulled.

Desperation transformed Nate into a

heaving, twisting dervish, but he remained stuck. When they paused to catch their breaths, he urged, "Get out of here! I mean it this time."

Puffing for breath, Shakespeare asked, "Has anyone ever mentioned that you resemble a beet when you're mad?"

Nate squinted at the sun-drenched vault above. "Why do they wait so long before firing more arrows?"

"They might not have many left," Shakespeare speculated. "Most warriors carry ten or so, and they lost some when they killed Niwot."

"Lucky for us." Nate did not relish dodging more shafts. He tried to move his hands and found he could shape them into scoops. Slowly at first, then with increasing speed, he clawed at the dirt.

With repeated glances at the forest, Shakespeare began clawing at the edge of the hole. "Notice anything about our friends in the trees?"

"You mean besides the fact that they want us dead?" Nate grunted between jabs and scrapes.

"They haven't let out a peep. Not once here, not once when they attacked down below." Shakespeare was accustomed to warriors who shrieked and whooped like banshees to scare their enemies and bolster their courage. "The only other Indians I've ever tangled with who fought this quietly were Apaches."

"I don't know who they are," Nate grunted, "but they sure as hell aren't Apaches." He had fought Apaches once, years ago, when Shakespeare and he decided to treat their wives to a trip to Santa Fe. Zach had been a mere slip of a boy, Evelyn not even born.

"I didn't say they *were* Apaches," Shakespeare noted. "I said they fight *like* Apaches."

"Small difference." Nate had other things on his mind, foremost getting the hell out of that hole. He could move both hands freely and was scooping as fast as he could, but his progress was much too slow. "Find a limb to use as a lever. Maybe you can pry me out."

"I'm not leaving your side."

"Consarn your thick skull," Nate growled. "I'll be fine."

"No."

"Damn it —" Nate began, then saw the red rivulets spreading outward from his friend's left foot. An arrow had sunk into McNair's leg a few inches above the ankle, from side to side. Nate's anger evaporated like dew under the morning sun. "Why didn't you say something?"

"You have enough troubles at the moment." It had been all Shakespeare could do not to scream. The pain had nearly caused him to black out. "Now stop pretending to be a gopher so we can get you out of there and you can remove this cussed arrow."

"You old goat," Nate said, his voice choked with emotion.

"Finally. You admit it."

"Admit what? That I care for you?"

"That I'm old. Now hush and help me. The sooner you're out of this fix, the sooner I can stop bleeding."

With renewed vigor they applied themselves to extricating him. Constant glances at the fringing woods betrayed their nervousness. Nate's right wrist came loose, and soon after, his left. Shakespeare made headway at loosening the talus that pinned Nate's upper arms.

"It's been minutes," Nate commented. "Why haven't they done something?"

"Like what? Rush us? We're out in the open. We can shoot them before they reach us. Either that or they have enough brains to stay away from talus. Unlike someone whose name I could mention but won't."

"We need the keg."

Shakespeare stared at the jutting hoof. "Alas, poor Yorick! I knew him, Horatio, a fellow of infinite jest, of most excellent fancy. He hath borne me on his back a thousand times. And now how abhorred in my imagination it is! My gorge rises at it. Here hung those lips that I have kissed I know not how oft. Where be your gibes now? Your gambols, your songs, your flashes of merriment that were wont to set the table on a roar?"

"You kiss horses?"

Shakespeare snorted and shifted his full weight from his wounded leg to his good one. "There is no hope for you, sir, no hope at all."

"Evelyn kisses her horse. I bet she picked up the habit from you. They say the young like to mimic their elders, no matter how silly their elders might be."

"I would shoot you but it would be a waste of lead."

They were joking to keep their spirits up but never for a second did either let down his guard. Since the arrows had come out of the trees on the opposite side of the slope, they focused their attention there. But Nate also scanned the nearby woods, and it was well he did, for just as he finally freed one arm and thrust it out of the hole, the vegetation parted sixty feet away, revealing a swarthy form with a barbed arrow notched to a sinew string.

"Behind you!" Nate cried, and pointed.

Shakespeare whirled, or tried to, palming a flintlock. His left leg gave out under him and he fired as he fell. In his haste he rushed his shot and the lead ball cored a fir next to the man.

The warrior jumped back, steadied his bow, and pulled the string.

There was no time for Shakespeare to reload, and at that range the warrior could hardly miss. Then Shakespeare saw Nate's Hawken, lying almost at his fingertips. Grabbing it, he pointed, thumbed back the hammer, and fired. He had no chance to aim. He was hoping to force the warrior to seek cover. But fickle fate smiled on him.

The top of the warrior's head burst in a shower of hair and brains. The man staggered, dead on his feet, and the arrow intended for Shakespeare or Nate left the string and imbedded itself in the soil. The bow fell from fingers gone limp, and was joined by the owner of those fingers.

"That was some shooting," Nate marveled.

"I cannot tell a lie," Shakespeare said as

he set to reloading. "Yes, it was."

"Give me a pistol and I will cover you. If that one snuck over here, the others might have, too."

Bending to the task, Shakespeare quoted, "To be or not to be, that is the question. Whether 'tis nobler in the mind to suffer the slings and arrows of outrageous fortune, or take arms against a sea of troubles, and by opposing, end them."

"I vote we oppose," Nate said. He had never been one to turn the other cheek. If he had, he would have died long ago. On the frontier it was kill or be killed. Only those willing to stand up for themselves had any hope of living to old age. The wilderness was no place for the weak of body or the weak of mind.

One of the great shocks of Nate's life had been the first time a man tried to kill him. His sheltered life as an aspiring accountant in New York City had not prepared him for the harsh reality of existence in the wild. It was one thing to sit in the warm comfort of an easy chair and read about the exciting exploits of Jim Bowie and the famous sandbar duel, and quite another to find oneself staring into the muzzle of a flintlock or at a gleaming blade held by someone bent on killing you.

Suddenly Nate became aware that McNair was talking to him.

"— a nap or do you want me to do all the work?" Shakespeare was tearing at the rocks and dirt. "A pair of very unfriendly gentlemen are still out there somewhere, in case you've forgotten."

Several minutes of steady digging resulted in Nate being able to climb out. He accepted his Hawken, and together they carefully crossed to the jutting hoof and knelt on each side of it.

Shakespeare scratched his white beard. "Appears to me the horse is upside down. It could take us forever to reach the keg."

"However long it takes," Nate said, and began digging.

Once again they were alert for the hostiles but the remaining two did not show themselves.

Nate had dug down about a foot and Shakespeare not quite as deep when McNair's knuckles rapped an object with a telltale *thunk.* "Can it be?" he said, and hastily scraped more dirt away.

It was the keg. Evidently it had come loose when the talus slammed into the sorrel, and ended up near the top of the mound rather than deeper down. Cradling it, Shakespeare inspected the seams. "In one piece," he chortled. "We can proceed as planned."

"First you let me doctor you." Nate in the lead, his Hawken leveled, they entered the vegetation. Nate made his friend sit. Gingerly hiking McNair's pant leg, he found that the arrow had missed the bone and gone through the fleshy part of the calf. "You are one lucky coon."

"If that were true, the arrow would have missed."

Nate gripped the shaft with both hands. "Grit your teeth. This might hurt. Are you ready?"

"You ask the silliest questions."

A quick *snap,* and Nate could pull the arrow out. "Want to save it as a keepsake?"

"Sure. Can you gather up the blood, too?" Shakespeare drew his knife and cut a strip from the bottom of his shirt for a bandage. He tied the strip himself, saying, "I'm better at knots." When he was done he slowly stood and limped in a small circle. "There. Now let's take a gander at the one I shot. Maybe he is from a tribe we'll recognize."

"I wouldn't count on it."

They stood over the dead man and stared. Not at the hole in his head or the pool of blood, but at the warrior's face and clothes.

"I'll be damned," Shakespeare said. "When I'm wrong, I'm really wrong. What in tarnation do we have here?"

Nate could not begin to say. The man was not a Blackfoot, or a Blood, or a Crow, or an Ute, or from any other tribe he ever had dealings with.

Stocky of build and swarthy of skin, the warrior wore buckskins notable for the absence of whangs, and for sleeves that flared from the elbows to the wrists. The leggings were ordinary except that on each hip, drawn in black, were peculiar symbols. On the right hip were three circles, one within the other. On the left hip was what appeared to be the sketch of a bear with extremely long canines. The man's moccasins were stitched in a cross weave and had buckskin laces at the front.

The truly remarkably thing, though, was the man's face. His low forehead sloped to a black thatch that was more gristle than hair. Thick, beetling brows hovered like twin caterpillars over dark pits with eyeballs as black as pitch. Thin lips and a jutting jaw were prominent but not nearly as prominent as the scars that covered every square inch of skin between neck and hairline in a mix of whorls and squiggles. Deep scars, they were, with thick ridges, the overall effect hideous in the extreme.

"Dear God," Nate breathed. "Do you

think he did that to himself?"

"Or someone did it for him," Shakespeare guessed.

"Why? What purpose does it serve?"

"What purpose do tattoos serve?" Shakespeare rejoined. "I never have been fond of marking up my body but some folks seems to think doodling on themselves is the reason they were given skin."

"This isn't doodling," Nate remarked, resisting an urge to bend down and touch the scar tissue. "It had to hurt like Hades and bleed like the dickens." He gazed at the nearby woods. "Do you suppose they are all like this? The women and the kids, too?"

"Since when did I become the Almighty?" Shakespeare asked. "To be honest, in all my years I have never seen anything like this."

The warrior's weapons drew their interest next. Nate picked up the bow. It was made of ash, the ends slightly curved. The workmanship, compared to the bows of the Shoshones, was crude. The same was true of the arrow. Raven feathers had been used, all of them applied unevenly. It was amazing they had been able to kill Niwot with one shot, and not surprising they had missed striking a fatal blow to Nate or Shakespeare.

A sheath dangled from a length of rope

that served as the warrior's belt. The knife had an antler hilt and an iron blade, the edge not nearly as sharp as the edge on Nate's Bowie.

"We should bury him," Nate said.

"Whatever for?" Shakespeare disagreed. "Coyotes and buzzards have to eat, too, don't they?"

"If his friends see us bury him, they might realize we are not the enemies they take us for."

Shakespeare extended his rifle so that the muzzle almost brushed the hole in the warrior's head. "Something tells me that after seeing me blow his brains out, it will take more than planting him to convince them we're friendly."

Nate was determined to do it anyway. He dug, scooping with a tree branch he trimmed and tapered at one end, while Mc-Nair stood watch. The sun was an hour above the western horizon when Nate patted the last of the dirt and stepped back from the grave. "There."

"Want us to erect a headstone and sing a few hymns?"

"You are not half as funny as you think you are."

"I could quote the Bard. How about this? Now cracks a noble heart! And flights of angels sign thee to thy rest."

"Show more respect for the dead," Nate said.

– Shakespeare snorted and said indignantly, "I refuse to shed false tears over someone who tried his best to turn me into a pincushion." He was beginning to worry about his prodigy. Nate was becoming too soft-hearted. Not long ago, Nate had tried to live in harmony, as he put it, with a grizzly, and nearly been slain when the griz figured harmony was the same as supper. "Let's head for the pass."

They did not have far to climb. Shakespeare held on to the keg, resting it on his thigh as they rode. Presently, the defile appeared. Since it ran from east to west, the rays of the setting sun bathed the high walls in a yellow glow.

Turning in the saddle, Nate remarked, "We still have time to blow the pass before dark."

"I would rather do it tomorrow and take our time," Shakespeare said. They had to do it right the first time or all the effort they had gone to would be wasted.

Nate was impatient to get the job finished. They could start down at first light if they set off the keg right away. By tomorrow evening he would be home with Winona.

"Let's at least have a look-see."

"Suit yourself."

The slope leveled. Before them loomed the opening. Drawing rein, Shakespeare dismounted and set the keg at the base of the south wall.

"Why not bring it along?" Nate asked.

"It's fine here," Shakespeare answered, inwardly chuckling at his devious stroke. They could not light the fuse if they did not have the keg with them.

Nate entered the pass. He had to squint against the bright glare of the sun. The thud of the bay's hooves sounded twice as loud. As he neared the west end of the defile, the wind intensified. From puffs and gusts it became an invisible buffeting fist, whipping the whangs on his sleeves. When he coughed, the sound was thrown back at him. He came out on a shelf that overlooked the next valley. Dense timber spread for as far as the eye could see.

"Your friend with the scar is from some-where out there," Shakespeare mentioned, coming to a stop.

"Any sign of a likely spot for the keg?"

"No." Shakespeare was telling the truth. They needed to find a crack wide enough to wedge the keg into, or make an opening that would suffice. Simply placing the keg at the base of either rock wall and igniting it would not be enough to bring the entire pass crashing down.

"I had high hopes," Nate said. Now they had to do it the hard way, which reminded him. "We lost our pick and shovel with the pack horse. How do we go about it without them?"

"Let me ponder some," Shakespeare said. "I should have an idea by morning."

Nate lifted his reins to wheel the bay and paused. Off to the west, past the valley and over the next range, more than a dozen smoky tendrils curled into the sky. "Their village, do you reckon?"

"That would be my hunch," Shakespeare said. A big village, too, he reckoned, if each tendril came from a single campfire or lodge.

"Let's hope the other two are on their way there," Nate said. It would take days to reach the village and return with more warriors.

"Maybe they are. There hasn't been any sign of them since you buried their friend. So much for gratitude."

"I still say it was the right thing to do."

The wind at their backs, they reentered the pass. Shakespeare assumed the lead. A third of the way in he spotted a crack midway up the left wall. He did not point it out to Nate. Plenty of time for that in the morning, he told himself. To keep Nate from glancing up and noticing it, he asked, "Do my buckskins have a rip in the back? I swear I can feel a draft."

"Not that I can see, no."

They were directly under the crack. Shakespeare needed to distract him for a few more seconds. "Ever have a hankering to give up this life and take your family and live in the States?"

"You know better."

Shakespeare reached out and patted the left-hand wall. An idea struck him and he asked, "Is there a way to the top?"

"I've only been up here a few times and never bothered to check," Nate responded. "Why? Are you thinking of setting off the keg up there?"

Shakespeare never answered the question. A shadow flitted across the gap, and he glanced up. Silhouetted against the sky were the two warriors. At least, he assumed they were the same pair. As they had done at the talus slope, each held a boulder over his head.

"Oh, hell."

CHAPTER EIGHT

"Nate! Above us!" Shakespeare McNair bawled, and dug his heels into the white mare. She was an exceptional horse, and always responded superbly. In a few bounds she was at a full gallop.

A quick glance showed Nate their peril. He saw one of the warriors lean out over the edge, about to drop a boulder on him. Instantly, Nate jammed the Hawken to his shoulder, thumbing the hammer back as he did, and fired. In the confines of the pass the blast was thunderous.

The warrior was jolted by the impact of the heavy lead ball. Gravity seized the boulder, and him, and both plunged over the brink.

Nate used his reins to pull the bay backward. But the boulder and the warrior crashed to the ground so close that one of the man's legs caught the horse a glancing blow across the nostrils.

The second warrior vanished, boulder and all.

Nate continued to goad the bay backward. When they had covered some twenty feet, Nate slapped his legs and the bay raced forward, gaining speed quickly so that when it came to the body and the boulder it vaulted them with ease. Nate watched the rim, but the second warrior did not re-appear.

Shakespeare was surprised the east opening was not blocked. He emerged from the defile and promptly reined around to cover Nate. He kept his rifle trained on the rim until Nate was out of the sun-drenched pass.

Nate brought the bay to a stop next to the mare and twisted. "Where did he get to?"

"Maybe they're gun-shy." Shakespeare had seen it before, especially during his early years in the Rockies. Tribes unfamiliar with firearms were cowed by them. He had once heard it said that the reason Cortez and his pitiful handful of soldiers defeated the Incas was because of the unreasoning dread in which the Incas held the Spaniards' weapons and armor.

In tense silence except for the breathing of their mounts, they waited. After several uneventful minutes, Shakespeare remarked, "I reckon we're safe."

"Until he tries to sneak up on us in the dark and slit our throats," Nate said. Yet more incentive to blow the pass before night fell, but he realized they must wait until daylight.

Common sense dictated they not camp near the pass. They descended a short way to a meadow and rode to the center. Stripping their saddles and packs, they picketed the bay and the mare to make it harder for the warrior to steal them.

Shakespeare deposited his packs and his saddle and sat with his back to the latter, saying wearily, "Well. This has been an interesting day."

Nate was about to imitate McNair when a slack-jawed look of astonishment came over him, and he froze.

"What is it?" Shakespeare snapped his rifle up and peered intently about them. "Did you see him?"

"We are dunderheads."

"How's that? Speak for yourself, Horatio. I pride myself on having a stray thought now and anon."

"You can't prove that by the keg of black powder."

Shakespeare's astonishment outdid Nate's. "We left it at the pass! How could we have been so careless?"

"In my case I had other things on my mind," Nate answered. "In yours, your rapier wit needs sharpening."

"You don't think —" Shakespeare began, and shook his head. "No. It couldn't be. We're dunces, is all."

"Don't think what?" Nate prodded, turning to the bay. "I'll go. You stay and rest those ancient bones of yours."

"You know better," Shakespeare chided. "We stick together. We can leave everything here and ride bareback, but we stick together."

By now twilight shrouded the upper tiers of the high country. At that altitude the air chilled quickly once the sun relinquished its rein to the stars and a crescent moon. They held to a walk, and, as much as possible, to open ground. Shadowy specters seemed to float about them, an illusion of the fading light and the whipping wind.

"I ever tell you the story of the headless horseman?" Shakespeare asked.

Steeled for an ambush, Nate was fingering his Hawken. "I have the book, remember? It's one of my favorite stories."

"This is the kind of night made for goblins and spooks."

Nate had thought the same thing but did not want Shakespeare to know. "Why bring that up? I swear. Sometimes you are worse than my kids."

"They're not kids anymore, Horatio. They're adults. Evelyn will be married before long, and between her and Zach, you and Winona will be up to your necks in grandchildren."

"My daughter is in no hurry to take a husband, and I don't blame her." Nate would not mind if she stayed single for another ten years.

"You will need to practice bouncing the tykes on your knee. Use a water skin. You can pretend they are infants or older, depending on how much water you have in the skin."

"Remember what I said earlier about your silliness?"

"I vaguely recollect you prattling on about something or other, yes," Shakespeare responded.

"You have outdone yourself."

"We should hush, son. We're getting close to the pass."

That they were. With the sun gone, the defile was an inky slit, the area around it mired in murk. Drawing rein well back from the opening, they sat and listened. A low moan from the pass caused the bay to shy and prance, but it was only the wind. Or so

Nate figured. "I'll go on foot," he whispered. "You stay with the horses."

"What part of stick together didn't you savvy?" Shakespeare asked. "You could take a knife in the back and I would never know."

Sliding down, they gripped their respective reins and slowly advanced. The writhing shadows worked havoc with Nate's nerves. The warrior could be anywhere. Twice he was willing to swear he saw a horribly scarred visage peering at them out of the darkness.

They came to the pass. The wind was stronger. The moans had become occasional shrieks.

Shakespeare stared at the spot where he had set the keg. "This makes the day complete."

The keg was gone.

Nate hunkered and ran his hand over the depression it had made. "They must have taken it before they sprang their ambush." Unfolding his body, he stated the obvious. "We'll have to wait until morning to track him."

Shakespeare reluctantly agreed. The warrior could be long gone by then. If the man traveled through the night, he would be miles into the thick timber in the next valley by dawn. Catching him would be on the order of a miracle.

"Let's get back to our gear." It angered Nate to think they had come so far, nearly losing their lives, and would be unable to do what they came for. Every day the pass stayed open was an invitation to the scar-faced tribe to send a large war party to wipe out his family and friends.

Neither spoke on the way down. They were too depressed.

Both drew rein at the edge of the meadow. Each had the same thought; the warrior might be waiting for them, crouched behind their saddles and packs. Nate bore to the left, Shakespeare to the right. Rifles extended, they advanced through the knee-high grass.

"No one," Shakespeare said, relieved.

Everything was exactly as they had left it. Nate picketed the bay, opened a beaded parfleche Winona had made, and took out a bundle of pemmican. Sitting cross-legged, he offered some to McNair. For a while they sat and chewed in silence, then Shakespeare cleared his throat.

"It occurs to me, son, that we better make damn sure that pass is plugged before more of those scarred devils show up. When they hear we've killed two of their friends, the entire tribe will want our scalps."

"We can't plug it until we recover the black powder." Nate mentioned the obvious.

"Which might not happen. Maybe we should give some thought to one of us heading back down for more."

"What about sticking together?"

"One of us needs to keep an eye on the pass. If more warriors do come through, our families have to be warned."

The logic, and the threat, could not be denied. Nate never hesitated. "I'll stay," he said.

"We should flip a coin." Shakespeare fished in a pocket, and then another. "Wouldn't you know it? The one time I want one."

"I'll stay," Nate repeated. He was younger, stronger, faster. But he gave a different reason. "Our move to this valley was my idea. You wouldn't be in danger right now if it weren't for me."

"You are too noble by half. But good reason must of force give way to better," Shakespeare quoted. "You can make it to the lake faster than I can. You should be the one to go."

"How do you figure? Your mare is as fast as my bay." Nate was not so gullible as to let himself be hoodwinked. "Either you go or neither of us does."

Shakespeare muttered something, then said, "Can it be that you and I are married and don't know it?"

"If I were drunk that might make sense."

"We squabble like a married couple," Shakespeare said. "But so be it. If you insist I go, I will, but I go under the duress of our friendship, and with the observation that there is no more faith in you than in a stewed prune."

Suddenly grinning, Nate declared, "I have it!" and snapped his fingers.

"Have what?"

"If the hostiles do attack, you can talk them to death."

Shakespeare sighed, and stood. "You are a knave, a rascal, an eater of broken meats, a base, proud, shallow, beggarly, three-suited, hundred-pound, filthy worsted-stocking knave."

"I like you, too."

"What a madcap hath heaven lent us here," Shakespeare grumbled, and set to work preparing to depart. Soon he had the mare saddled and his parfleches tied on. All but one, which he dropped next to Nate. "Inside is the fuse I made. Light it and run like hell, and I hope you trip and get blown to bits."

"Be careful on your way down," Nate said. Riding at night was risky enough; riding down a mountain in complete darkness taxed the best of horsemen.

Swinging up, Shakespeare clucked to the mare. He glanced back as the night enfolded him, and waved. His parting admonition was, "Keep your eyes skinned, hoss!"

Nate did not sit back down until the hoof falls had faded. He chewed on a piece of pemmican without really tasting it. Now that he was by himself, unease gripped him. He tried to shake it off as nerves. He was alone at the top of the world near a portal to another time, to the wilderness as it had been before the first white man stepped foot on the continent. Who wouldn't be nervous?

The Indians had many accounts of the early times. Legends, the whites would say, and give them little credence. But to the various tribes, the stories of their ancestors were descriptions of real events.

Nate was reminded of the tales of the redheaded cannibals. He was glad the scarred warriors did not have red hair. Where they came from, why they disfigured their faces, were mysteries. He vaguely recollected hearing about a tribe that did something similar, but it had been so long ago, he could not recall the particulars.

Nate went to take another bite and froze. To the north, in the vicinity of the glacier, rose a ululating cry. It was not the staccato yipping of a coyote or the wavering howl of a wolf, but something entirely different, entirely new. It had a forlorn, mournful quality, like the wail of a lost soul in the throes of torment, and yet the throat that voiced it was that of a beast. The wail rose and fell and rose again, then abruptly ended.

Nate placed the pemmican in a parfleche. He was not all that hungry. He folded his forearms across his knees and leaned against his saddle. It would be a long night. He doubted he would sleep much.

Nate disliked being away from Winona. When he was younger and ran a trap line, he did not mind. He was often gone for weeks setting traps and adding to the collection of prime peltries he sold at the annual rendezvous for more money than most men earned in two or three years. But that was how he had made his living, and he accepted the separations as a necessary.

Not anymore.

Nate no longer trapped for a living. The beaver trade had died, the victim of new fads in fashion. The rendezvous ended. Nate stayed home and grew to like it. There was no one he cared more for than his wife, no one in whose company he would rather be. Some men were the opposite. They would rather do anything *but* be with their wives, which always struck Nate as peculiar. Why say *"I do"* if what they really meant was *"I will but don't crowd me"*?

The bay had been cropping grass but now raised its head and pricked its ears.

Pretending not to have noticed, Nate looked toward where the bay was staring so intently. It could have been anything from an owl to a mountain lion. When a minute went by and nothing appeared, he concluded it was not worth being concerned about. The very next moment he was proven wrong.

A squat shape materialized out of the gloom. Whether man or beast was hard to say but one thing was immediately apparent.

Whatever the creature was, it was stalking him.

"What do you think Pa is doing right about now?"

Winona King was washing the supper dishes in a bucket on the counter by the window. She looked out and saw the distant peaks silhouetted like jagged fangs against the canopy of stars. For some reason she shivered. She held a hand to the window, but there was no draft.

"Ma?" Evelyn said. "Didn't you hear me?"

"I imagine your father and Shakespeare are swapping tall tales," Winona said. "Without us there, they can exaggerate to their hearts' content."

Evelyn was in the rocking chair by the fireplace. They had let the fire burn down after cooking their stew and only a few red coals remained. Slowing her rocking, Evelyn imagined that two of the embers were glowing eyes. "I hope they make it back safe."

"Your father is a hard man to kill," Winona said by way of praise, "and your Uncle Shakespeare did not get all those white hairs by being puny."

"Maybe so, but those Indians who killed Niwot worry me." Evelyn was sure she would be haunted by the image of the arrow slicing into his throat for as long as she lived. "Why can't Indians just let us be? It's not right, them always trying to kill us."

"I trust, daughter, that you realize *I* am an Indian."

"Oh, Ma."

"My point is that not all Indians try to kill us. The *Sosoni* have always tried to get along with the whites. They have adopted your father and your brother and you into the tribe."

"I know that."

"Then you know that not all Indians are your enemies. The *Sosoni* are your people as much as mine. They care for you, *baide,* as they do for any of their own. They would die for you."

Evelyn had noticed that her mother was using certain Shoshone words instead of English. She mentioned it, adding, "Are you doing that on purpose?"

"Haa."

Which was Shoshone for "yes," as Evelyn well knew. "Why?"

"To remind you that you are a woman of two worlds. You speak two tongues, the white tongue and *Sosoni.* Or you can, if you want to, but you almost always speak English."

Belatedly, Evelyn realized her mother had just referred to her as a *woman.* It shocked her. Half-jokingly, she said, "So I'm not a little girl anymore, *bia."* The Shoshone word for "mother."

Winona placed the last of the plates on the counter, and turned. Folding her arms, she regarded her daughter a bit before saying, "No, you are not. I have thought of you as a girl, but I see now that was wrong. Niwot was not here to play tag with you. He was here to court you."

"Niwot," Evelyn said softly, wishing her mother had not reminded her. Again the image of the shaft imbedding itself in his throat seared her, and she shuddered. "I can never forgive myself. His death was my fault."

"That is preposterous," Winona said.

"As you pointed out, he was here courting me. If I had told him months ago that I could never be his wife, he would still be alive."

"Gia, baide."

"No, daughter?" Evelyn repeated. "How can you say that? He was here because of me. He died because of me."

"Was the arrow that killed him yours? *Gia.* He was killed by enemies. Do you understand that word? No matter which tongue I speak it in?"

"I know what an enemy is," Evelyn said in mild resentment.

"Do you? An enemy is someone who wants to kill you. It is that simple. You can try to be nice to them and talk to them but they will still want to kill you. It is what they do. It is why they are an *enemy.* Put the blame for Niwot's death where it belongs. Their hands are stained red with his blood, not yours."

"I can't help how I feel."

"Yes, you can. You are a woman now, not a little girl," Winona said. "Little girls live by their emotions. A woman must temper her feelings. She must control them, not let them control her."

Evelyn was about to comment that she resented being lectured when it struck her that her mother was not lecturing her; her mother was talking to her as one woman to another. "I'm not as grown-up as you would have me be."

"Only because you do not want to grow up. Grown-ups have responsibilities. They must do that which is best for those they love and not just what is best for them. They shoulder the burden of their actions without making excuses."

"One minute you say I'm not to blame for Niwot's death; the next minute you say I am."

"That is not what I said at all, daughter. The men who chose to be our enemies are responsible. You must not wallow in misery. You will have an unhappy life if you do."

One of the embers that Evelyn had imagined was an eye had blinked out. "I don't want to talk about it anymore."

"That is the little girl talking. Girls do not

like that which is unpleasant. They hide from it rather than confront it."

"I've never seen you so serious before," Evelyn remarked.

"Yes, you have. And it is fitting. Niwot's death is serious. Your being a woman is serious. You must cast off the perceptions of a little girl and look at the world as the woman you have become."

Evelyn did not respond. She was too deeply troubled.

"Nothing to say? Avoiding it will not make it go away."

"What is it, exactly, that I am avoiding again?" Evelyn sullenly asked.

"Please, Blue Flower. I respect you. You should respect me."

Evelyn felt her eyes moisten. "But I don't want to start thinking like a woman. Once I do, I will never be the same."

"None of us are," Winona said. "Some of us try to put it off longer than others, but eventually we must grow up whether we want to or not."

"Why are you telling me all this now?"

"A fruit ripens in its time. So does a person. You are on the threshold, as the whites would say. You must embrace that which you fear."

"I am not ready. It is too much for me."

Evelyn slumped in the rocking chair. She felt sad and tired.

Winona walked over and tenderly placed her hand on her daughter's shoulder. "You need not give up being a girl right this minute. It is enough, for now, that you know what is before you. When the time comes, you will choose the right path."

"How can you be so sure?"

Winona smiled warmly. "You are a King, and as your father is so fond of telling us —" she did her best to imitate her husband's deep voice, "— the Kings stand on their own two feet, by God!"

Despite herself, Evelyn grinned. "How will I know when it's time, Ma? How will I know when to give up the one and be the other?"

"It will happen without you being aware. One day you will wake up and look around you and you will look through the eyes of a woman." Winona bent and kissed Evelyn on the cheek. "Do not let it worry you. What will be, will be."

"How did you get so smart?"

Before Winona could answer, they were surprised by a knock on the door. Automatically, Winona started for her rifle, propped against the wall. "Who is it?" she called out.

"The wife of a certain white-haired lunkhead," came the answer.

Immensely pleased, Winona scooted to the door and threw the bolt. Blue Water Woman was not just her neighbor but her best friend. "Come in. Come in. What brings you over so late?"

"I was hoping you would not mind company for the night," Blue Water Woman said. "I get lonely when that tub of hot air is gone. But if you ever tell him that, I will deny saying it."

Winona laughed. "Of course you are welcome. I will make hot chocolate and we will stay up late talking about the silly things our men do."

Blue Water Woman smiled at Evelyn. "What have the two of you been up to?"

"Nothing much," Evelyn said.

CHAPTER NINE

Nate King opened a parfleche and rummaged inside as if searching for something. From under his brow he watched the squat shape in the grass. Melting onto its belly, it snaked toward him with infinite care.

Try though Nate might, he could not see the face clearly. But it had to be the scarfaced warrior. Nate had to hand it to him. The man's stalking skill was considerable. Not once had Nate heard him. A glint of metal told Nate the warrior had a knife.

By rights Nate should shoot him. Just set the parfleche to one side, pick up the Hawken or draw a pistol, and put a lead ball into the middle of the shape. The parfleche in his lap, he slid his hand to a flintlock, but he did not draw it.

Nate would not kill if he could avoid it. In his younger days he had not had any qualms about squeezing the trigger, but now things were different. He was older and wiser. Killing was no longer a means to an end. He only slew as a last resort.

So there Nate sat, seemingly unaware of the stalking death, awaiting the right moment to try something other than killing. He was aware of the risk. Shakespeare would say he was being a simpleton, but Shakespeare was not there.

Time passed with awful slowness.

Twice Nate gazed about him but he made it a point not to look directly at his stalker. Each time the warrior froze and did not move again for several minutes. Nate wanted to give the impression he did not suspect anything. Once, he even stood and stretched and stifled a yawn, then walked in a circle around his saddle and packs while gazing at the forest that hemmed the meadow. When Nate sat back down, he positioned himself so that while he was not facing the warrior, he could still watch him out of the corner of an eye.

The deadly stalk continued.

Nate let his chin dip a few times and each time jerked his head up, to give the illusion he was having a hard time staying awake. Finally he pretended to doze off, his arms crossed in front of him in such a way that his hands happened to rest on his flintlocks.

The warrior did not take the bait. He did

not move any faster. He was taking no chances, this one.

Finally, the moment Nate had been waiting for; the scar-faced warrior was within a few bounds, girding his legs under him to spring. Nate was ready when the warrior suddenly exploded into motion and sprang for him. Whipping sideways and rising onto his knees, Nate trained his pistols on his would-be slayer, cocking them as he rose.

The warrior had seen both of his companions fall to firearms. He knew what guns could do. Stopping short as if he had slammed into a wall, the warrior glared at the twin muzzles, then at Nate, his grotesque scars lending him an inhuman aspect.

"Drop the knife," Nate said. To convey his meaning, he pointed a flintlock at the man's hand, then at the ground.

The warrior was loath to part with his weapon. He held on to it.

Nate aimed at a spot in front of the warrior's feet and fired into the ground. The blast and the flash of flame and smoke caused the scar-faced warrior to flinch. Again Nate pointed at the man's hand and then at the ground.

The knife fell.

Nate sidestepped and motioned for the

warrior to sit near his saddle. He prudently kept space between them, picked up the knife, and threw it into the darkness.

"Do you speak English?" Nate asked. As he expected, he received no response. He tried Shoshone. He tried Flathead. He tried Crow. He was not a linguist like Winona, but he possessed a smattering of words from over half a dozen tongues, and the scar-faced warrior responded to none of them.

Stymied, Nate stepped back another couple of steps, and hunkered. His prisoner's features were inscrutable.

"I wish you would help me out here," Nate said. The man had to guess he was trying to communicate. Placing the pistol on his leg and keeping his hands next to it in case the warrior tried to jump him, Nate resorted to the well-nigh universal hand language of the plains and mountains tribes. "Question. You talk sign language?"

The warrior blinked.

Nate's fingers flowed, repeated the question.

After a moment's hesitation, the scar-faced warrior slowly raised his right hand to chest height, his index finger pointing straight up, his other fingers clenched with his thumb on his second finger, and moved his hand to the left and then down.

It was sign for "yes." Elated, Nate nearly forgot himself and started to move closer but stopped. "I no enemy," he signed.

"You talk two tongues," the warrior signed, which was the same as saying Nate was a liar.

"I talk true," Nate insisted.

"Your friend kill Ghost Walker. You kill Stands On Moon. You talk two tongues," the warrior insisted.

"They try kill us," Nate reminded him.

The warrior's hands went still. Then he signed, "Question. You called?"

"Grizzly Killer." Nate signed the name by which the Shoshones and other tribes knew him, a name bestowed on him by a Cheyenne warrior years ago after the warrior witnessed a fight between Nate and a grizzly in which Nate miraculously slew the giant bear.

The scar-faced man began to quake slightly, as if he were shivering. Peering intently, Nate realized, with mild shock, that the warrior was laughing. Silently, inwardly laughing.

"Question. Why you laugh?" Nate signed.

"Your name," the man replied.

"I not know," Nate signed, which was the same as saying, "I not understand."

"You Bear People. Your friend Bear

People. But you kill great bear."

It took a minute of mulling for Nate to comprehend. The warrior thought that Shakespeare and he, with their beards and large size, resembled bears, and it struck the warrior as humorous that a bear man would slay the creature he resembled. Nate expressed his hunch in sign language.

"My people think your people Bear People," was the reply.

Nate's brow knit. The implication was that the warrior's tribe had dealings with whites in the past. "Question," he signed. "Your people called?"

The warrior said something in his tongue, rather proudly, then signed, "Heart Eaters."

Usually, the name of a tribe, whether their own or what they were called by other tribes, was based on a distinguishing trait or tribal practice. The signs for the Cheyenne were Finger Choppers. The signs for the Blackfeet were Black Moccasins, since that was the color the Blackfeet favored. The signs for the Shoshones were Sheep Eaters. It prompted Nate to sign, "Question. Your people eat hearts?"

"Yes."

"Question. Deer hearts? Buffalo hearts? Bear hearts?" To Nate those seemed the logical choices.

"All hearts," the warrior signed.

A chill seized Nate, a chill that had nothing to do with the brisk wind. "Question. Your people eat people?"

"Eat people hearts," the warrior signed.

The distinction was a minor one to Nate. "Question. Why Heart Eaters eat hearts?"

"Make strong. Make fast. Make —" The warrior's fingers stopped moving. He seemed to be trying to come up with just the right way of saying it. "— make good medicine."

Nate thought he understood. The tribe ate the hearts in the belief that in doing so they acquired the special power of whatever, or whomever, the heart belonged to. Thus, eating the heart of a bear lent them the strength of a bear. Eating the heart of a deer made them fleet as deer. And so on. "Question." Nate amended an oversight on his part. "You called?"

"Drinks Blood."

Figuring the warrior was confused, Nate signed, "Question. Your people drink blood?"

The warrior placed a hand flat on his chest. "I drink blood."

Nate sat back. *Drinks Blood. Ghost Walker. Stands On Moon.* All were unusual names, but then, everything associated with this new tribe was unusual. "Tell me, Drinks Blood," he signed. "Why cut face?" He ran his fingers over his cheeks to signify running them over the warrior's scars.

"For medicine," Drinks Blood answered.

Nate was at a loss. "Medicine" was used by many tribes to allude to the Great Mystery, as they called it. Some whites considered the Great Mystery the same as God. Nate had divined a subtler context. The Great Mystery was God and yet more or other than God. To the Indians, the Great Mystery was not a wrathful deity but more akin to a living force. "Question. Great Mystery medicine?"

Drinks Blood seemed surprised that Nate knew of the Great Mystery. "Yes," he signed.

Nate digested the information. Medicine was extremely important to most Indians. It had nothing to do with healing herbs or the like, but rather referred to the mysterious power of the Great Mystery. Not power in a physical sense but power in a deeper, spiritual context. Among some tribes, it was common for warriors to go on what were called Vision Quests in pursuit of that power. Among other tribes, the power was believed to be reserved to the medicine men. "Question. All Heart Eaters medicine men?"

Drinks Blood cocked his head in puzzlement. "All Heart Eaters have medicine." Using his right thumb, he touched the center of his chest. It was the sign for himself, for him personally as opposed to the rest of his people. "Drinks Blood have medicine. But Drinks Blood no medicine man."

So the power could be acquired by anyone, Nate reflected. "Question. Heart Eaters have chief?"

"Yes. Him eat most hearts be chief."

"Question. People hearts?"

"Yes."

Nate suppressed a shudder. Small wonder the other tribes in the central Rockies considered the region taboo. "Question. Many Heart Eaters warriors?"

Drinks Blood did not respond.

"Question. Where Heart Eaters villages?"

Again the scar-faced warrior did not acknowledge the question.

Nate did not want Drinks Blood to clam up when he was learning so much. He tried a different tack. "Question. Why kill Ute near lake?"

"Him enemy."

"But you not eat heart."

"Kill enemy. Always kill enemy. Eat hearts no always."

So they did not kill just for the medicine alone. Nate found that interesting. "Question. Many tribes enemy?"

"All tribes enemies. Bear People enemies."

"Question. Heart Eaters no have friends?" Nate asked, hoping to learn if the tribe had dealings with any other.

"All people enemies," Drinks Blood clarified, thereby revealing that his tribe had another trait in common with the Apaches.

There was so much Nate wanted to ask, but he was hampered by the limitations of sign. The Shoshones had about seven hundred signs they used in sign talk. Other tribes used a few more, some fewer. Nate knew about five hundred. He was capable of asking most anything, but he had to take care in how he strung the signs together or his meaning would be lost. He was debating how to pose his next question when Drinks Blood apparently decided it was time to ask a few of his own.

"Question, Grizzly Killer. Why you live Heart Eaters land?"

Nate had been hoping the tribe did not claim his valley as theirs. Now he knew. "I no know your land."

"Heart Eaters land," Drinks Blood repeated.

"Live many moons near lake. No see

191

Heart Eaters before you," Nate pointed out.

"Heart Eaters no come lake often." Drinks Blood used the signs for "many times" but it meant essentially the same thing.

"Question. Why no come lake?"

Drinks Blood gazed to the north, in the direction of the glacier. "Bad medicine here. Much bad medicine."

Other tribes believed the same thing. Nate had asked Niwot why the Utes shunned the valley and been told that long ago, longer than the memory of the oldest living Ute, an Ute hunting party had visited the valley to hunt elk. They had camped on the lakeshore. Their hunt had been successful, and the night before they were to leave, they were in camp, celebrating, when they were attacked and slaughtered by what Niwot could only say was a "creature of the old times." When Nate pressed him, the young Ute had said that was how the older Ute warrior described it. "Question. You know bad medicine?"

Once again Drinks Blood stared northward. "Come when sun gone. When moon full. Come outside ice. Kill and kill and kill. Arrow no hurt. Knife no hurt. Go in ice and sleep."

Forgetting himself, Nate said in English, "You're saying that something lives *in* the glacier? That's ridiculous." It was a mistake. Some of the friendliness went out of Drinks Blood's expression, and he stiffened. "Tell me all," Nate signed.

"No."

Nate changed to a different subject. "Question. Drinks Blood have wife?"

"Yes."

"Question. Drinks Blood have children?"

"Yes."

"I have wife. I have children. We much same." Nate was trying to impress on him that they had more in common than Drinks Blood might imagine, and thus had no real reason to be enemies.

"We much not same," the warrior disagreed. "You white. I Heart Eater. You bad. I good."

"People be people," Nate signed.

Drinks Blood held his right hand out, palm up. "Heart Eaters," he signed, and held the hand flat again. Then he held his left hand out, palm up. "People no Heart Eaters." He placed his left hand in his right hand and then closed his right hand and shook it to signify the right was squeezing the life out of the left. "Question. Grizzly Killer understand?"

"Yes." Nate was getting nowhere. The other still regarded him as an enemy who must be slain. He tried one last time. "Question. We be friends?"

"No."

"Question. Friends time in front?" Nate was asking if there was any chance they could be friends at some point in the future.

"No."

"Why?"

"You be dead," Drinks Blood signed, and smiled. "You be dead now."

Something in the way the warrior signed the words, and in his expression, gave Nate pause. It was almost as if Drinks Blood were gloating — or knew something he did not. Then Nate saw that Drinks Blood was staring past him, into the dark at his back. An awful premonition seized Nate and he started to turn, but he was too late and too slow.

Heavy forms slammed into Nate from behind. He was nearly bowled over, and wound up on his knees with his arm gripped by iron hands. Twisting, he discovered he was being held by not one but two Heart Eaters. He realized that Drinks Blood had kept him talking sign so the pair could sneak up close without him being aware.

Nate had taken it for granted there were three warriors and only three warriors. He had seen three crossing the meadow; he had seen three at the talus slope. It did not occur to him there might be more, an oversight that might now prove his undoing.

Growling like the bear the Heart Eaters thought he resembled, Nate sought to wrench his arms free. Although the Heart Eaters were short, they were stocky and strong, and while he caused one to trip and nearly lose hold, he failed to shake them off. And while he was struggling, Drinks Blood had pushed himself erect.

They were going to kill him.

The certainty fired Nate with fury. He refused to die, refused to accept that he might never set eyes on Winona again. Or Evelyn. Or Zach. Surging to his full height, he whipped halfway around, the power in his shoulders and right arm sufficient to lift the warrior holding that arm clear off his feet and swing him like a sack of flour. Nate whipped him straight into Drinks Blood and both men went down in a tangle, Drinks Blood bellowing angrily in a guttural tongue.

The third warrior still had firm hold of Nate's left arm. Shifting, Nate started to point the flintlock at the man's forehead with the intention of blowing his brains out. Nate glimpsed a streak of metal, and his own forehead burst with pain and bright pinpoints of swirling light.

Nate's knees slammed into the ground. He tried to aim the pistol, only to find it was no longer in his hand. Another blow to the head rocked him. He dived for his Bowie, but his hand seemed to move in slow motion. It was taking forever for his fingers to reach the hilt. Something or someone rammed into the middle of Nate's back and he was knocked flat. Dimly, he felt hands clamp on to his wrists. He bucked upward, only to have the back of his head cave in.

That was the last thing he remembered.

Pain was the first sensation.

Nausea the second.

The third was jarring brightness when Nate opened his eyes and beheld the sun directly overhead. It was noon. He had been unconscious more than twelve hours. Blinking, he went to shield his eyes with his hand, but his arm would not move. He looked right and then left, and scowled. His wrists were secured to stakes. Glancing down, he saw that his ankles had been accorded the same treatment. He also found that his shirt was gone.

A shadow fell across him. Several shadows, each resolving into a hideous scarred face and a stocky body in buckskins. One of the scarred faces hovered over his, then dipped down.

Drinks Blood regarded him intently. His hands moved in sign language. "Question. You surprise you alive?"

"How do you expect me to answer with my wrists tied?" Nate snapped in English. He was mad. Not at the Heart Eaters, for they had done what every hostile tribe did to an enemy. No, he was mad at himself for letting them take him so easily.

Drinks Blood grunted. "Question. You want know why alive?"

"I can guess." Nate's missing shirt was the clue. They were called *Heart* Eaters, after all, and apparently they preferred to carve the hearts from still-breathing victims rather than dead flesh.

As if Drinks Blood could peer into Nate's thoughts, he signed, "More medicine when alive. Much strong when alive."

"I hope you choke to death on the first bite." Nate tested the ropes that bound his arms. They had done a good job.

Drinks Blood placed his hand on Nate's chest above his heart. Grinning, he produced a knife. Not his own knife with the crude bone handle, but Nate's Bowie. He placed the razor tip against Nate's skin and a tiny drop of blood appeared.

Nate braced himself for the fatal thrust. He had always known this day would come, the day when his luck played out. Life in the wilderness was fraught with peril, and over the years he had survived countless dangers. But no one survived indefinitely.

The thrust did not come. Drinks Blood, his hand resting lightly on the hilt, touched the tip of a finger to the drop of blood, then touched the drop of blood to his tongue. He smacked his lips and grinned.

"Like to play with your victims, do you?" Nate growled.

While Drinks Blood did not understand the words, he seemed to guess their meaning. "No kill now, Grizzly Killer," he signed.

"You plan to torture me first, is that it?"

Drinks Blood straightened and slid the Bowie into Nate's sheath, which now hung around his waist. "No eat hearts when day. Eat hearts when night. You understand, Grizzly Killer?"

Yes, Nate did. Some tribes conducted certain ceremonies at night. Fortunately for him, the Heart Eaters did their heart eating under the stars and the moon.

"Much medicine when night," Drinks Blood signed.

Nate was getting tired of hearing about medicine. He lay quietly as the three war-

198

riors filed past. Shifting, he surveyed his surroundings. He was still in the meadow. His saddle and parfleches were off to his right. The parfleches had been opened and upended and the contents strewn about. No doubt, the Heart Eaters had helped themselves to whatever caught their interest.

The bay was where Nate had picketed it. In going past, the three warriors gave the horse a wide berth and gazed at it as if apprehensive it might rear or try to kick them. Their reaction told Nate as surely as words that the Heart Eaters did not have horses, an interesting tidbit to keep in mind for the future.

Nate smiled grimly. *The future?* He had no future if the Heart Eaters had their way. He must ensure they didn't.

Drinks Blood and one of the other warriors spread out blankets — Nate's blankets — and lay down. The third warrior went off toward the pass.

Nate was perplexed by how completely they ignored him. Maybe they felt he had no hope of freeing himself. Maybe they thought they were close enough to stop him if he did.

"We will see about that," Nate said to himself. He gripped the right stake. He gripped the left. They were solidly imbedded. But it would be another seven to eight hours before the sun went down. A lot could happen in that amount of time.

His face set in grim lines, Nate began trying to rock the stakes back and forth. They would not budge. He tried again and again and again, always with one eye on the Heart Eaters. Over and over and over until his skin blistered and bled and his fingers and wrists were in torment. But he did not stop. He *must* not stop.

His life was in the balance.

CHAPTER TEN

The afternoon crawled by on turtle's feet.

Nate King sweated and tugged and sweated and wrenched. Smears of scarlet streaked both stakes. The ropes had rubbed through his skin and into his flesh so that every movement was agony. He clenched his jaw and bore it. He had endured worse. He could endure this.

Nate had once read a newspaper account that said mountain men were a hardy breed. The journalist who wrote it did not know the half of it. The weak and the squeamish never lasted long in the wild. It took a kind of fortitude that few men had. The ability to withstand blistering heat and frigid cold. The stamina to go without food and water for days. The readiness to fight for one's life. Unless a man was hardy enough to do all that, he had no business living in the mountains.

A weaker man would have succumbed to

the pain by now. But Nate's will had been tempered on the whetstone of the raw edge of existence and forged in the furnace of adversity. He could no more give up than he could stop breathing.

The afternoon waned. The sun was half an hour shy of abandoning its throne when the third Heart Eater appeared out of the woods below the pass and made for his friends. Both rose to greet him and an excited exchange took place. There was a lot of gesturing at the pass.

Nate did not like the looks of that. Placing his cheek against his arm, he adopted what he hoped was a look of utter despair. He also shifted his wrists so his hands hid the blood-spattered stakes. The precaution proved timely.

Drinks Blood approached. Whatever news the third warrior had brought pleased him. His fingers flowed in sign. "Many Heart Eaters come, Grizzly Killer."

"Must make for small portions," Nate said.

"We make smoke talk," Drinks Blood signed. "Warriors come village."

The warrior who had gone up to the pass, Nate realized, had sent smoke signals. Now more were on their way. "So you only have the one village? Thanks for the information."

Paying no heed to Nate's muttering, Drinks Blood signed, "Make smoke talk you. Make smoke talk bear man white hair."

"You told them about me and my friend," Nate said. "Yes, I got that much."

"Make smoke talk your woman. Make smoke talk your daughter. Make smoke talk Bear People near lake."

Going rigid, Nate raised his head. "You did what?"

"Many warriors come," Drinks Blood signed, smirking as he moved his hands. "Many warriors come lake."

"You bastard." Nate was horror-struck. Drinks Blood had relayed the news about his family and friends to the Heart Eater village. Winona and Evelyn and the rest would be taken prisoner and subjected to the same fate he would see come nightfall; they would have their hearts cut out while they were still alive. "You miserable, stinking bastard."

Nate seldom indulged in cursing but calmly and bitterly he called Drinks Blood every foul name under the sun. He stopped only because Drinks Blood laughed, showing that he enjoyed Nate's dismay.

"If it is the last thing I ever do, I will kill you," Nate vowed.

"Your heart eat short time," Drinks Blood gloated. "Tomorrow night eat heart your woman." He paused as if waiting for Nate to throw a tantrum, and when it did not happen, he frowned, turned on his heel, and rejoined the others.

It was with heightened urgency that Nate renewed his assault on the stakes. When he flagged, when he tired or the pain became too great, he had only to think of Winona and their children having their hearts cut out, and a fresh flood of vitality flooded through him.

The sun came to rest on the peaks to the west. Then, by gradual degrees, the blazing orb slid from sight, growing smaller and smaller until only bands of pink and yellow remained to mark the fading of the day.

The Heart Eaters became more animated than Nate had heretofore seen them. They were excited at the prospect of eating his heart. Excited by the power they believed it would give them, the special medicine they valued more than anything else.

Nate watched them, and he watched the sky. A lot depended on how dark it became before they performed their grisly ritual. Stars blossomed, pale against the twilight. The crescent moon hung poised like a scimitar.

It was the moon they were waiting for. One of the warriors pointed and said something, and all three drew knives and held them in front of them while slowly advancing on Nate. They did not whoop or laugh. A grave solemnity marked their features. The eating of a heart was their holy of holies, and they took part with the utmost seriousness.

Nate squared his shoulders and girded himself.

Drinks Blood came up to him. The others moved to each side. They were holding their knives close to their chests, the blades pointed at the heavens.

Staring at the moon, Drinks Blood spread his arms and gave voice to a singsong chant that went on and on. Now and then the other two chimed in, in unison. Like Shoshone ceremonies, this one had to be conducted in a certain way, at a certain pace. They would not rush things.

Take as long as you want, Nate thought. He would gather his strength and be ready.

The chant ended. Drinks Blood held the Bowie over Nate and turned the blade from side to side so that it gleamed in the moonlight, while he intoned words that must have special meaning. The other two stood with their knives aloft and pointed at the spectral moon.

Then came the moment Nate had been waiting for.

Raising his voice, Drinks Blood sank to his knees. A look of near ecstasy came over him as he held the Bowie with its tip on Nate's chest, above the heart. He did not look at Nate. He stared fixedly at the knife, at the spot he would open to reach the heart. His dark eyes glittered with inhuman hunger.

None of the Heart Eaters noticed Nate grip the right stake and then grip the left. None of the three seemed to think it strange he showed not the least bit of fear. Frozen with fright, they probably assumed. They were about to learn differently.

Drinks Blood raised the Bowie, his voice rising higher as he raised the knife. When the Bowie was at its apex, Drinks Blood stared at the moon and uttered a piercing shriek echoed by the other two.

With a mighty heave of Nate's powerful frame, both stakes came out of the ground. He twisted at the waist. The Bowie nicked his back but sank into the earth instead of into his body. Astonishment held the Heart Eaters in momentary paralysis, enabling Nate to slam the stake in his right hand against Drinks Blood's head. Drinks Blood folded, and the next instant, Nate had replaced the stake with the Bowie.

Nate had to end it quickly, before the warriors thought to skip back out of reach and slay him with arrows. He spun, slicing deep into the legs of the warrior on his right. Almost in the same breath he spun the other way, arcing the Bowie at the abdomen of the man on his other side. The warrior had started to throw himself backward and his body was bent like a bow. The blade bit into his groin instead.

All three were down but they were alive.

Lunging, Nate slashed at the rope binding his right ankle. The hemp parted like strands of wax. He turned to do the same to the rope around his left ankle but had to parry a stab by the warrior he had cut in the groin. Steel rang on iron. Hissing like a serpent, the warrior stabbed again. Nate parried, feinted, and opened the warrior's arm from wrist to elbow.

Not once had any of the Heart Eaters cried out in pain.

The warrior on Nate's right turned to crawl to the packs — and a bow and quiver. Nate could not let him reach them. He drove his Bowie into the man's leg. The big blade went all the way through, glancing off bone. Stiffening, the warrior opened his mouth wide, but made no sound. The force of will it took impressed Nate tremendously.

Drinks Blood lay dazed. The third warrior had drawn back and was bent over, clutching his forearm to his waist, striving to stanch the blood that showered the grass like red rain.

A swift slice, and Nate had freed his other ankle. He pushed up off the ground, or tried to as much as he could with his stiffened legs. The Heart Eater on the right sliced at his chest. Nate blocked the stroke. Then, before the man could recover his balance, Nate grabbed his wrist and pulled so hard, the warrior tumbled forward. A lightning swing, and one of the Heart Eaters was disposed of.

The warrior on Nate's left had risen. Although severely wounded, he struck again, aiming a terrific blow that, had it landed, would have cleaved Nate from his shoulder to his sternum. But Nate got the Bowie up in time. Their blades met and locked. The warrior seized Nate's other wrist. Straining, each sought to unbalance the other. The Heart Eater was shorter, but his muscles were as hard as rock, and for a span of some seconds the outcome was undecided. Then Nate shifted and kicked out a sore leg. The warrior stumbled to one knee. Before he could straighten, Nate swung, half severing the man's neck so that the head flopped and blood gouted in a torrent.

Sucking in deep breaths, Nate stared at his fallen foes. They were formidable fighters, these Heart Eaters. Once again they reminded him of Apaches, and he wondered if there might be a link between the tribes. But no, that couldn't be, he told himself. Apaches did not scar their faces, or eat human hearts.

A slight sound was Nate's first inkling he had blundered. He spun, and beheld Drinks Blood almost at the packs. Almost to the bows. Nate could not possibly reach him before Drinks Blood grabbed one. He whirled and raced for the forest. To his horror, he discovered the circulation in his legs had been cut off for too long. The best he could do was lurch woodenly, like a puppet with its strings severed.

Nate willed his legs to go faster and shot a glance over his shoulder. Drinks Blood had notched an arrow to a bow. Even as Nate looked, Drinks Blood loosed the shaft. It was a blur in the night.

Bending, Nate heard the arrow whiz past his ear. It motivated his reluctant legs into doing what they needed to do. He looked back again. Drinks Blood was notching another arrow. This time the warrior wanted to be sure, and took his time.

Nate began weaving as best he could. His legs were regaining their strength but not quickly enough. He looked back, wanting to be ready when Drinks Blood released the shaft.

Drinks Blood already had.

The arrow was nigh invisible in the gloom. Nate threw himself to one side in the hope it would miss. It didn't. Searing pain racked his side. He nearly fell. A few more loping strides brought him to the timber, and he was in among tall firs. Stopping, he leaned against one.

Burning waves of pain assailed him. Nate reached down, expecting to find the barbed tip of the arrow sticking out of his body. But all it had done was graze him, leaving a furrow above his hip. He was bleeding, but only slightly.

Movement in the moonlight gave Nate a few moments of forewarning that Drinks Blood was after him.

Nate had three choices: stand and fight, knife against bow; run; or do what he did, namely, bound to a cluster of close firs, squirm in among them, and curl into a ball with his arms wrapped around his legs and his cheek tucked to his chest. He acted not a moment too soon.

An onrushing shadow acquired form and substance. Drinks Blood came to a stop near where Nate had leaned against the tree. He raised his head, listening intently, and sniffed several times like a bloodhound seeking fresh scent. He turned left, then right. Moon glow showed his scarred features scrunched in puzzlement. He peered about him, then seemed to come to a decision and sped off into the woods, evidently convinced his quarry was somewhere up ahead.

Nate stayed where he was. He had been lucky. Damned lucky. Winona would never learn how close she came to being a widow. Thus it ever was in the wild. A man never knew from one minute to the next when a new threat would abruptly bring him to the brink of oblivion, or beyond.

Nate slowly raised his head. He hoped to hear a sound, any sound, that would confirm Drinks Blood was still moving east, but except for the wind, the forest was unnaturally still. He must take a chance.

Slowly rising, but staying low, Nate eased from between the firs and glided toward the meadow. The Hawken and his flintlocks should be somewhere near his packs and saddle.

A slight rustle to his rear caused Nate to spin. He thought Drinks Blood was sneaking up on him but the warrior was nowhere to be seen. Hurrying on, he paused just long enough to establish that the two he thought he had killed were lying where he had left them. Then he flew on Mercury's wings, his back prickling at the prospect of taking an arrow. He passed one body and then the other, spied his shirt, ammo pouch and powderhorn, and hunkered. *Give me a little more time,* he prayed.

Nate felt like a target painted on a wall. At any moment Drinks Blood might return. He groped about, sure his weapons were there, but he could not find them. Acutely conscious he was squandering precious time, he searched among the contents of his upended parfleches.

Where could his guns be? Nate fumed. Surely, the Heart Eaters had not destroyed them. He looked under a parfleche. It was then he noticed that his saddle was on its side and not propped up as he had left it. He lifted it and came close to whooping for joy. The flintlocks were underneath.

Never in his whole life had Nate reloaded so fast. It was with an elation akin to pure joy that he held a pistol in each hand and wished Drinks Blood would show himself. Placing the saddle as he had found it, Nate sank to his knees behind it. It was not big enough to hide him, but in the dark Drinks Blood might not notice he was there.

Nerves tingling, Nate watched the tree line to the east. That was where Drinks Blood would appear. Nate would let him get close, so close he could not possibly miss, and squeeze off both pistols.

To the south a wolf howled in lonesome lament and was answered by a kindred spirit to the southwest.

The stars in their celestial orbits moved faster than the passage of time in the meadow. It was taking Drinks Blood much longer than Nate reckoned. He did not understand it. Drinks Blood would not blunder about in the dark forever. The warrior would guess he had been tricked and come on the run.

Nate's wounds and fatigue began to tell. His eyelids grew leaden. He could scarcely hold up his head. It was possible, just possible, that Drinks Blood had been watching him the whole time and was waiting for him to pass out. The chilling notion erased Nate's fatigue as effectively as an eraser did chalk on a slate.

Going by the position of the Big Dipper, it was two in the morning when Nate first entertained the thought that Drinks Blood was not going to show. He stayed behind the saddle a while longer, though, because he refused to believe Drinks Blood had given up. There had to be a reason Drinks Blood had not reappeared, but for the life of him, Nate could not imagine what it was.

Finally Nate stood. His legs were stiff again but not as bad as before. The first thing he did was don his shirt against the biting wind. Then he slid his powderhorn and ammunition pouch across his chest.

Taking a blanket, Nate entered the woods to the west. As soon as the foliage closed about him he bore to the left until he came to a thicket. With it at his back and the blanket draped over his shoulders, he sat and watched the meadow until the first pink flush of dawn painted the eastern horizon. Not once was there the slightest suggestion, by sound or movement, that Drinks Blood was anywhere near.

More mystified than ever, Nate tried to put himself in the Heart Eater's moccasins. He worried that Drinks Blood had gone down the mountain to the valley floor. If so, he must warn Winona and the others. Or was that merely what Drinks Blood wanted him to think? Nate remembered Drinks Blood signing that more warriors were on their way. Could it be that Drinks Blood had gone to hurry them along?

The possibility brought Nate to his feet. He went to the center of the meadow and in the growing light of the new dawn conducted another search. The Hawken had been there the whole time, partially covered by one of the packs the three warriors had opened and emptied, and by trampled grass. He hugged it to him as if it were Winona.

His natural impulse was to gather everything up, but as soon as he found his moccasins and possibles bag, he saddled the bay, climbed on, and made for the pass at a trot. The rising sun was warm on his back.

Since the pass ran from west to east, it was aglow in sunshine. When he came to the body and the boulder, he dismounted and advanced on foot. At the west end the wind was stronger.

The valley below was plunged in shadow. Out of it rose gray wisps from a campfire.

The Heart Eater war party was less than a mile away. As soon as the valley flooded with sunlight they would be on the move.

Nate had an hour, probably less. He retraced his steps to the bay and led it to the east end of the pass. A game trail revealed how Drinks Blood and the other two had climbed to the top. Nate swiftly gained the summit.

Boulders were strewn in a chaotic jumble. Threading through them, Nate came to where the warriors had stood on the rim. Only a few of the boulders were small enough to lift. Nate's hope of rolling down enough to block the pass was dashed.

Nate turned to continue to the west end. His foot bumped something that moved. He looked down, and was thunderstruck.

Drinks Blood and his friends had done Nate a favor. Not knowing what the keg of black powder was, they had left it lying there instead of breaking it open and scattering the powder. He had a chance now. Tucking the keg under his left arm, he prowled the rim, seeking a crack or crevice. He came to the west overlook.

The sun had banished the shadows to the undergrowth. Smoke no longer rose skyward. The campfire had been extinguished. The Heart Eaters were on their way.

Nate considered dropping the keg on the warriors when they reached the pass. But some might survive the explosion.

It was tempting, oh-so-tempting, to get on the bay and fly to his loved ones so he could be by their side when the war party arrived.

Then Nate came to a boulder about the size of the bay, perched an arm's-length from the edge. He walked around it, noting how it tilted toward the gap. The angle and proximity suggested an idea. On the side opposite the defile, he knelt and dug in the dirt until he had a hole wide enough and deep enough for the keg. He wedged it tight against the boulder and sat back. If he calculated right, the blast should send the boulder over the side and perhaps bring down part of the wall, as well. All he had to do was light it.

Consternation coursed through Nate with the jolt of a physical blow. He had not brought the fuse! In the time it would take to run to the bay and gallop to the meadow to find it, the war party would be there.

Nate had one recourse, and one only. Removing the keg from the hole, he set the keg upright and drew his Bowie. The *thunk* of the tip biting into the wood was much too loud for his liking but he kept at it, slivers flying, until he had a hole about the size of his middle finger. Replacing the Bowie in its sheath, he rose partway, carefully cradled the keg, and tilted it so that black powder trickled out. Backing away from the boulder, he created a trail of powder some fifteen feet in length. Longer would be safer, but he sensed he was running out of time.

Quickly, Nate wedged the keg back in the hole. Grabbing the Hawken, he retreated to the end of the powder trail, opened his possibles bag, and took out his fire steel and flint. Hunching over the powder, he struck the steel against the flint. Sparks flew, but none landed on the powder. He tried again. A spark fell where he wanted it to, but the powder did not ignite.

Was it Nate's imagination or did he hear voices? Harsh gutturals were borne on the breeze. The war party was almost to the pass. Or maybe advance scouts. Either way, he must stop them from making it through.

Beads of sweat broke out on Nate's brow. From his possibles bag he slid his tinder box and placed a wedge of tinder on top of the black powder. The tinder consisted of a piece of bird's nest. He held the flint and steel over it. A few sharp strokes, and an ember alighted atop the dry material. A wisp of smoke blossomed. Bending, Nate puffed lightly. The wisp grew, fed by a red ember.

Someone was shouting.

Nate raised up. The shouts were coming from the east end of the pass, not the west. It sounded like Drinks Blood. Was he urging the others to hurry?

Bending low again, Nate puffed a few more times and the ember became a tiny flame. Licking higher, the flame devoured the kindling, giving off more heat in the process. Suddenly the black powder hissed and crackled. Fingers of flame leaped along the trail of black grains toward the keg.

Nate ran. The press of boulders slowed him. He did not look back. A misstep now courted disaster. He covered twenty feet. Thirty. He had put several boulders between him and the one he hoped would plug the pass when the keg exploded. Twin sledge-hammers buffeted his ears. The ground heaved and the pass walls shook.

Nate stumbled, recovered, stumbled again. Careening off a boulder, he pitched onto his side. He saw it.

A great roiling column of smoke and dust and earth and rocks had mushroomed skyward and outward. In the blink of an eye it engulfed him, the dust swirling into his eyes and nose and mouth. Coughing and sputtering and blinking, he tried to rise. Stones and bits of stone pelted him like hail, stinging his head and face and shoulders. He covered his head with his arms.

A tremendous crash shook the pass. More dust and dirt and bits of rock filled the air.

There followed a series of gradually smaller crashes, each adding to the choking cloud. Last came a loud clattering and rattling that faded to a sound that reminded Nate of sand being poured from a bucket.

The cloud began to settle. Slapping dust from his buckskins, Nate stood and edged to the rim for a look. Not only had the blast propelled the giant boulder into the pass, but the section of wall below the boulder had shattered and caved in, filling the defile with tons and tons of debris.

The pass was effectively blocked. To clear it would take months of back-breaking labor.

Of Drinks Blood there was no sign.

Within the hour Nate was leading the pack horse down the mountain, anxious for hearth and home. He had done it. His valley, and those he most cared for, were safe.

But as subsequent events were to prove, he could not have been more wrong.

■ ■ ■ ■

BETWEEN TWO
WORLDS

■ ■ ■ ■

CHAPTER ELEVEN

A motley collection of hovels that called itself Boomburg had sprouted on the east bank of the Mississippi River well south of St. Louis. Shabby cabins, poorly constructed shacks that looked fit to blow away in the next strong wind, and a few tattered tents and leaky lean-tos fleshed out the scarecrow community of misfits, malcontents, and cutthroats.

Boomburg was a nest of vipers. Decent citizens avoided it like the plague. In a sense, its inhabitants spread a plague of a different order, the social disease of crime and all its many ills. Indeed, it was Boomburg's reputation as a haven for those who lived outside the law that accounted for the presence of so many two-legged vipers.

Unwary travelers were considered fair game by Boomburg's conscienceless gentry. Every rider, every wagon, was scrutinized and assessed as ripe for plucking, or not, as the case might be.

It was pushing nine o'clock and darkness had descended when a pair of riders brought weary mounts to a stop at the hitch rail in front of The River Rat, Boomburg's one and only tavern. As the sole watering hole for miles around, it drew the thirsty in droves. This night was no exception.

The locals studied the two newcomers with the predatory manner of hunting hawks, and decided the game was not worth the blood that would be spilled. For the pair were armed for bear. They strode straight to the bar, and the burlier of the duo, a muscular slab of a man, surprised everyone by climbing on the counter.

"Hold on, there!" the tavern keeper rumbled. "Who do you think you are? My customers behave themselves or they get tossed out on their ear."

"Interfere and I'll shoot you," the burly man warned, to the delight of some of the patrons. Many thought the tavern keeper had a habit of being too high-handed. Then, motioning for quiet, the newcomer raised his voice for all to hear. "I'm Arthur Forge from New Albion."

"That means nothing to us!" an unkempt customer snarled. "Why don't you toddle along and leave us to our liquor?"

"How would you like money for more than you can drink in a month?" Arthur Forge asked.

Raw greed spread like wildfire on every face. "What are you on about, mister?" called out a man at the back of the room.

"Justice," Forge said. "I'm after the stinking savages who killed my son. They call themselves the Nansusequa. My hounds lost their scent in the marshy country east of here."

"I hate Injuns," a man declared.

"Makes two of us, Humphrey," a red-nosed sophisticate grunted. "Old Andy Jackson had it right. The only good redskin is a dead redskin."

"I'll drink to that!" a hulking river pirate exclaimed, and did so.

Arthur Forge impatiently tapped his rifle until quiet fell, then said, "I have reason to believe they will try to cross the river by any means necessary. You have a ferry here, and boats. Need I spell it out?"

"There was mention of money," someone said.

"That there was," Forge confirmed. "There are five of these Nansusequa. Two men, two women and a girl. I'm offering a hundred dollars a head."

"Dead or alive?" came an excited query.

"I'm not fussy," Forge said. "Although I'll pay extra for alive if only so I can whittle on them before I kill them."

Murmurs spread. Five hundred dollars was more than most of these men had ever had in their possession at any one time in their entire lives. One of the more distrustful by nature hollered, "How do we know you're good for the money, stranger? We don't know you from Adam."

"I'm good for ten times as much," Arthur Forge boasted, adding, "Ask any of the dozen men with me." He counted on the mention of the extra guns to cool the monetary ardor of those who might entertain notions of bashing him over the head and helping themselves to his poke.

"Mr. Forge is as good as his word!" piped up the man who had accompanied him. "He's one of the leading citizens of New Albion."

"That's good enough for me," a man at the bar asserted.

"And me!" hollered another.

Forge smiled as vicious a smile as any of the assembled cutthroats were capable of. "I knew I could count on the likes of you. At daybreak I will be here with my posse, ready and willing to pay out to those who have earned it."

Ten seconds after the tavern door closed, the denizens of the The River Rat scurried in a mad rush to be the first to exit, only to be brought to a stop by a snarl from the most seasoned member of their pack.

"Not so fast, clods and dimwits! Or would you rather the bounty money slips through your fingers?"

"What are you on about, Silas?" the tavern keeper demanded.

When Old Silas spoke, the others listened. It was said there wasn't a law Silas hadn't broken, a commandment he hadn't trampled. He was generally conceded to be the shrewdest of their criminal brotherhood if by no other measure than he had lived so long without having his neck stretched.

"Just this, lads," Old Silas said. "It's Injuns you're dealing with, and those red devils are crafty."

"So?" demanded a ruffian.

"So where are you all off to if not to stand guard over your boats and canoes and skiffs in the hope the redskins will waltz into your gun sights?" Old Silas snapped. "Them, with their eyes that can see in the dark better than ours, and their ears that can pick out a whisper at a hundred paces."

"How else would we snare them?" a man asked.

"Simple. You lay a trap. You make it so easy for them, they can't resist." Old Silas tipped his ale to his lips and wiped his mouth with his sleeve and did not say anything else.

Finally a stalwart took the bait. "How do we do that?"

"You hide most of the watercraft," Old Silas answered. "Leave a few out in plain sight, with half a dozen men hid nearby to watch each one."

"It's brilliant," a man marveled.

"But those in on the catch will have to share the bounty," another noted.

"A share is better than none," opined a philosopher.

Old Silas motioned with his stein. "Brilliance doesn't come cheap. I get twenty dollars if they're caught."

Everyone agreed that was fair, which in itself was remarkable. Groups were chosen, and out they barreled. Boomburg saw more hectic activity over the next half hour than it had seen since its inception, with the result that all but two canoes and a small boat vanished into sheds and shacks and under nets. One canoe was placed along the bank at the north end of the settlement, the second canoe at the south end, while the small boat was tied to the dock that normally berthed the ferry. The ferry was hauled across to the other side of the river.

Pleased with their devious trap, the riffraff hid themselves and waited for fate to smile on them.

In the marsh to the east of the settlement, on a hummock of dry land that jutted above the snake and alligator-infested waters, huddled five weary figures. A clammy fog had formed, a ghostly mantle imbued with moon-induced pallor. The surface of the water was a dark mirror that offered no clues as to the presence of the swamp's deadlier residents.

The five had been laboring across the swampland for days. Creepers and vines hung in profusion, impeding their way. Slippery moss was constantly underfoot. The marsh was a morass of vile, dank water, quicksand, mosquitoes, leeches, spiders — the list was legion. Whites usually shunned the marsh, which was largely why the five surviving People of the Forest had intentionally plunged into its fearsome fastness.

Tenikawaku had never been so exhausted. Sprawled on her side, her head and one arm resting across a moldy log, she yearned for the pristine greenery of her beloved forest.

She and her green buckskin dress were splotched with mud, her dress damp in spots. She would gladly sleep for a week if she could. "How much farther? Does anyone know?"

Degamawaku was the only one on his feet. He had lost considerable weight, and his buckskins hung on him more loosely than before. His moccasins were caked thick with marsh mire, a consequence of always breaking the trail. "It cannot be far," he hazarded. "What do you think, Mother?"

Tihikanima had lost her bearings their second day in. She knew north from south and east from west, but the monotonous sameness of their surroundings rendered distance a nebulous concept. "I hope the river is near, my son," she said, and looked at her husband. Hope flared in her eyes but as promptly died.

Wakumassee stared numbly at a rotting stump. He seldom spoke unless spoken to, and when left to himself would sit slumped in despair, unmoving, until they were on the go again.

"Are you all right, husband?"

"I will never be all right again."

Tihi switched her attention to the other one who worried her. Little Mikikawaku was skin and bones. "How are you, daughter?" Tihi asked. "Any pains I should know about?"

"I am fine, Mother," Miki lied. The stink, the muck, sickened her. Her legs ached so much at times, she feared they were rotting away. Time and again her brother had to hoist her to his shoulders and carry her, or she would have collapsed.

To the west, a break in the fog gave Dega a glimpse of something other than slime and moss. "Lights! It must be a white settlement. I will investigate."

"Not alone," Tihi said, thinking her husband would echo her precaution and offer to go along. But Waku said nothing.

"The two of us will investigate," Teni offered, although every muscle in her body yearned for rest.

Dega squatted next to her. "One of us must watch over the others," he whispered. "They are weak and worn."

"And we still have far to go," Teni said. "The prairie stretches forever, the whites say."

"It cannot stretch forever if there are mountains on the other side," Dega responded. "We will reach those mountains. We will have a new home." He offered her the rifle. "Take this to protect them while I am gone."

"Only you know how to use it," Teni reminded him. "I have my knife and my bow." Her mother and father had bows, too, fashioned while on the run from a band of whites who had been on their trail since that terrible day the village was destroyed. Countless times they had tried to shake their pursuers and failed. Only recently did they find out why; the whites had dogs, great bristly brutes trained to track.

Dega squeezed Teni's shoulder, smiled encouragement at Miki and his mother, and quickly stepped over the side of the hummock and into a tepid pool. He remembered to hold the rifle over his head in case he slipped. It would not function wet. But the water only rose as high as his waist.

The thickening fog clung to Dega in wet folds. They had encountered a lot of fog since entering the marsh, which helped as well as hindered. The fog made it harder for the whites to find them, but it also made it harder for them to find their way out of the quagmire.

Plus, it made it difficult for Dega to spot alligators and snakes. He stayed alert for the telltale bumps of alligators' eyes and the sinuous ripples that marked the passage of serpents.

The marsh was alive with sounds. Bird

cries. Shrieks. The croak of frogs and the chirp of insects. At night the *yeonk-yeonk-yeonk* of young alligators bleated without cease, except when they were drowned out by the less frequent booming bellows of the adults.

A mosquito stung his cheek, but Dega did not slap at it. Sharp sounds drew unwanted attention.

Fingers of dry land alternated with the marshy tracts. In spots the vegetation was so thick, Dega had to hack a path with his blade. Once he gripped what he took to be a vine and it hissed and slithered from his grasp.

At length the fog thinned. Across a last rivulet of foul water stood the settlement Dega had spotted. It lay quiet under the stars. Signs of life were few. Lights blazed in a score of windows, and somewhere a woman sang softly, as if to an infant.

Dega circled to the north. He intended to find a safe way around the settlement and go back for his parents and sisters. By dawn they would find a spot to hole up, and, after they rested, push on afresh to the west in search of the waterway that some tribes called the Father of Rivers and the whites called the Mississippi.

Dega was past the last of the marshland

and crossing a field grown high with grass when a scent stopped him in his tracks. It was the scent of water, but not the foul water of the marsh. This was the unmistakable smell of a large body of water, a lake or a river. He continued on and soon heard gurgling and velvety rippling. Silently scrambling over a bank, he came to a flat fringe of shoreline.

It was a river.

Rising, Dega tried to assess its size. He could see lights perhaps three arrow flights distant, which he took to be a house. The reflection of the moon was no help as it was too low in the sky. He was bending to grope for a rock when he realized the lights he thought to be a house *were moving.* Not toward him, but from north to south. He had never heard of a moving house, but he would not put any absurdity past the whites.

Belatedly, Dega perceived that the river and the moving lights were cause and effect. The house must be a boat. White boats regularly plied the Albion River. The speed with which the current carried the craft suggested a river much larger than the Albion.

Dega's mouth grew slack with amazement. Squatting, he dipped a hand in the water and splashed his shoulders and chest. *Was* this *the Mississippi?* he wondered. The boat was almost to the settlement, but it did not veer to the dock. He watched until the craft was swallowed by the darkness; then he crept along the shore.

An untended canoe caused Dega to stiffen with excitement. It had been drawn up out of the river and turned upside down. Beside it was a pair of paddles. Nearby was a plank building.

Dega started forward, then stopped, wary. He had noticed the canoe was in a circle of light cast by a lantern. The lantern itself sat on — Dega had to struggle to remember the word his father said the whites used — a crate. But of the person to whom the canoe belonged, and to whom, conceivably, the lantern also belonged, there was not a trace.

The canoe was exactly what Dega's family needed to cross the Mississippi, if the river, was, in fact, the one they sought. He should be overjoyed. But he could not help wonder why the canoe was in the circle of light, like a fawn staked out to attract a marauding bear. And why, farther down the shore, was there another watercraft in another circle of light?

Dega sank onto his belly. The situation smacked of a trap. Yet that was preposterous. The whites in the settlement had no way of knowing he was in need of a means to cross the river. They had no way of knowing *anything* about him. He was exercising caution where none was called for.

Dega started to crawl but once again stopped. He could not shake the feeling that something was amiss. Coming to a sudden decision, he stripped off the powderhorn and ammo pouch and placed them with the rifle. Then he angled to the right, into the water. His belly scraping the bottom, he wriggled along the shore until he was abreast of the canoe.

From here Dega had a better view of the settlement. All appeared quiet. In fact, the streets were empty. That, too, was strange. It was early yet, by white standards. Yet he heard none of the lusty sounds he had always associated with the watering holes, as the whites called them, in New Albion.

With only his nose and eyes showing, Dega waited. The water was chilly but not uncomfortably cold. He was just beyond the circle of light, so if someone did spot him, he might mistake him for an alligator.

Dega thought of his sisters and his parents, alone and exhausted in the terrible marsh. They were counting on him. He must not take forever. He slid his right hand toward solid ground to pull himself out of the river, then turned to stone.

A door in the plank building near the canoe had opened a crack. Someone whispered. The door opened wider and out crept a grizzled white man in dirty clothes, who turned and hurried into the settlement. The door closed again.

So it *was* a trap. Dega suspected that their relentless pursuers were somehow behind it.

Dega had not told Teni or the others, but one night he had snuck back and climbed a tree to spy on them. He had seen the great shaggy dogs with their powerful jaws rimmed with sharp teeth. He also saw Arthur Forge, the father of Byram Forge. Arthur had vowed to take revenge for Bryam's death, and evidently he intended to fulfill that vow.

Dega studied the situation. The canoe was a quick dash from the water. It would only take a few moments to turn it over and push it into the river. But the whites would spill out and shoot him. Unless —

Dega smiled as an idea was born.

Rocks littered the shoreline. Several the size of grouse eggs were within easy reach. Dega slid closer and lined up several in a row.

Footsteps heralded the return of the man

who had gone into the settlement. He carried a bottle. He knocked lightly on the shack door and it opened to admit him.

As soon as the door closed, Dega snaked along the water's edge until he was past the shack and in shadow. He crawled out onto dry land and lay there waiting for his body to stop dripping. Then he crawled to the side of the shack and rose. A number of implements leaned against the wall. He chose one with a stout handle and metal tines.

From within came whispers and chuckles. Dega put an ear to a plank and heard a sloshing sound, as of the bottle being upended. He crept around the corner and froze. A small hole in the center of the door enabled those inside to see the canoe. Keeping low, avoiding the hole, he carefully and silently wedged the long-handled tool against the door. Returning to the river, he eased into the water and moved north until he was near the canoe again.

Dega hefted one of the rocks. As a boy he had practiced dropping birds until he could hit one on the wing. Cocking his arm, he threw the rock at the lantern. His aim was accurate. He struck the base, not the glass, and it upended and fell from the crate. But it did not go out, as Dega had hoped. There was a *crunch* and a *phffttt,* and flame spouted in a bright flare.

A loud yelp came from the shack.

The smart thing for Dega to do was to get out of there. Instead, he bounded to the canoe, flipped it over, threw the paddles in, and began dragging it toward the river. Angry shouts filled the shack. Furious pounding shook the door, but the stout-handled prop held.

The canoe was heavier than those the People of the Forest used but not so heavy that Dega could not handle it with relative ease. He slid the bow into the river and climbed in. The shack door was splintering under heavy blows as he grabbed one of the paddles and stroked westward.

More loud voices came from down the shore.

With a loud *crack* the whites spilled from the shack. They saw him. Rifles and pistols spewed lead and flame.

Dega bent low as lead balls chopped the water on either side and whistled above his head. He was far enough out that he was in near complete darkness. He stroked a little farther, then turned the canoe north. The current proved stronger than he anticipated but not so strong that it defied him.

The whites were in a frenzy. Others had

come from the second circle of light. Some scurried about like decapitated chickens. A boat and another canoe were brought and shoved into the water. Men piled in. Both craft were propelled to the west.

Dega turned east, toward shore. For a moment he feared the current would take the canoe and sweep it out of control but he came to a slight bend and brought the canoe in. The bottom scraped as he dragged the canoe onto dry land, but he was far enough from the buildings that the whites did not hear the sound.

A crowd had gathered and was making a considerable racket.

Dega crawled through the high grass. He found the rifle and was slipping the leather strap to the ammo pouch over his shoulders when the grass parted and shadowy shapes closed in. He jerked the stock to his shoulder, then saw who they were. "You were supposed to stay where I left you," he whispered.

"The dogs were too close," Teni whispered. "We could not stay."

Waku put a hand on Dega's shoulder. "I saw what you just did, my son. You make me proud."

"We must not linger."

Little Miki had to sit on Tihi's lap, but

the five of them fit in the canoe. With Dega in the bow and Waku in the stern, they paddled for the far shore. The river was wider than they imagined any river could be. All went well until they were near the middle. Dega and Waku stroked furiously, making slow headway against the strong current. They were fortunate the river was not at flood stage or they would never have made it across.

As it was, the night was almost over when they gained the shelter of an inlet on the west shore. Nearly spent, their arms and shoulders aching, Dega and Waku concealed the canoe and the family sought the cover of a stand of trees.

South of them at a small dock was the ferry. Whites scoured the brush but none came anywhere near their hiding place.

"You did well, my brother," Teni said, and tenderly clasped his blistered hand. "You led us through the marsh. You outwitted the whites. We could not have done it ourselves."

"Manitoa has been with us," Tihi said.

"Was Manitoa with us when our people were slaughtered?" Waku bitterly asked. "I never want to hear of Manitoa again."

"You do not mean that, husband," Tihi said.

"We should sleep," Dega suggested. They

needed the rest. They had made it across the Mississippi but they still had a long way to go to the mountains. Come sunset, they would push on into the dark heart of the unknown.

CHAPTER TWELVE

Grass. So much grass. Day after day after day, before them and behind them and all around them. So much grass, Dega began to think his sister had been right, and the sea of grass *did* stretch forever.

The prairie was not completely flat, as they had been told. Hollows and gullies were common, and now and again solitary hills broke the monotony. Dega always climbed them, and always saw nothing but grass and more grass.

At first, game was abundant. Rabbits were their staple. Rabbit stew. Rabbit on a stick. Rabbit roasted. Rabbit rare. While they were still close to the Mississippi they saw deer but could not get close enough to bring them down. They had white hunters to thank for that. The deer had learned to flee from humans as they would from ravening wolves.

The farther from the Father of Rivers they

traveled, the fewer animals they saw. Then they came to a stream, and for a while wildlife was abundant again. It was a pattern that repeated itself over and over.

Where there was water, there was life.

And where there was life, there were predators. Dega came across signs of foxes, coyotes, bobcats, wolves, cougars and bears.

For a long while, the family paralleled the rutted tracks made by whites bound for the mountains and beyond. The tracks led from one source of water to the next, from stream to river to spring to the next stream.

The plains were home to many Indian tribes, some hostile to travelers of every hue. Now and then Dega came across the tracks of unshod horses, and once upon the charred embers of a camp. But of the hostiles themselves, thankfully, the family was spared an encounter.

Dega did not use the rifle to kill game for fear the shot would be heard. Why he held on to the weapon, he could not say, beyond the fact that it held a deep fascination. He would stare at it at night while he kept watch and everyone else slept. Stare and ponder, seeking an answer to a riddle, an answer that proved elusive.

Dega practiced loading the rifle until he could do it with his eyes closed. It helped that he had, on occasion, seen whites from New Albion use their rifles. He remembered that the powder went in first, and that the whites had wrapped the lead ball in a patch before shoving both down the barrel using the ramrod in its housing under the barrel.

Dega did risk firing the rifle four times for practice. He recalled hearing somewhere that too much powder would burst the barrel, so he poured down what he considered a safe amount. It still proved almost too much, as the blast nearly tore the rifle from his grasp. He used less after that. He could not get used to the smoke and the flash; they always amazed him.

The truth be told, much about the whites amazed Dega. They were so different from the People of the Forest. So different, as well, from every tribe he had ever met or heard about.

Since Dega believed that all living things stemmed from Manitoa, it stood to reason the same applied to the whites. Therein lay the riddle to which he could not fathom an answer. For if That Which Was In All Things was also in the whites, then the very nature of That Which Was In All Things was not the nature he had imagined it to be.

The Nansusequa belief in Manitoa had a twofold foundation. Manitoa, the elders taught, was not only *in* all things, but maintained all life in a state of balance. Manitoa did this because to Manitoa, and Manitoa's children, the Nansusequa, the purpose for life was to live in harmony with all other life.

Balance led to harmony. Harmony brought about balance. This was the creed by which the People of the Forest lived, the goal for which they continually strived.

⚜ Harmony. Balance. They were part of a great, grand cycle. The Nansusequa saw it reflected all around them. Rain, for instance, nurtured the soil, which, in turn, nurtured plant life, which, in turn, nurtured the plant eaters, which, in their turn, were nourishment for the meat eaters. Harmony throughout, balance throughout. Just one example among many.

The Nansusequa believed that for their people to thrive, or any people for that matter, they must become part of the grand cycle. They must nurture as Manitoa nurtured. They must achieve a balance with all living things.

They were an old tribe, the Nasusequa. They had been in the world longer than any other. It was why the other tribes called them the Old Ones. They attributed their longevity to one thing: the harmony and balance they maintained with the world around them.

Yet now, except for Dega and his family, the People of the Forest were no more. Their devotion to harmony and balance had not saved them from being slaughtered. Ironically — and herein was the heart of the riddle — they had been wiped out by people who, as far as Dega could see, possessed no sense of harmony or balance whatsoever.

It flew in the face of all Dega believed. So he sat and stared at the rifle and sought to make sense of that which was senseless. The whites defied reason. They were chaotic creatures who spread chaos wherever they went. They knew nothing of Manitoa, nothing of harmony, nothing of balance. They were the opposite of all Dega valued, the living embodiment of everything the Nansuseqa regarded as wrong to think and wrong to do, and yet the whites were spreading across the land in an unstoppable wave.

Where was the harmony? The balance? Again and again Dega asked himself those two questions. Again and again he could not provide an answer.

But Dega did perceive one thing. If the whites, who were chaos in human form, could defeat the Nansusequa, the caretakers of harmony and balance, then white medicine was more powerful than Nansusequa medicine, and their chaos more powerful than harmony and balance.

It turned Dega's world upside down. It took everything he believed and rendered it meaningless.

Dega refused to accept that. There *had* to be an answer. There *had* to be a reason chaos prevailed. If he could discoverer what it was, if he could solve the riddle, his world would be restored to the way it should be. If not — Dega did not like to think about that, for it meant that that which he had taken to be evidence of the balance and harmony in all things was nothing more than a hideous emptiness.

Now, sitting by the fire on yet another night under the stars in the midst of the vast grassland, Dega heard a buckskin dress rustle, and Teni sat next to him.

"Do you mind company? I cannot sleep. I have that problem often."

"You are not alone," Dega assured her.

Teni tucked her legs and wrapped her arms around her knees. "Will we ever sleep through the night again?" She shivered, but not from the cool breeze. "I hear them, brother. Hear their screams. Hear the cries of the young. I hear them when I am awake and cannot fall asleep. I hear them when I am asleep, and they wake me up. What am I to do?"

"If you find out, let me know," Dega said. "For I hear them, too."

Teni stared at the sleeping forms of their mother and father and little Miki. "They have no problem."

"I have heard our sister cry out in her sleep," Dega mentioned. "Our mother whimpers and gnashes her teeth."

"Father?" Teni asked.

Dega made no attempt to smother his scowl. "Nothing. Ever. He does not cry. He does not become mad."

"We Nansusequa have always prided ourselves on our self-control," Tenikawaku said. "Father's control has always been better than ours."

"It is more than that," Dega said. "He is lost inside himself and cannot find his way out."

Teni leaned toward him. "Mother says she has never seen Father like this. At times he does not answer when she talks to him. At other times he talks to himself and ignores her if she says something."

Dega had witnessed both behaviors. He was afraid for his father, afraid his father's mind had gone elsewhere.

"I never thought Mother was stronger than Father," Teni said.

"He will recover. You will see," Dega said, but he said it without conviction. An entire moon had passed since the attack on their village, yet their father showed little improvement.

Teni leaned back and gazed at the myriad of stars. There were far more than she ever remembered seeing. "Father is not the only one who has changed."

"Miki is much more quiet than she ever was," Dega said.

"It is not her I am talking about, brother. It is you."

"What have I done?"

"You have cast off the moccasins of a boy and put on the moccasins of a man," Teni said.

"It is good I have, is it not?"

"Yes. But it is not that to which I refer." Teni looked at him. "You have changed in other ways as well."

"I am listening."

"I notice you have not made a bow for yourself, or a lance. Yet once you would not go anywhere without one or the other."

"I use Father's bow when I hunt game."

"But you always take the rifle, too. The weapon of the whites. The weapon of our enemies. No Nansusequa has ever used one. Strange that you do so now, after the whites have wiped out our people."

"You make more of it than there is."

"Or is it that you make less?" Teni placed her hand on the barrel. "Feel this. Feel how cold it is, feel how hard. As cold and hard as the whites. This is their weapon. It is not a fitting weapon for a Nansusequa warrior."

"You talk nonsense."

"I tell you true, brother. You are not the same as you were. I am worried for you, as I am worried for Father."

Her comments gave Degamawaku much to think about as they forged westward. On several occasions water became scarce. When that happened, the wildlife became scarce, too, and they had to go without both for days at a time.

Two incidents occurred that none of them would soon forget.

The first was toward the end of the Heat Moon. They had come on a winding, shallow river, more mud than water. As they filed along a gravel bar, they heard grunts and snuffling sounds and repeated heavy thuds. Thick cottonwoods and undergrowth prevented them from seeing whatever was responsible, and they cautiously advanced until they beheld the prairie. Prairie that

251

crawled with an incredible multitude of huge hairy beasts.

"Buffalo!" Teni breathed.

The first they had seen. Larger than horses, more powerfully built than bears, buffalo were the lords of their domain. Males were as high at the shoulders as Dega was tall, the females slightly less. Manes, beards, tails that ended in tufts, were common to both sexes. So were curved black horns, wicked weapons of death that could disembowel anyone or anything with deceptive ease. Some of the buffalo were rolling in bowls of dust. Others grazed. The young nuzzled their mothers. Bulls snorted and pawed the ground.

"We will never make it through them," Teni said.

As it turned out, they did not need to try.

An hour before sundown, as they sat among the cottonwoods debating what to do, a low rumble shook the ground. They ran to the edge of the trees and saw a spectacle few people, white or red, were ever privileged to witness; the enormous herd was on the move. Long into the night and most of the next day, the migration continued; so many buffalo, counting them was impossible. Dega estimated the total to be hundreds of thousands. His mother was of the opinion there were more than a million, a number so high as to induce awe.

Only after the last stragglers had vanished in the distance did Dega lead the family into the open. Buffalo droppings were everywhere, almost as numerous as the blades of grass the buffalo had trampled in their passing.

That night, with no wood and scant grass to burn for fire, Dega collected an armful of dry droppings. He recalled that white farmers sometimes burned dry cow and horse droppings, so why not buffalo? He broke the droppings into chips and soon had a nice fire blazing. It gave off an odor not to Tihi's liking and caused young Miki to pinch her nose, but they stayed warm, and that was the important thing.

The second incident of note occurred shortly after the Heat Moon had given way to the Thunderhead Moon. The Nansus-equa had twelve moons: the Ice Moon, the Hungry Moon, the Cold Wind Moon, the Warm Wind Moon, the Planting Moon, the Flower Moon, the Heat Moon, the Thunderhead Moon, the Hunters Moon, the Yellow Leaf Moon, the Blood Moon and the Snow Moon.

They were following a ribbon of a river through country broken by islands of vegetation, a welcome change to the sameness of the grass, when Dega's sharp eyes spied smoke. Three previous times during the course of their trek they had spotted the smoke from distant campfires, and had avoided them. This time was different. Maybe it was because they had gone so long without contact with other people, maybe it was simple curiosity, but by silent consent they spread out and crept through the brush until they could see the source.

A band of warriors had camped in a clearing. Teni counted fourteen. They were tall, these men, with long arms and long legs and craggy faces with large noses and wide mouths. Odd markings had been painted on their bodies, brows and cheeks. Their horses bore similar markings. They were armed with lances and bows and knives, and had a fierce demeanor that frightened her.

They also had prisoners.

A man and a woman were on their knees, their wrists bound behind them. Their buckskins were of fine quality. Both were shorter than their captors, and more heavily built. Heads high, they awaited their fate.

Dega took a liking to the couple. They had a quiet nobility about them that reminded him of his own people.

The painted warriors ringed their prisoners. One drew a knife and held it close to the face of the bound man and spoke, and the bound man answered him. Whatever the bound man said was not to the warrior's liking. Suddenly he seized the bound man by the hair, bent the man's head, and with a single swift stroke, sliced off the man's right ear.

Teni covered her mouth with her hand.

Miki buried her face in Tihi's dress.

The bound man did not cry out. He sagged, with blood pouring down his neck, then raised his head as high as before.

The warrior with the knife moved to the woman. He addressed her as he had the man, and she replied in a haughty manner laced with contempt. The warrior gripped her chin so she could not move her head, smiled down at her, and cut off her nose.

Tihi turned away, cradling Miki. She motioned for Waku to go with them but Waku stayed where he was.

So did Dega. The warriors and their captives were from tribes his family might have dealings with in the future. The more he learned about them, the safer his family would be.

Torture was not new to Dega. The Nansusequa never practiced it, but other tribes in the region had tested the mettle of those they caught by seeing how much pain the captives could endure. Apparently, something similar was taking place here. Other body parts joined the ear and the nose on the ground. The painted warriors took turns chopping off fingers and toes, gouging out eyes, cutting off tongues, and more. When they were done, the bound couple had been reduced to quivering vestiges of ravaged flesh, barely recognizable as human.

"I wish they would put them out of their misery," Teni whispered plaintively. She got her wish shortly thereafter.

The pair had their throats slit. The man was scalped.

Dega nodded at Teni to withdraw and she did so without complaint. He sidled to his father and touched his father's arm, whispering, "We should go."

Wakumassee did not move.

"Father?" Dega urged.

"Did you see, my son?" Waku whispered. "Did you see what they did?"

"It is not safe," Dega whispered. The warriors were astir, preparing to leave, and Dega was worried one might spot them.

"The world is not safe, my son," Waku responded. "Manitoa has the taint of madness. We should tell these men, that they may know the fault is not entirely theirs."

Panicked that his father would give them away, Dega gripped Waku's wrist. "They would not care."

"What about you, son? Do you care?"

"We should talk about this later," Dega suggested. Preferably when the painted warriors were leagues away.

"What good is talk?" Waku asked. "We talked to Stilljoy. We talked to other whites in New Albion who said they were our friends. All that talk, and they slaughtered our people. No, talk is empty air."

"Then talking to those warriors would not help them or us."

Waku considered that. "You speak with a true tongue. I am sorry, my son. I was not thinking."

"What is wrong with you, Father?"

"I do not know. I feel —" Waku looked down at himself. "I feel empty inside. I am not the man I was."

"You can be so again if you try," Dega ventured.

"Do I want to try? That is the question."

"For our sakes," Dega said. "You were a great man of peace. You can be so again."

"In a world tainted by madness, what use is there for peace?" Waku asked. "The whites do not believe in peace. Those warriors do not believe in peace. Their answer to everything is to kill."

"Our answer need not be."

Waku smiled and whispered tenderly, "Son. My son. Once that would have made me so proud. But we have both seen what those who kill do to those who value the path of peace."

"Should we judge all men by the actions of a few?" Dega had been casting furtive glances at the painted warriors. Most had mounted. They would soon leave. All he had to do was keep his father talking a while more.

"Once I would have said no," Waku responded. "But perhaps we must if we are to survive."

"We will find a new home. Our life will be as it was."

Waku's features clouded. "Am I five winters old? Our life will never be as it was. All those we loved, all our brothers and sisters, are gone. Our land has been taken from us. We have nothing left."

"We have each other," Dega said. "We have our family. That is the one thing no one can take."

Horses nickered and hooves drummed. The painted warriors were leaving. They headed to the northwest and were soon swallowed by their dust.

Dega rose. "I will get Mother and the girls." He found them seated on a log, their expressions glum. Not that long ago, his mother had been perpetually happy, and Miki had always worn a smile. "It is safe," he announced.

Teni fell into step beside him. "Maybe we should only travel at night until we reach the mountains."

"The meat eaters are abroad at night," Dega reminded her. Of late, some nights the roars, grunts, shrieks and howls of the predators were a constant cacophony from dusk until dawn. Of particular worry to Dega was the amount of bear sign. Black bears he was familiar with. But much of the sign he found was of bears many times larger. Their footprints suggested a size bordering on the gigantic.

Dega had heard stories about the great silver bears, so-called, even though they were shades of brown in color, because the tips of their hairs were supposedly silverish. He had heard they were the most formidable creatures alive, but after seeing buffalo, that seemed doubtful. Whether true or not, he did not want to encounter one. If only half the reports of their ferocity and hardiness were to be believed, they were still next to impossible to slay.

"Dega," Teni suddenly said.

Dega looked up. His father was not where he had left him. Waku had gone to the clearing and was standing next to the remains of the couple who had been tortured.

"What is he doing?"

Just standing and staring, as near as Dega could tell. "Take Mother and Miki around the clearing." He hurried forward. "Father?"

"Their faces are gone," Waku said. "It is sad to die without a face."

"We should not be out in the open like this." Dega took his father's wrist but Waku did not move.

"I had a face once."

Dega tugged on his father's arm. "Please. The warriors might come back." He deemed that unlikely, but why take the chance?

"I had a strong face. Now I see my reflection in the water and all I see is fog. Is that not strange?"

Dega refused to answer. It would only upset him. "Mother and the girls are waiting."

"Our people were too proud," Waku said. "We thought we would last forever. We thought we were special. We thought we were in harmony with Manitoa and Manitoa was in us. But we were wrong."

"We must go, Father."

Waku seemed not to hear. "We thought we could persuade the whites to be as we were. We had been told how the whites destroyed tribe after tribe, but we refused to believe the whites would do the same to us."

Dega gave up trying to get him to listen.

"Our people learned an important lesson, but they learned it at the point of white knives and to the sound of white guns." Waku turned from the gory remains at his feet. "You and I have been more fortunate, son. We learned an important lesson, and we survived. Never again will we trust a white man. Never again will we offer the sign of friendship to anyone white. We will find the mountains we have heard so much about and make them our new home. If any whites dare to try to take our new home away from us, we will do to them as the whites did to our people. We will kill them and mutilate them and leave their carcasses for the coyotes." Waku raised his arms to the sky. "To this do I, Wakumassee of the Nansusequa, so vow! To this do I, Waku-massee of the Nansusequa, give my sacred pledge! Are you with me in this, my son?"

"I am with you," Dega said.

CHAPTER THIRTEEN

Finding the Rocky Mountains proved to be ridiculously easy. All they had to do was continue west far enough and there the mountains were.

First to spot them was Degamawaku. He was studying what he took to be a massive thunderhead on the far horizon, trying to figure out why parts of the cloud bank appeared white instead of the usual ominous black, when it dawned on him that the thunderhead was a mountain range and the white was snow that crowned the highest of the peaks. He informed the others.

Teni clapped her hands in glee and exclaimed, "At last!"

"I had begun to think they did not exist," Tihikanima said, her eyes filling with tears of happiness. Clasping Miki to her, she said, "Do you see them, daughter? Our quest is almost at an end."

Wakumassee bowed his head.

Soon the plain began to slope gradually upward to a high rise. The climb taxed them. From the crest they saw that it was but the first of more to come. Beyond lay the foothills. Beyond them, the mountains.

It was the middle of the afternoon when they came to a broken crest overlooking a wooded waterway and saw seven riders heading from north to south perhaps five flights of an arrow distant.

"Down!" Dega barked, and flung himself flat. He took it for granted the rest would do as he had said, which compounded his shock when he saw that his father was still standing. "Father! They might see you!"

"Let them," Waku declared. "They are white men, and I am at war against all whites."

Dega looked at the riders again. They wore buckskins, as Indians would. But there was no mistaking their bushy beards and beaver hats.

"Where are they bound?" Tihi asked.

"Who can say?" Dega responded. They knew nothing of this country other than one fact which now appeared in dispute. "There are not supposed to be many whites here."

"Maybe there are," Waku said. "Maybe there are as many here as there are east of the Father of Rivers. Maybe we have come all this way only to die at the hands of more white locusts."

"Please do not talk like that," Tihi said, with a meaningful nod at Miki. Her husband had grown so unpredictable of late, she did not know what to expect next.

"Fire your rifle, son," Waku said. "Attract them to us so we may slay them."

"There are too many," Dega said, and watched that his father did not shout or do something equally reckless.

Once the whites were out of sight, Dega hustled his family to the stream and the woodland that bordered it. "We will stay here until dark, then try to reach the foot-hills before dawn."

"Are we rabbits that we cower in holes?" Waku dripped sarcasm. "I am not afraid."

"You should be," Dega said. He was afraid for all of them, but most of all for the kind, gentle man who had once been supremely devoted to peace but who now acted more bloodthirsty than the whites he reviled.

Tihikanima took her youngest's hand. "Miki and I will go wash. Are you coming, Teni?"

"You go ahead, Mother."

The stream was the width of two bows laid end to end, and came midway to Tihi's knees at its deepest. She was hoping to find a deeper spot and pushed on until they rounded a bend and startled a pair of ducks from a broad pool that glistened in hues of green and blue. "This will do, little one."

"I do not want to," Miki said.

"You never want to," Tihi countered. "At your age I did not want to, either. But our dresses are dirty. We are dirty. A bath will be nice."

"You first."

Tihi squatted and dipped her hand in. "The water is cool. Undress and we will go in together." She sat and began to undo her moccasins. She felt fingers tug at her dress and said, "Do as I say. We must not be at this all day."

"Mother?" Miki said.

"Do not argue." Tihi pulled off one moccasin and tugged on the other. She shrugged her daughter's hand off her shoulder, saying sternly, "Enough. If you do not undress I will throw you in as you are."

"That would be mean."

Tihi rarely lost her temper. Like the rest of her people, she prided herself on her self-control. But she was losing it now. "You will wash, and you will do so without talking back."

"But what if we go in the water and it attacks us?"

"It?" Tihi glanced at Miki and then gazed in the direction Miki was gazing. A gasp tore from her throat. Her hand flew to Miki and she pulled Miki to her even as she swept to her feet.

On the other side of the pool, intently regarding them, was a bear. Not a black bear, like those that roamed the verdant forests after which the Nansusequa took their name, but a bear that dwarfed black bears as black bears dwarfed dogs.

"A silver bear!"

"Should we run?" Miki timidly whispered.

"No!" Tihi answered much too loudly, provoking a growl. The monster would overtake them before they took ten steps. "Stand still and do not speak."

"I am scared, Mother."

So was Tihi. So scared her legs trembled. But she did not give in to her fear. She must be brave for her daughter's sake.

The monster took a ponderous step. Its huge triangular head lifted and its black nostrils flared. Thin lips curled from teeth as long as Tihi's fingers. It opened its maw as if to roar but closed its mouth again after uttering a snuffling snort. It was as tall as Tihi at the front shoulders. Above them rose a pronounced hump that added to its height. The body was incredibly massive, and as long as a Nansusequa canoe. Raw brute strength radiated from the beast like heat and light from the sun. Its claws were knives.

"Mother!" Miki said again.

"Quiet." Were it a black bear, Tihi would slowly back away. Black bears usually left people alone. But the thing in front of her had a reputation as a man-eater. The slightest movement might incite an attack. She had her bow and quiver slung across her back, but her arrows would do little more than sting.

The silver bear huffed and dipped a paw in the pool.

Certain it was about to cross, Tihi swung Miki behind her, putting herself between her daughter and the danger. "When it attacks, run to your father and brother."

"Not without you."

The bear stopped. It batted its paw at the water a few times, then abruptly wheeled and ambled off into the cottonwoods without a backward glance.

Tihi held on to Miki to keep from collapsing. Her legs would not stop shaking; her heart hammered in her chest. That had been as close as she ever wanted to come to being eaten alive.

"Do we wash now?" Miki asked.

"Bathing is not as important as I thought it was," Tihi said, and retreated along the stream without taking her eyes off the spot where the bear had vanished.

One glance at his mother and younger sister warned Dega something was amiss. He listened to his mother's brief recital. Before she was done, he had the family on the move.

Unknown to the others, Dega had seen several of the gargantuan brutes on the journey west. Once, he had come on one as it rooted at a prairie dog burrow. The bear was so intent on treating itself to a tasty morsel that it did not notice as Dega slunk quickly and quietly away.

Their size stunned him. But then, the size of the wildlife here in general had become a source of wonderment.

It was Dega's settled opinion that animals west of the Mississippi were larger than their cousins east of it. Rabbits, squirrels, deer, coyotes, bears, it was the same with all of them. Dega thought he had an answer as to why. Because there were fewer people, both red and white, there was less hunting. Because there was less hunting, the animals lived longer. The longer they lived, the bigger they grew. A good explanation, except that it did not explain the buffalo and the silver-tips.

They hiked all night. The sun was painting the eastern sky pink when they came to the foothills. Dega brought down a doe with his father's bow and they spent the entire day and night resting.

That night, Dega was startled to behold not one, not two, but three campfires. All were at a safe distance.

Dawn broke bright and clear. Before them reared the Rockies, breathtaking in their sweep and grandeur, several peaks mantled in the ivory of deep-packed snow.

"How will we ever climb them?" Teni wondered.

"There will be trails," Dega predicted.

Little Miki had her head tilted so far back, she was about to topple. "From up there," she marveled, "we can see to the ends of the world. We could even see our village."

Waku had been sitting with his arms wrapped around his chest. Now he stirred and asked, "Why would you want to, young one? There is nothing left of it. Nothing left of the Nansusequa."

"I still think of it," Miki said. "I still think of our people."

"Better if you stop," Waku advised. "Dwell in the past and it will bring you misery and sorrow."

Tihi came to her daughter's defense. "Not all memories are sad ones. Are we to forget all those we loved? All our relatives and friends?"

"If you want to sleep at night, yes," Waku said.

"Your worry me, husband," Tihi remarked. "You are not the man who fathered my children. You look like him, but you do not act like him. You are a stranger to me."

"I am a stranger to myself," Waku said.

"My husband of old would not try to lure white riders in close that he might slay them, as you wanted to do."

"Your husband of old was a fool."

"Not in my eyes," Tihi said. "He was kind and gentle, and I loved him dearly for those qualities."

"A fool," Waku repeated, "whose kindness blinded him to the violence in others. He advocated peace with the whites, remember? Peace with those who wiped out his people."

"You did what you thought best for the good of all," Tihi said. "Why must you be so hard on yourself?"

Waku uttered an angry hiss. "How can you sit there and ask that? *They are all gone!* Our way of life is no more. We have nothing left."

"We have each other."

"Waugh!" Waku said in disgust. "You have eyes, but you do not see. You have ears, but you do not hear."

"Yet another way you have changed," Tihi said sorrowfully. "My old husband never talked to me as you do."

Waku looked away and then back again. "I love you as deeply as ever. Never think for a moment I do not."

"I do not like the new you," Tihi said. "I want my old husband back."

"He died when our people died. It is good he is gone. Your new husband will protect you much better than the old ever did."

"I am a grown woman. I do not need protecting."

"Tell that to the Nansusequa women who died that day. Tell it to their children." Waku shook a clenched fist. "The person who does not learn from a mistake will repeat it. I will not be found wanting twice."

"I never found you lacking in any manner," Tihi said affectionately. "Nor did my father."

"Do not remind me."

Dega was tempted to say something, but it was regarded as the height of rudeness to intrude on one's elders, especially one's parents. He was glad when his mother lapsed into silence. The bickering between

271

the two had become much too common.

— Dega's prediction about a trail was borne out shortly after they began to climb. Deer and elk tracks were conspicuous. So were the prints of shod and unshod horses. The most recent looked about a week old.

They climbed all day. And the next day. And the one after that. On past the emerald foothills, to the threshold of the timbered heights.

Eventually they came to a rocky gorge bisected by gurgling rapids. The gorge brought them to a crag-rent escarpment. They were not accustomed to the altitude, and their lungs strained for air. Miki was so red in the face and breathing so raggedly that Tihi and Teni took turns carrying her.

As usual, Dega was in the lead. He negotiated a switchback and plodded up a steep incline. At the top he stopped as abruptly as if he had walked into a tree.

"It is beautiful," Teni breathed.

"Is this where we will live?" Miki asked.

Before them spread a valley. Roughly oval, much of it was thick forest. A small lake was home to scores of ducks, geese and brants. The racket the waterfowl were making explained why Dega did not hear the two men and the dog before he saw them. They came out of the woods to the south of the lake and walked west along the shore, their backs to him, the dog scampering about the two buckskin-clad figures and frolicking in the water.

Dego motioned for his family to seek cover. He could not say whether the men were white or red until one turned to pick up a stick and threw it for the dog to fetch.

"More whites!" Waku said angrily. "Will there never be an end to them?"

Dega did not admit it, but he was thinking the same thing. Had all they had gone through been for nothing? Was the safety they sought an illusion?

"What do we do?" Teni asked.

"What else?" Dega responded. They skirted the lake and a cabin they spotted in the trees. Several more large dogs gamboled about but did not spot them or catch their scent.

By dark they had gone half the valley's length. They made a cold camp in the recesses of a thick.

"I'm hungry." Miki voiced one of her few complaints.

"Tomorrow we eat," Dega promised. He dared not rove about with the dogs in the vicinity. All it would take was an errant breeze and they would have more whites baying at their heels.

With the setting of the sun, the temperature dropped and kept on dropping until the air was uncomfortably chill. At that altitude the Hunters Moon would start early, a prelude to ever colder days and nights. Their threadbare buckskins could ill keep them warm.

An uncomfortably brisk dawn broke on their worn, shivering forms. Dega roused the rest and they plodded westward.

They had finally reached the Rockies, but that was only the first step. Now they must find a suitable home, a valley like the one they had just passed through, a haven for them and them alone.

Toward noon, Waku downed a doe. They dragged it into a ravine and Tihi kindled a fire. They were famished. No sooner did the mouth-watering aroma of the haunch fill the air than they tore at the red, dripping meat, and stuffed themselves until they could not swallow another mouthful.

Tihi wanted to save the hide to use in making a dress but Dega assured her she would soon have more and better hides to chose from, as many as she needed to make new clothes for all of them.

Ridge after ridge, valley after valley, fell behind them. Everywhere, game abounded. Now and then they came across hoofprints, but nowhere was there a trace of human habitation.

Three nearly identical snow-crowned peaks fell behind them. They followed a stream to where it forked to northwest and southwest. After talking it over, they took the former. It brought them to a hump-backed ridge. They followed the ridge to where a portion had buckled, leaving a fir-choked gap.

Curious, they entered the gap and discovered a hidden canyon.

A sense of excitement gripped them. They hiked faster, eager to see where the canyon led.

It ended at the rim of a magnificent bowl-shaped valley, one of the largest they had come across. Entirely ringed by mountains, it was a world unto itself. On one of the peaks glistened a mass of greenish-white ice. A sparkling blue lake, only partly visible, was the final factor that compelled Dega to say, "We have found our new home."

"I agree," Waku declared. "Here we will be safe from all our enemies."

"A new home!" Miki said breathlessly.

Tihi clasped her hands to her bosom. "Land of our own. A lodge of our own. A lake for us and us alone. It is a dream."

They were halfway to the valley floor when the pines thinned enough to permit a clear view of the lake. Shock brought them to a stop.

Dega threw back his head and nearly shrieked in rage.

"It cannot be," Teni said softly.

Tihi bowed her head and said forlornly, "More whites. Everywhere we go, there are more whites."

Little Miki turned away, covered her face, and began sobbing softly.

To their mutual surprise, Waku did the last thing they would expect him to do; he laughed. The cold, hard, brittle laugh of a man who had been pushed as far as he was willing to be pushed. "I warned you. I warned all of you. The whites are everywhere. There is no getting away from them."

"We must go on," Tihi said.

"There will be other valleys." Dega tried to soothe them.

"No," Wakumassee said.

"Husband?"

"There will not be other valleys. We have come far enough. It is this valley we like, and this valley we will claim."

Teni pointed at the lake, at the three cabins along its shore. "They were here before us."

"So?"

Tihi absorbed the full meaning of his retort. "What you suggest is not the Nansusequa way."

"You keep forgetting. We must cast off the old ways and adopt new ones if we are to survive in this new land."

"What would you have us do, Father?" Teni bluntly demanded.

"Kill them."

In the silence that fell, they could hear the beat of a raven's wings as it flew overhead.

Tihi was the first to break the spell, saying guardedly, "Kill people who have done us no harm?"

"They are white."

Tihi stared at the cabins. Smoke rose lazily from two of the three chimneys. She imagined families inside, families like her own. "Has it come to this? That is not reason enough, and you know it."

"Whites wiped out our people. Whites destroyed our village."

"But not *these* whites," Tihi stressed. "You would punish them for the actions of others?"

"Did those other whites do less to us? They punished all the Nansusequa because of something Dega did."

"That was different," Tihi insisted.

"Lives for lives. Homes for homes. I see nothing different about it," Waku disagreed. "What do you say, Dega?"

Degamawaku was deeply torn. He agreed with his mother that the whites below had done nothing to merit the fate being contemplated, but he also agreed with his father that whites were their enemies. All whites, not just the ones who attacked their village.

"Is your tongue caught in thorns?"

"Why not drive them off instead of killing them?" Dega proposed. He was not sure how, but there must be a way.

Waku snorted. "You have become as soft as your mother. Do you think the whites will give up this valley without spilling blood? Would you give it up if you were them? No, you would not."

"We can find another valley," Tihi said.

Gesturing at Miki, Waku said, "Look at your youngest. Look at her clothes. Do you see how thin she is? Do you see the holes in her dress?"

"I see them."

"Hasn't she suffered enough?" Waku demanded. "Would you put her through another moon of this?"

Tihi did not answer.

Until that moment Teni had been silent, holding her own council. Now she cleared her throat and said, "I side with Father."

"What?" Tihi could not credit her ears.

"I am tired, Mother. Tired in my body. Tired in my spirit. I want to eat regular meals again. I want to wear clean clothes. I want to *be* clean. I want a lodge roof over my head at night, and the crackle of a fire to keep me warm. I want all that. I want it here. I want it now."

"See?" Waku crowed.

"It is wrong."

"No more so than burning our village to the ground," Waku said. "But we will not burn the cabins. The Snow Moon is not far off. We will need to keep warm when it is cold. The cabins will do nicely."

"You have everything worked out," Tihi said, and she did not intend it as a compliment.

"You will thank me when this is over." Waku grinned. "Whoever these whites are, they must die so that we may live."

■ ■ ■ ■

PARADISE FOUND

■ ■ ■ ■

Chapter Fourteen

Nate King found the strange tracks on a brisk autumn morning when the mountain air cracked like a whip at every sound. The horses had been skittish the night before, and at first light he was dressed and went out to the corral. They were all there, huddled in a corner.

Nate suspected a mountain lion was to blame. The grizzly that had ruled the valley was gone, black bears seldom bothered horses, and the wolves that haunted the range to the south usually announced their nocturnal visits with howls and yips. But though Nate scoured the ground around the corral and the cabin long and hard, he could not find a single cougar track.

Mystified, Nate gazed across the lake at the rising sun. The lake surface was perfectly still and reflected the blazing orb as clearly as a mirror. It gave the illusion there were two suns. Shouldering the Hawken, he pivoted on his heel to go back inside — and was struck cold. Not by a lead ball or a barbed arrow, but by what he had failed to notice because the light was not quite right.

"What on earth?" Nate turned left and then right. Everywhere he looked, he saw strange tracks, if tracks they were. Whatever was responsible had circled the cabin not once or twice but many times, and apparently crept close to the window and the door to listen.

Nate's skin crawled. Hunkering, he examined them closely. They were not in any way human. They were not animal tracks. Nor were they bird tracks. But exactly what they *were* was beyond him.

They were in pairs. Roughly circular, each no bigger than a walnut, they were spaced about the length of Nate's forearm apart. Whatever made them left the faintest of impressions, suggesting the creature was as light as a feather.

Nate had his nose practically touching the dirt and he still could not make sense of them. He traced a few with his fingertip. He sniffed at them. They were a complete and bewildering mystery.

Nate decided to go in and tell Winona. As he rose, his gaze strayed past the woodpile. He had spent hours every day over the course of the past week stockpiling firewood for the upcoming winter, and yesterday he had left the axe imbedded in the log he was chopping.

The axe was gone.

Nate ran to the log. All around it were more circles. The logical conclusion was that whatever made them had taken the axe. The circles led toward the forest. Once among the trees the trail disappeared. The hard ground and thick undergrowth were to blame.

Stumped, Nate sat on the log. He was still there a quarter of an hour later when the cabin door opened and Winona came out, looking as lovely as the day he had become her husband.

"There you are. Your breakfast is getting cold."

"Do you believe in leprechauns?" Nate asked her.

"In what?" Winona had to think before she remembered him telling her once about little men in a land far across the great saltwater sea. The subject came up while they were discussing the Shoshone belief in a race of deadly dwarves that lived deep in the mountains. "Do you mean the green men with the pots of gold?"

"That's them," Nate said.

"Have you seen one?" Winona asked, and laughed.

"No, but I've seen something that has me flummoxed." Nate clasped her hand and led her to the corral. He did not say anything. He simply pointed at set after set of the peculiar circles and saw her eyes widen and her mouth drop.

"What are they?"

"You tell me and we will both know." Nate told her about the axe. "Has anything else gone missing I might not know about?"

Winona gave a start and glanced at the cabin. "It can't be."

"You saw a little green man with a pot of gold?"

"No. I was chopping onions for your supper two days ago. I left the knife on the counter and came out to close the chickens in the coop for the night. When I went back in, the knife was not there."

"And you didn't think to tell me?" Nate chided. It was rare for her to be so forgetful.

"You were at Shakespeare's and Evelyn was at Zach's. I heard no one. I saw no one. I figured I imagined leaving it on the counter and it must be somewhere else."

"You searched, though, and couldn't find it," Nate guessed.

"Haa," Winona answered. In her bafflement she forgot herself and spoke in Shoshone.

"I'm going to have a look around," Nate said. "Maybe we've been bigger dunderheads than we think."

"Haggai enne?"

"Whatever it is has been skulking about longer than a few days." Nate said. He estimated that some of the tracks were a week old or more.

"I will keep your breakfast warm," Winona promised.

"Keep Evelyn inside, too," Nate suggested. "I don't want her wandering around until we get to the bottom of this."

The lake was the likeliest place to start. Or, rather, the soft soil at the lake's edge, where wind-whipped waves lapped the shore. Sure enough, Nate found more circles, some old, some recent. He examined them as closely as he had the others, and was thus engrossed when a shadow fell across him.

"I hesitate to ask what you are doing, Horatio. Did you lose a nose hair? Or do you have a newfound fascination for dirt?"

Nate arched an eyebrow at his mentor. "Didn't you boast once that you could track anything, anywhere, anytime?"

"I might have," Shakespeare said. "Was I drunk?"

"Let's see you make sense of these." Nate again pointed out the circles without saying anything.

Shakespeare blinked, then blinked some more. He had, in fact, drunk too much red wine the night he made the boast, but it was no idle claim. Red men and whites alike widely regarded him as one of the best trackers alive, if not *the* best. But the circles stumped him. He ranged along the shore from Nate's cabin to his own, finding new circles as he went. "I'll be damned," he said when they reached his place.

"The tracks go right up to your door and window, just like they do mine," Nate mentioned.

"There are more things in heaven and earth than are dreamt of in our philosophies," Shakespeare paraphrased, "but this is deuced bizarre."

"I wonder if we'll find some at Zach's?"

"Fetch your bay. I'll throw a saddle on my mare and join you."

About to turn, Nate paused. "Hold on. Have you lost anything lately?"

Shakespeare snickered. "My nose hairs are intact, thank you."

"I'm serious, you ornery goat. Has anything gone missing? Anything at all? Anything that disappeared and you couldn't explain it?" Nate shared an account of the axe and the knife.

"This is getting spooky." Shakespeare pulled at his beard, a habit of his when he was deep in thought. "About a week ago I left a rope on a peg by my corral and when I went to get it, it was gone."

They looked at one another, and Nate summed up both their sentiments with, "What in hell is going on?"

From his vantage in the woods to the west of the lake, Degamawaku of the Nansusequa had watched the two white men in growing puzzlement. He had seen the big one with the black beard scour the ground as if reading sign, and then the reactions of the woman and the white-haired man. Dega would very much like to know what they had found.

Crouched behind a spruce, Dega absently fingered his rifle and reviewed all he had learned about the valley's inhabitants over the course of the seven sleeps his family had been spying on them.

His father still insisted killing was the answer. But these whites were not like the whites from New Albion. For one thing, the two white men had taken Indian wives. For another, the white men showed by their attire that they had adopted Indian ways, additional proof, in Dega's opinion, that they were not bigots like the hateful whites in New Albion.

There was a third man, the youngest, half white and half red, who had the cabin on the north shore. Based on the young one's features and build, Dega suspected he was the son of the white man with the black beard. Although a half-breed, he had a white wife.

Then there was the girl.

The first time Dega saw her was six days ago when she came out of the cabin carrying a basket and entered a much smaller structure that, as near as he could determine, served no other purpose than that of a chicken lodge. When she came back out, the basket was filled with eggs. She had paused to gaze at the sky and then at the woods in which Dega lay hidden.

Something unexpected happened to Degamawaku of the Nansusequa. A pleasant tingle coursed through him from head to toe. He had been struck by the beauty of her features and by the graceful manner in which she carried herself. He noted, too, that she was about his age.

The girl had turned and gone in the cabin, and for the longest time Dega had stared fixedly at the cabin door, hoping she would reappear. Eventually she did. She emerged carrying a rifle and with a pair of pistols wedged under a belt about her slender waist. She came straight toward the woods, and him.

For a few brief moments of panic, Dega thought she knew he was there. But no, she passed within a few arm's lengths of his hiding place and hiked on into the forest.

Waku had warned Dega not to do anything that would give their presence away, yet Dega found himself rising and padding on cat's feet in the girl's wake. Partly, he was curious as to what she was up to. But a larger part was his desire to see more of her.

The girl's face and eyes betrayed a keenness of mind that intrigued Dega. Her eyes, in particular, fascinated him. They were green, the color the Nansusequa associated with Manitoa, the nurturer of all things. They were the color of the forest, his home. Green was special, apart and above all other colors — and it was the color of her eyes.

Dega liked the confident air she had. He had met white girls in New Albion who were as timid as fawns and never ventured from the settlement without a man along to protect them. But this girl needed no protector. She was at home in the woods. She walked with a confident stride. Once, the underbrush to her left crackled and she whipped around, her rifle ready, but it was only a long-eared rabbit. She laughed as it bounded off, and went on.

Dega could not shake the sound of that laugh. It stuck with him. He would hear it in his head when he lay under the stars at night, or during other quiet moments.

He almost gave himself away, that day he followed her. She had gone over a rise and he had hurried so he would not lose sight of her. He was almost to the top when he heard soft humming and realized she had stopped. Quickly, he ducked and backpedaled, circling once he was sure she had not heard him.

The girl was picking flowers. Amid a rocky area grew slender plants with striking blue-to-purplish blooms unlike any flower with which Dega was familiar. There was much about the mountains that was new to him, but his interest in the flowers paled compared to his interest in the girl.

She had drawn a knife, and cut a stem down low before adding it to a growing pile. Still humming, she sheathed the blade, gathered up the bouquet, and stood. She held the flowers to her nose and sniffed, smiling happily, then retrieved her rifle from where she had leaned it against a boulder.

Suddenly the girl stiffened. Her head jerked up and she peered about her as if she suspected she was being spied on.

Dega imitated a log, his eyelids hooded to slits. For tense heartbeats she seemed to stare right at him, but then she cautiously backed down the rise into the trees. He was impressed. She had sharp senses as well as beauty. That she came all this way for a handful of flowers said much about her character.

Dega had seen the girl several times since, and the more he saw of her, the more he liked what he saw. He did not tell anyone. It was the first time he had ever kept a secret from his family. Since childhood he had been taught he must always be open and honest, but this was too personal to share. Besides, he was convinced they would not understand. Not that he could blame them. He did not fully understand, either, why he felt as he did.

Now, as Dega turned to shadow the girl's father and the white-haired man as they trotted on horseback toward the cabin on the north shore, he was given pause by the appearance of the one he could not stop thinking about.

X The girl and her mother came out and stared after the men. Their expressions bore mild concern.

Dega would very much like to know why the whites were — He caught himself. He must stop thinking of them like that. Only the two men and the wife of the son were white. He must think of them as people, as individuals.

The mother went back in. The girl walked to the corral. A sorrel came over and she patted its neck and spoke softly.

To Dega's consternation, he found himself imagining what it would be like to have her do the same to him. Warmth spread through his body, and he self-consciously shifted his weight from one foot to the other and willed himself to think about something else. But he couldn't.

Faint rustling came to Dega's rescue. He whipped around, hiking the rifle. Since he was not due to be relieved until the sun was overhead, he was mildly surprised to see his sister hurrying toward him. Teni was supposed to be with the others. They had agreed among themselves that at no time must any of the family be separated from the others unless it was to take a turn spying on the people in the cabins.

"You are early," Dega whispered.

Teni was nearly out of breath. She had run all the way from their camp, which was a considerable distance into the forest. "Mother and Father sent me. You must come right away. It is Miki."

"What about her?" Dega envisioned their little sister being attacked by a bear or a big cat.

"She is missing."

"She probably wandered off and is lost."

Teni motioned for him to hurry. "We are not sure. That is why they want you to come. You are the best tracker."

Casting a reluctant glance at the girl by the corral, Dega said, "Let us go." Side by side, they loped to the west.

"When did you see Miki last?" Dega asked. "How long has she been gone?"

"I cannot say how long," Teni answered, "but I saw her last shortly after we ate breakfast. She was playing with the doll Mother made for her."

Miki loved dolls. Dega remembered she'd had seven or eight of them at one time, all destroyed when their lodge was burned. The other day, their mother had skinned a rabbit and stuffed the skin with grass. A carved wooden head, tiny strips of buckskin for hair, and Miki had a new doll to play with.

"Have you searched for her?"

"Of course."

"You found no sign at all?"

"We found —" Teni hesitated, "— something."

"What?"

"You must see for yourself."

Teni would not say more, even though Dega pressed her.

They had camped in a clearing near a stream fed by the gigantic block of greenish-white ice. It was far enough from the lake that there was little risk of being discovered.

Their parents were anxiously waiting.

"Still no sign of her," Tihi said.

Waku gripped Dega by the arm. "Are all the whites accounted for this morning, my son?"

"They are not all white —" Dega began, then said, "What do you mean, Father?"

"Have any of them left their wooden lodges?"

Dega related what he had seen, leaving out the part about the girl rubbing his neck. "What do they have to do with Miki?"

"Come with me and I will show you."

All four of them went, Waku in the lead, jogging along the stream for a stone's throw. On a grassy bank Waku stopped and pointed. "There."

Some of the grass was flattened, as if a struggle had taken place, and in the center of the trampled patch lay the large axe Dega had last seen the black-haired white man use to chop wood. "What is that doing there?"

"It must belong to whoever took Miki," Waku said.

Dega squatted and examined the grass and the area around it. "There are no footprints."

"I told you there were none," Waku said to Tihi.

"But that is impossible," Teni remarked. "The axe did not fly there."

Dega examined the grass a second time, more thoroughly. "No tracks," he repeated. There were scuff marks where Miki had briefly struggled, then nothing.

"Whoever it was carried her off," Waku speculated. "When she fought, he dropped the axe."

Dega disagreed. The axe was not that heavy. A grown man would have no difficulty holding it and Miki both.

"Why did Miki not cry out?" Teni wondered. "Why did we not hear anything?"

Waku had an answer for that, too. "The man had a hand over her mouth so she could not scream."

"There has to be sign," Dega said. People did not disappear into the air. He commenced to search in earnest, in ever-widening circles. The others followed, relying on him to do what they could not. But although he hunted long and diligently, in the end he held up his arms in exasperation and said, "Nothing. At all."

"It is the whites, I tell you," Waku said. "They found out we are here and want to drive us out."

"So they abducted the youngest of us?" Dega said skeptically.

"To force us to do their bidding," Waku said. "They will demand we leave their valley or else they will harm Miki."

Dega could not imagine the black-haired man being so vicious, not after he had witnessed the affection and tenderness the man showed to his daughter. "I do not think it was them."

"You defend the whites?" Waku asked in astonishment. "Have you not learned they can never be trusted?"

Teni had a proposal. "We should go to them and ask if they have her."

"That is the one thing we must definitely *not* do," Waku said sternly. "They will only deny it."

"But you said they want to force us to

leave by threatening to harm her." Teni pointed out the contradiction.

"Who can predict what whites will do?" Waku responded. "The thing for *us* to do is to strike back at them before they expect."

"Strike back how?" Tihi asked. She had not contributed much to the discussion, but she was hanging on every word. She could not bear the idea of losing her youngest as she had lost the rest of her relatives and friends. "By attacking them?"

"If we do that, they might kill Miki out of spite," Waku said. "No, we must be smart. We must force them to bow to our will as they would have had us bow to theirs."

"You speak in riddles," Tihi said angrily.

"It is simple. They took one of us. We will take one of them."

"What?" Dega said.

"We will abduct one of the whites," Waku proposed, "and demand they return Miki in exchange for the one we take."

"But what if they do not have Miki?" Dega said. "We would be in the wrong."

"Who else can it be?" Waku countered. "We have not seen anyone but the whites since we arrived."

Tihi said hopefully, "If you have another explanation for your sister's disappearance, I am happy to listen."

"I do not," Dega admitted.

"Then it is settled," Waku said. "We must strike quickly before Miki is harmed, and take the whites by surprise."

Before he could stop himself, Dega said, "I wish you would stop calling them that. Some of those people are Indians, like us."

"You surprise me," Waku said. "Yes, they are Indians, as the whites call anyone with red skin. But they are not like us. They are not Nansusequa. They are not People of the Forest."

"That makes them our enemies?" Dega asked more harshly than he should. But he could not help it.

"It does not make them our friends," Waku responded. "Were the Hurons friends to the Iroquois? Were the Sauk friends to the Dakota? Were the Fox friends to the Chippewa?"

The tribes Waku mentioned had all been bitter enemies, as Dega was well aware. "No."

Waku was not done making his point. "We are the People of the Forest. But that does not make us brothers to the People on the Hills or the People of the Standing Stone or the People of the Mucky Land. It does not make us brothers to the women in those cabins, or to the tribes those women are part of."

"Do you really think this plan of yours will work, husband?" Tihi anxiously asked. She was consumed with worry for Miki.

"There is only one way to find out. We leave now to take a white captive."

"One of the women?"

"No," Waku said. "I have been giving it some thought. They took our youngest, did they not? It is fitting, then, that we take their youngest." He paused. "We will abduct the daughter of the black-haired man, and if he does not return Miki, we will kill her."

CHAPTER FIFTEEN

Evelyn had always loved flowers. In their old valley flowers had grown in great numbers in the spring and summer. Many a lazy afternoon she whiled away lying in beds of wild flowers, breathing deeply of their fragrance.

Evelyn loved having flowers in her room. They added splashes of color and scent. It was not unusual for her to have half a dozen vases scattered about, brimming with various flowers.

Early on, Evelyn had discovered an interesting fact about flowers. The Shoshones had a name for every flower in the mountains, but the whites did not. Part of the reason was that many were not found east of the Mississippi. Then, too, the early trappers had been more interested in beaver and plews. Naming flowers was not high on their list of priorities.

When she was eight, Evelyn had asked her

father if he could find a book on flowers, and to her delight he returned from St. Louis with a volume by a noted botanist. It included paintings of every known flower. She had read it avidly, and been disappointed because so many of the flowers she knew and liked were not represented.

There was the bright yellow flower, with five petals, which was common above timberline. Also rife that high up were small blue flowers that grew on plants with leaves covered by silvery strands, like hair. Less common was a purplish-green flower that resembled a bell. Marigolds grew along the waterways. Primrose grew close to streams and rivers, but while the pinkish-purple flowers were lovely, they smelled exactly like a skunk. That always perplexed her. Why have a flower so lovely that stank so bad? There was a large red flower the Shoshones called Red Sun. Deep-blue larkspur was yet another that favored moist areas.

On dry hillsides grew purple flowers that arched outward from their stems. So did a plant that produced bright pink flowers with a honey scent.

But it was the mountain meadows where most flowers thrived. Daisies, columbines, and a host of others: a creamy white flower that grew in pods; a purple flower with a tiny hood, which the Shoshones said was poisonous; a yellow, fuzzy flower with a minty odor; a type of flower so red, it resembled globes of blood; and a large orange-yellow flower with a red center that always made her think the flower was on fire.

These, and many more, Evelyn enjoyed and collected. Some bloomed early in the year, others in the heat of summer, still others in the cool of fall. In her diary she noted the types and seasons.

A particular favorite of hers was a bluish-purple flower that grew in rocky areas. Usually it thrived near the timberline, but she had discovered a patch only a few minutes' walk from their new cabin.

The last handful she had gathered was starting to wither, so she decided to go for more.

Winona was at the counter cutting up potatoes and carrots for the stew they were having for supper.

Easing her bedroom door open, Evelyn quietly slipped out. Her father and Shakespeare had gone to talk to her brother about the strange tracks they had found. To Evelyn, it looked as if someone had gone around poking the ground with a stick. They were hardly cause for worry, although her father seemed to think so. When her father worried, her mother worried. They had asked that she stay inside until they decided it was safe.

But Evelyn wanted those flowers.

She started for the door. She had her Hawken and her pistols, so it was not as if she couldn't defend herself. The real challenge would be slipping by her mother. On cat's feet she tiptoed past the rocking chair and the fireplace and neared the table. She remembered a floorboard that creaked and stepped over it. The front door was open a few inches. All she had to do was lightly pull on the latch.

"Where are you going, daughter?"

Startled, Evelyn almost dropped her rifle. Her mother's back was to her. "How did you know it was me?"

"You and I are the only two here." Winona scooped up a handful of chopped potatoes and dropped them into the stew pot.

"No, I meant, how did you know I was going out?" Evelyn had lost count of the number of times her mother had done something like this. "I didn't make a sound." She quickly added to justify being so quiet, "I didn't want to disturb you."

"How considerate," Winona said dryly,

and turned. "It is no great mystery. I can see out of the corners of my eyes as well as straight ahead."

"Oh," Evelyn said, feeling foolish. "Well, I won't be long." Again she reached for the latch.

"You have not told me where you are going."

"I just want to walk a bit," Evelyn fibbed. "I don't like being cooped up on a nice day like today."

"Do not go far from the cabin," Winona directed. "Not until your father says it is safe."

"I don't see what the fuss is about," Evelyn groused. "It's not as if he found grizzly tracks or the tracks of hostile Indians. All they are is circles in the dirt."

"They are out of the ordinary," Winona said with her usual maternal patience, "and the out of the ordinary can be dangerous."

"Those little circles?" Evelyn said, and laughed.

"Be that as it may," Winona said in her flawless English, "you will stay close to the cabin until your father returns or you will not go outside. Agreed?"

"I promise I won't go gallivanting up to the glacier," Evelyn said, and skipped out with guilt riding on her shoulders. She disliked misleading her mother. But in ten minutes she would be back with fresh flowers.

Evelyn was careful to close the door after her. She did not make for the woods right away in case her mother was watching out the window. Playing it canny, she went to the corral and petted her sorrel. Then, keeping one eye on the window, she quickly crossed the cleared space and was soon in among the pines. As soon as she was out of sight of the cabin, she went even faster.

Evelyn was pleased with herself. She supposed she was being immature, but what harm could it do? The flowers were only in bloom for another few weeks.

Thus preoccupied, Evelyn had gone a hundred yards when it occurred to her that the woods were much too still. Normally, the sparrows and juncos and warblers were merrily chirping. Chipmunks would chitter at her and scamper away with their tails raised in alarm.

Evelyn stopped and looked about her. Not so much as a leaf stirred. She debated going back and shrugged off her unease as nervousness. All because of a bunch of silly circles. Chuckling, she ran on.

The rise where the flowers grew came into sight. Evelyn smiled. But the smile faded the very next moment when she heard her mother calling her name. Stopping, Evelyn turned. She cupped a hand to her mouth to answer and was transfixed with shock. Converging on her from out of the vegetation were four green-clad figures. She had turned so unexpectedly, they did not have a chance to conceal themselves.

"What on earth?" Evelyn blurted.

The four rushed her.

"Ma! Help!" Evelyn cried, even as she brought up her Hawken. She fired when it was nearly level, but as the rifle went off a warrior in green swatted the barrel and the lead plowed a furrow in the earth.

Evelyn thrust the muzzle at his face, at his eyes, but the warrior ducked and grabbed at her dress. Skipping backward, she dropped her rifle and stabbed for the pistols wedged under her belt. She had the flintlocks half out when the warrior's iron arm looped about her waist and she was bodily lifted off the ground. A hand clamped over her mouth.

Then an older warrior shouted something in a tongue Evelyn had never heard, and the next instant the four bounded into the forest with her as their captive.

Winona King stiffened at the rifle blast. She

heard her daughter's cry for help, and, spiked with fear, she whirled and raced into the cabin. Her pistols were on the table, her rifle propped in a corner. In a twinkling she was armed and slinging her ammo pouch and powderhorn across her chest.

Winona practically flew back out and toward the trees. To the north, Nate and Shakespeare were standing near Zach's cabin, talking to Zach. All three had heard the crack of the rifle and were staring in her direction. They had to see her. Pumping an arm, Winona screeched her husband's name. Then she was in the forest and streaking to the west.

"Evelyn!" Winona shouted in English. "Blue Flower!" she hollered in her own tongue. Neither was answered.

Her fear mounting, Winona glanced wildly about. She had told Evelyn not to go far but Evelyn did not always listen as she should. Winona vaulted a log, avoided a thicket, and saw, up ahead, wisps of gray that might be lingering tendrils from the shot. Past the tendrils was a rise. The very rise, Winona recalled, where Evelyn sometimes came to pick flowers.

An acrid odor proved Winona right. So did the glint of metal. Stopping so suddenly she nearly fell, Winona snatched her daughter's rifle off the ground. That it was Evelyn's there could be no doubt. The Hawken brothers had custom made it for Evelyn at Nate's request. The barrel was shorter than most Hawkens, the stock not quite as thick.

"Evelyn!" Winona yelled again, without result. Rather than plunge blindly on, she searched for tracks. She was not the tracker her husband was, but she was no slouch, either, as the whites would say. She found partial prints and scrape marks, indicating several attackers had swarmed Evelyn and carried her off.

The tracks led to the northwest.

Winona sprinted in pursuit, her fear palpable, fear bordering on terror, terror that one of her worst nightmares had come true and her daughter was in the hands of hostiles who would hurt her in ways no human being should ever be hurt, or force Evelyn to become the unwilling blanket mate to a warrior whose only interest in her was as a trophy.

Spurred by her terror, Winona neglected to scan the ground. When she remembered, she halted, aghast. She had lost the trail.

Frantic, Winona spun. She must find the prints, and quickly. Every second of delay made it that much more likely Evelyn's kidnappers would escape.

"Gai, gai, gai," Winona said aloud in Shoshone, which was the equivalent of "No! No! No!" *"Haga u ahti?"* She had gone farther than she thought. There were no tracks anywhere. She ran to one side and then the other, shouldering through high grass and brushing low tree limbs aside.

Lodgepole pines reared ahead. Winona did not recall passing them. She turned to the southwest, in the direction of the rise. A whisper of sound and a hint of movement caused her to snap her head up. Unwittingly, she made what happened next easier.

A noose settled over Winona from behind. She dropped Evelyn's rifle and grabbed at the rope to tear it off but whoever held the other end gave a powerful tug. The noose constricted around her throat and she was wrenched backward. Stumbling, she let go of her own Hawken and gripped the rope with both hands, but she could not tear it off.

Winona fell onto her back. The rope dug deep and choked off her breath. She pried and pulled but could not loosen it. In desperation she tried to get to her knees and was violently yanked back down. Her vision swam. Her chest was on fire. Gasping for air that was not there, she rolled onto her side and succeeded in heaving onto her right knee. It did no good. The rope did not grow slack.

Winona stabbed for a pistol. Another wrench on the rope made her sprawl face-down. Odd sounds fell on her ears. Through the blur the world had become hurtled a burly figure, moving in an ungainly fashion. It did not look quite human. She blinked and saw the apparition clearly, and thought she had gone mad.

A club arced at Winona's head. She evaded the first blow and the second, but, hampered as she was by the rope, the outcome was inevitable.

Agony filled the space between her ears.

Then came blackness, and nothing more.

The sound of the shot filled Nate King with alarm. He recognized the lighter boom of his daughter's rifle. It was distinct from the heavy-caliber rifles he and his wife used. Then he glimpsed Winona flying toward the trees. Her faint shriek was all that was needed to galvanize him into swinging onto the bay and riding like a madman to the south.

Nate could not begin to guess what had happened. Evelyn rarely fired her rifle except for practice. She was not fond of hunting and always left that chore to them.

It could be she had been attacked by a wild animal. Images of her body, torn to pieces, nearly paralyzed him. Shaking them off, he lashed the reins and jabbed the bay with his heels.

"Winona!" Nate shouted. "Evelyn! Where are you?"

Nate had complete confidence in his wife. Winona would get to Evelyn and save her, whether from beast or man. No frail female, his woman. In defense of her loved ones she was a she-cat unleashed, as fierce as any four-legged predator could ever hope to be. On occasions without number she had proven her mettle. She would do so again now.

Yet it compounded Nate's worry that she did not reappear before he came to the cleared area near his cabin. He did not slacken his speed but rode pell-mell into the pines, reckless in his bid to find them. Again he called their names, and was mocked by silence.

About fifty yards in, Nate reined up. He strained to hear the slightest sound, but heard none that would point him in the direction he should go. He rode on, more slowly, and had gone a dozen yards when the undergrowth crackled and popped to the passage of other riders.

Shakespeare and Zach had caught up to him. Zach was riding bareback. They came up on either side and drew rein.

"Any sign of them, Pa?"

Nate shook his head.

"Lou is saddling her horse. I told her to wait at your cabin until she hears from us." Zach began seeking tracks, and suddenly pointed sharply. "There, in that dirt. Those are Ma's. I'd know them anywhere."

So would Nate. He read the sign as readily as he would a page in one of his cherished books. When he spied the rise, and the flowers that grew among the rocks, he drew rein. "I wonder."

"Wonder what?" Shakespeare asked. He was being uncharacteristically quiet, a trait of his when he was worried.

"That daughter of mine and her flowers," Nate said. "Let's climb down and look around."

Between them they reconstructed the series of events: Evelyn alone, Evelyn set upon by four Indians, Winona rushing to help, Winona racing to the northwest.

Shakespeare was hunkered over a clear track left by one of the four. "Have you taken a gander at these? I've never seen the like, and I know most every kind of moccasin made by most every tribe in these mountains."

"Heart Eaters, do you reckon?" Ever since blowing up the pass, Nate had lived in dread of a Heart Eater war party paying them a visit.

"Their tracks were different." Taking his reins in hand, Shakespeare began tracking on foot. The prints wound around the rise and into the verdant forest. Presently, Shakespeare halted, and frowned. "Damn."

"What?" Zach asked.

"The four who grabbed your sister changed direction and went west. Your mother never noticed. She ran to the north-west." Shakespeare walked in a circle. "There's no sign she caught on to her mistake and came back, either. Mighty strange, that. Winona has a keen eye."

Nate shifted toward his son. "Find her and bring her as quickly as you can. Shakespeare and I will keep after your sister."

Zach opened his mouth to argue. He would never admit it in front of others, but he cared for his sister, cared deeply, and he wanted to get his hands on the sons of bitches who had snatched her. But quibbling would not help rescue her, and that came before all else. "On my way, Pa," he said, and applied his reins.

Shakespeare was climbing onto the mare.

"Whoever these four are, they're making no attempt to hide their trail."

"Think they are setting a trap?"

"Possibly. Or they're just in an all-fired hurry to make themselves scarce," Shakespeare postulated.

"They're not shaking me this side of the grave," Nate vowed. He would not rest until Evelyn was safe.

Shakespeare clucked to the mare, but he only went a short distance. Sliding down, he squatted. "They've split up. Probably to throw us off the scent. Two have gone to the southwest. The other two are still headed west."

"Which two have Evelyn?"

Shakespeare extended an arm to the west.

"Then you take the other pair. I want the ones who have my daughter." Without waiting for a reply, Nate took up the chase. He leaned first to one side and then the other, alert for sign. Crushed grass here. A broken twig there. A bent bush at another spot. There a partial print. The trail was faint in spots but not so faint that he lost it. He had the advantage of being on horseback. He could travel faster.

The pair were making a beeline for somewhere. Nate noticed that one had a long, even stride, the second a shorter pace with the feet spaced more to either side. It suggested the second one was female. But that made no kind of sense. War parties rarely included women.

Not that it mattered. Male, female, they had abducted Evelyn, and for that Nate would see them dead. He was not violent by nature, but there were certain things he would not abide, and harming his family was at the top of the list.

Nate came to a stream. The tracks showed where the pair had stopped and turned. They had heard the bay. They knew he was after them. The man's prints continued west. The woman's angled to the south. Nate was set to gig the bay in pursuit of the man when he saw that the woman's tracks were deeper than before, more clearly defined, as if she now bore extra weight.

It could be, Nate mused, that the man had given Evelyn to the woman in an effort to shake him.

Nate went after the woman. Presently ranks of firs hemmed him and he rode in shadow. He was so intent on the woman's tracks that he did not pay attention to his surroundings. Suddenly the bay nickered. Nate snapped his head up — just as a lance flashed out of the gloom toward his chest.

Shakespeare McNair knew better than to rush. He assumed the pair he was after were armed, and he had no hankering to ride into an ambush. Nice and slow was called for, so nice and slow he rode.

The pair were jogging shoulder to shoulder, which Shakespeare thought was touching, given that one was a man and the other a woman. He tried to recollect if he had mentioned to Nate that they were chasing two of each gender. In the excitement he might have forgotten.

Given his druthers, Shakespeare would have stayed with Nate. Usually, Nate had a level head, but when his family was in danger he tended to be reckless. Not as reckless as Zach, whose fits of fury transformed him into a berserker. But Nate had his moments.

The pair had changed direction again. They swung more south than east and were running faster.

Shakespeare wondered if they knew he was hard on their trail or if they had some deviltry in mind. His opinion inclined toward the deviltry when he spied the rise.

They had gone in a circle.

Shakespeare slowed. He held the Hawken across the pommel, his thumb on the hammer, his finger curled to the trigger. He discovered the pair had gone up the rise instead of around it as they had done before.

It reeked of a trap, and Shakespeare had not lived to have a head of white hair by ignoring his nose. He drew rein and gazed from tree to tree and boulder to boulder. Nothing.

Stumped, Shakespeare stayed where he was. If they planned to jump him, he would not make it easy. Let them come to him. Let them show themselves and he would blow them to Hades and back and sort out the mystery of who they were later.

The seconds crawled into minutes.

The mare began to fidget. Shakespeare grew impatient himself. Against his better judgment he reined to the right and rode slowly along the base of the rise. Either the pair were extraordinarily well hidden, or they were not up there. He came to the opposite side, and swore.

Their tracks came down off the rise and pushed east.

Shakespeare started after them, wondering where they were bound. There was nothing in that direction except the lake — *and the cabins.* Louisa and Blue Water Woman were there. As if seared by a bolt of lightning, Shakespeare jolted to life and goaded the mare into a gallop.

"How could I have been such a lunkhead?" Shakespeare castigated himself aloud. Of course the pair had circled back! They must be looking to abduct someone else, or maybe they intended to burn down the cabins. His delay at the rise had given them plenty of time to get there ahead of him.

"Damn me!"

The mare became a streak of white amid the green.

Shakespeare prayed he was not too late. Lou was supposed to be at Nate's cabin, and Blue Water Woman was at theirs. Both should be safe if they kept the doors bolted, but neither was scrupulous in that regard. Blue Water Woman, in particular, seldom used the bolt or the bar Shakespeare had installed. When he took her to task for it one day, she had retorted, "All the years I lived in a teepee, I got by just fine. And all a teepee has is a flap."

"You lived in a village, surrounded by your people. There was little danger of an enemy trying to sneak into your teepee," Shakespeare had noted.

"Even so, I refuse to live in fear. Were it

up to me, I would have you take off the door and replace it with a flap."

There was no arguing with female logic.

Just then patches of blue appeared through the trees. Shakespeare smiled. He was almost there.

Suddenly the morning air was rent by a war whoop. A rifle imitated thunder and was punctuated by a scream.

CHAPTER SIXTEEN

Decades in the wilderness, decades of clashes with wild beasts and savage men, had honed Nate King's reflexes to the quickness of lightning. He had that to thank for his narrow escape from eternity, for as the lance flashed toward his chest, Nate threw himself to one side and left the saddle in a headlong dive. The lance cleaved the space Nate had occupied, struck a fir, and pierced the bole. Caught fast, it quivered.

As Nate fell, he contrived to roll so that his shoulder bore the brunt of his weight. He grunted from the pain of impact but did not let it slow him. Rising into a crouch, he aimed his Hawken at the spot the lance had come from. He did not shoot.

A slim figure in a green buckskin dress was running off with the speed of a bounding doe.

Nate raced after her, determined not to let her get away. She glanced back and saw him. Her features did not betray fear. Rather, they mirrored grim determination to match his own. He poured on extra speed, and then an iota more, but only narrowed the gap by a couple of yards.

The woman glanced back again. Inadvertently, because the firs were so closely spaced in somber phalanxes, it proved her undoing. A trunk loomed directly in her path. Too late, she faced front, saw her peril, and tried to swerve. The *thwack* of her body striking the tree was loud even to Nate, ten yards back.

Slammed off her feet, the woman clutched at her bosom and thrashed about in torment. A trickle of blood seeped from her lower lip.

Nate came to a stop above her. For the first time he beheld her face clearly. She was much younger than he thought, not a grown woman at all, but a girl barely older than Evelyn. He bent to help her.

A knife swept up and out from the girl's hip. She caught Nate flat-footed. If she had stabbed at his throat, he would be through. But she did not try to cut him. She pumped backward on her elbows, swinging the blade from side to side to keep him at bay.

Nate made no attempt to grapple with her. Straightening, he stepped back, placed the Hawken's stock on the ground and leaned on the barrel. "Make up your mind. Do you want to kill me or not?"

The girl backed against a fir and stopped, breathing heavily, still in pain, and if her expression was any indication, as confused as Nate. Still wagging the knife, she tried to stand but sank down again. The collision had knocked the breath out of her and she had yet to recover.

"I don't savvy this," Nate said. "I don't savvy any of this. Do you speak English by any chance?"

Her blank look was eloquent answer.

"Do you speak *Sosoni?*" Nate tried in that tongue.

Again, only puzzlement.

Nate tried sign language. Invariably, that worked. Sign was used by virtually every tribe on the plains and in the central and northern mountains. Yet once again, incomprehension. Which suggested to Nate she was from a tribe east of the Mississippi, where sign was not as common, or else from a tribe along the far west coast of the continent. Going by her green buckskins, he favored the former. He had been born and raised in New York, and recalled that a tribe or two back East dyed their garb in a similar manner.

"Well, this is a fine pickle," Nate said in exasperation. "Where's my daughter, damn it? Does the other one have her?"

The girl slowly sat up. She dabbed at a split lip with her sleeve.

"My daughter?" Nate repeated. He pointed at her, held his hand at chest height. "A girl about your age, only so high." It was hopeless. She stared up at him in bewilderment. With a sigh, he offered her his hand. "Here. Let me help you up."

Suspicion flared, and she tensed, as if to spring at him, or to bolt.

Hunkering, Nate locked eyes with hers, attempting to take her measure by her reaction.

The girl met his gaze unflinchingly. She acted more curious than scared. She plainly did not know what to make of him.

"You're no killer," Nate said, and unfurled. Again he held out his hand, and when she stayed where she was, he shrugged and made haste to reclaim the bay. He had only taken a few strides when he heard her dress rustle. She was following him. When he stopped, she stopped. When he went on, she went on. So long as she stayed far enough back that she could not reach him with the knife, he did not care what she did. He was thinking only of Evelyn, of finding her as quickly as possible.

The bay was nipping grass. Nate snagged the reins and swung up. The girl had stopped and seemed more confused than ever. She stared at his rifle, then at the pistols at his waist. "What's the matter with you? Haven't you ever seen guns before?" Nate went to ride off but she suddenly raised her hand as if appealing to him not to.

"What is this?" Nate asked suspiciously. "Are you stalling so your friend can get away with my daughter?"

The girl in green pointed at the rifle, then at the flintlocks.

"I have no idea what you are trying to get across," Nate informed her. He tried something else. He touched his chest and said, "Nate." Then he pointed at her and arched his eyebrows. He repeated the pantomime several times.

The girl's eyes widened. She placed a finger to the same spot on her chest and said, "Tenikawaku."

"That's some mouthful." Nate smiled and repeated her name slowly, hoping he had caught all the syllables. He touched his chest once more, and waited.

"Nate," the girl said.

"It's a start," Nate said. He indicated her

knife, then leaned down and held his hand out to her. "Let's try this one last time."

The girl hesitated but only for a few seconds. Abruptly sheathing her blade, she grasped his hand and permitted him to swing her up behind him.

"Hold on," Nate said, hoping to God he had not just made the biggest mistake of his life.

Tenikawaku of the Nansusequa was awash in a flood of confusion. Too much had happened too swiftly. She was lightheaded, but she attributed the feeling to running into the tree.

Teni was amazed the white man had not killed her. He could have, easily. He had the rifle and the short guns. He had a knife and a tomahawk. But he had made no attempt to use them when she lay dazed and next to helpless. This, after she had tried to impale him with her lance.

Something was wrong, Teni mused. Something was very wrong. The white man was not as she expected him to be. Any man who would abduct a young girl, as this man had supposedly taken Miki, would not hesitate to kill someone who had tried to kill him.

Teni's hand drifted to the hilt of her knife.

She could kill him now if she wanted. All it would take was a quick plunge of the blade low in his back and the deed was done. But she could not bring herself to draw it.

For the moment Teni was content to go with the white man and see what developed. She suspected he was after Dega. The man must know Dega had his daughter. The urgency with which he rode showed how worried he was, which, in turn, showed him to be a devoted, caring father. Suggesting, even more, he was not the kind of person who would take Miki.

The bay flew like the wind. Teni had only ever been on horseback twice in her life and neither experience left her wanting to own one. Horses were too big, too terrifying. As it was, she was so scared being on the bay, she forgot herself and wrapped her arms around the man. He looked back and smiled.

Teni would not have been more shocked if he sprouted wings and flew off. Was the smile relief that she no longer appeared to want to kill him? She met his look, but promptly averted her gaze. He had what the Nansuseqa called *strong eyes;* eyes that bored through her into her innermost being. They could not, of course, but she sensed in them a wisdom and a kindness that was at odds with everything she had come to believe about whites.

In time they came to a stream. The white man swung his mount upstream, in the direction Dega had gone. The vegetation was not as thick along the bank, and he rode with a speed that left Teni breathless.

Suddenly the white man drew rein. Vaulting to the ground, he searched right and left. Seeking tracks, Teni realized. He found where her brother's footprints went into the water. They did not come out on the other side.

Teni admired her brother's cleverness. To elude the white man, Dega would stay in the center of the stream for as long as his feet and legs could stand the cold water.

The white man gazed upstream and then downstream. He was unsure which direction Dega had gone.

Teni knew. It was upstream, toward the clearing and their camp.

Placing a hand on her foot, the white man gestured in both directions, then quizzically regarded her.

"You want *me* to tell you?" Teni marveled in the Nansusequa tongue. He was incredible, this white man.

Again he gestured.

Teni felt sorry for him. She wanted to

help. She sincerely did. But helping him meant defying her father, and while she no longer believed this white man was the enemy her father believed him to be, she refused to betray her father.

The white man's eyes were on her in mute appeal.

Sadly, counting on him to divine her meaning if not her words, Teni said, "There is nothing I can do. Your daughter's fate is not mine to decide."

The man bowed his head.

In a thunderous flurry of pounding hooves, the white mare exploded out of the woods and into the clearing near Nate's cabin. Shakespeare half dreaded he would find Louisa or Blue Water Woman lying in a pool of blood, with the pair of Indians gloating over her body. But the situation was the exact opposite.

Louisa was framed in the doorway to her in-laws' cabin. In her right hand was a Hawken, smoke curling from the end of the barrel. In her left hand, as steady as a rock, was a cocked flintlock. Louisa was slight of frame but tougher than steel. Short sandy hair gave her a boyish aspect. Her eyes, as blue as the lake, were lit with fierce fire. "Stay right where you are!"

She was addressing the pair Shakespeare had spent the better part of an hour tracking. The warrior's green buckskins and the woman's green buckskin dress showed evidence of much wear and tear. The man was on his knees, his left hand pressed to his right shoulder, glaring defiantly at Louisa. A bow and arrow lay next to him. The woman in the green dress was at his elbow, supporting him.

Shakespeare trotted around in front of them and brought the mare to a stop. "What have we here, Lou?"

"That's what I'd like to know," Lou said. "Zach told me to hurry over and keep an eye on the place. I was looking out the window, wondering where in creation all of you got to, when these two came running out of the woods. I opened the door and that damned fool tried to put an arrow into me."

Smothering a chuckle, Shakespeare slid down. It took a firebrand to marry a firebrand, and Lou was a match for Zach. "So you winged him? Nice shooting."

"I can't claim any credit. I was aiming for his heart, but I rushed my shot." Lou stepped into the sunlight. "Suppose you tell me who these green rascals are?"

"I would like to know myself." Covering

them, Shakespeare moved closer. Both wore masks of defiance. "My conscience has a thousand several tongues, and every tongue brings in a several tale, and every tale condemns the pair of you for villains," he quoted.

The warrior in green licked his thin lips. "What you say, white beard?"

"By my troth!" Shakespeare exclaimed. "The King's English or some semblance thereof. How now, sirrah, and what is your cognomen?"

"You not talk white tongue?" the warrior asked.

Louisa laughed. She had lowered her pistol but held it trained on the twosome. "That will teach you to babble the Bard."

For all of ten seconds Shakespeare was at a loss for words. Then he parried with, "Go to, woman. Throw your vile guesses in the devil's teeth from whence you have them. Old William S. possessed an eloquence of which you can scarcely conceive."

The wounded warrior looked at Lou. "What white beard say?"

"Even he doesn't know."

"That is too much presumption on thy part," Shakespeare quoted, and turned back to their prisoners. "Permit me to try again. I am Shakespeare McNair. Who might you two folks be?"

"Where daughter, Mc-Nair?" the warrior demanded.

"That's what we would like to know," Shakespeare responded. "Why did your friends make off with Evelyn King?"

"Evelyn King?" the warrior said with some difficulty. "You mean white girl?"

"She's half and half, although you would never know it to look at her," Shakespeare said. "Why did you and your friends jump her?"

"Not friends," the man responded in a strained tone. The wound was taking its toll. "Son, daughter, wife, me."

"So this is a family affair?" Shakespeare said. "That's well and good but still begs the question, why?"

"We want daughter."

"I always wanted a son, but you don't see me going around stealing one from someone else."

"No," the warrior said. "Want own daughter."

"Sorry, but Evelyn King already has a ma and a pa. You can't have her," Shakespeare said gruffly. Their gall was beyond belief.

"Not King girl. Want own daughter."

Louisa had been listening with great interest to the exchange. "I think he means he has a daughter of his own in the mix somewhere."

"Is that true?" Shakespeare asked.

Excitement seized the warrior. "Yes! Have own daughter. Want back. Give you King girl."

"Hold on there, hoss. You think we have your daughter and you stole Evelyn to force us to give your daughter back?" Shakespeare was inclined to regard it as a preposterous lie intended to trick him into lowering his guard, but there was no denying the other's sincerity.

"Yes! Yes!" The warrior stood and swayed. His wife had to hold him to keep him from falling.

"Before we go any further, do you have a name? And what tribe do you and your missus belong to?"

"My name Wakumassee. Wife Tihikanima. Our people Nansusequa."

A tribe Shakespeare had never heard of. "Well, I have good news and not so good news. The good news is that neither me nor my friends have your daughter. The not so good news is that I have no idea where she is."

"You talk two tongues. Wakumassee see axe."

"Axe?" Shakespeare said, and remembered

Nate had mentioned his was missing. "One of ours was stolen."

The woman in green had been silent this whole while, but now she spoke to Wakumassee and he talked at length. Her repeated glances at Shakespeare hinted that Wakumassee was translating everything that had been said so far. When Wakumassee was done, it was the woman's turn. "Wife have questions," he translated.

"First things first." Shakespeare lowered his rifle. "How about if we patch up that shoulder of yours before you bleed to death?"

Wakumassee did not hide his surprise. "You do for me?"

"Why not? You haven't hurt anyone yet, and something tells me there is more to this than meets the eye." Shakespeare went up to them and bestowed his friendliest smile. "What do you say? Truce?"

"What mean truce?" Wakumassee asked.

"I won't try to kill you and you won't try to kill me," Shakespeare explained. "How about it? Come inside and we'll tend you."

Louisa interjected, "Are you sure it's wise? We don't know these two from Adam and Eve."

"That works both ways," Shakespeare said. "I believe them about their girl, and if

I were wearing their moccasins, I would be as anxious as they are to find her."

"Taking Evelyn wasn't too bright," Lou remarked. "If any harm comes to her, my husband will be out for blood. We both know what Zach is capable of. He won't give them a chance to explain or apologize. He'll kill them before they can so much as blink."

"Let's hope it doesn't come to that."

Wakumassee listened to their exchange in growing confusion and alarm. Confusion because the white woman could have finished him off after she shot him, yet she had not done so, and because the white-haired white man impressed him as being sincerely friendly. Alarm because it sounded as if the one called Zach was a formidable warrior who would not hesitate to kill Dega and Teni if he found them.

Waku let the white-hair help Tihi bring him into the cabin. But he was not as helpless as he let on. His wound hurt, but he had known worse pain, and the bleeding had about stopped. It would be simple for him to grab the white man's knife and plunge it into the pair before they could stop him, but if the white man was telling the truth, and they did not have Miki, then he had made a great mistake.

Waku's first mistake had been to trust Reverend Stilljoy. It had cost his people their lives. He naturally blamed Stilljoy and the other whites, but part of the blame must fall on his shoulders. His desire for peace had warped his reasoning. He had trusted without making sure the person was worthy of his trust. Now he wondered if he was not doing the same thing again, only in reverse.

The seed of hatred planted in Waku's heart by the massacre had grown into a hatred for all whites. A hatred he had nurtured during his family's long journey to the mountains. Hatred motivated him to lay claim to the valley. It was hatred that fed his lust to kill those already here.

In that respect, Waku realized, he was no different from Reverend Stilljoy. He wanted to kill out of blind hate. Kill people who had done him no harm, just as his people had done no harm to the bigots of New Albion.

Waku was torn inside. Part of him still wanted to slay the one called Mc-Nair and the young, dangerous woman, but another part of him, the old part, the part that had always sought peace rather than war, the part he thought dead, wanted to hear them out and then decide what to do.

They seated Waku in a chair. While the young woman heated water, Mc-Nair had Waku shed his buckskin shirt, then examined the wound. Waku noted that the older man took great care not to cause him any more pain than was necessary.

Tihi, who had been quietly standing to one side, said, "Ask him, husband. It is important we find out."

Waku chose his words slowly so as not to make mistakes. "You say not take our daughter?"

"As God is my witness," McNair said while daubing at the bullet hole. "We don't make war on children."

"Then who?" Waku pressed him.

"That is what I would very much like to find out," Mc-Nair answered. "There are a lot of folks in this world who think no more of making life miserable for everyone else than they do of stepping on a bug."

Once again Waku had to mentally wade through a morass of shades of meaning to get at the right one. The white tongue was hard enough for him to understand. Mc-Nair, with his unusual use of many words Waku had never heard before, made it that much harder. "Have enemies?"

"Who doesn't?" Mc-Nair rejoined.

That was not much of an answer but Waku

relayed it to Tihi. He should have listened when she said it was too dangerous for them to go from cabin to cabin looking for Miki. He thought the whites and their women and the half-breed and his woman were off searching for the girl. But he had been wrong and Tihi had been right. He should listen to her more.

Coincidentally, Tihi said, "Ask him about their wives."

Waku grunted. She had been curious about them since she first saw them. "Your woman," he said to Mc-Nair. "She Indian."

"Through and through. She's the kitchen wench, and all grease, and I know not what use to put her to but to make a lamp of her, and run from her by her own light."

Once again Waku struggled to make sense of the answer. "Sorry?"

"She would have made Hercules have turned spit, yea, and have cleft his club to make the fire, too."

"I not understand," Waku admitted.

"Don't feel bad," the white woman said. "No one else understands him, either. But that doesn't stop him from prattling."

Mc-Nair scowled and leaned down as if to confide in Waku. "I will fetch you a toothpicker now from the furthest inch of Asia, bring you the length of Prester John's foot, fetch you a hair off the great Cham's beard, do you any embassage to the Pygmies, rather than hold three words' conference with this harpy."

His confusion at a peak, Waku said, "You give me foot?"

The young woman laughed merrily. "He'll give you his nose and his ears, too, if you ask real nice."

"Pay her no mind," Mc-Nair cautioned. "She hath more hair than wit, and more faults than hairs."

"And more lead than both," the young woman said.

"Good sooth, she is the queen of curds and cream," Mc-Nair declared. "If she lives till doomsday she'll burn a week longer than the whole world. She speaks poniards, and every word stabs."

"I wouldn't want my blade to rust," was the woman's response.

"See? Did you hear? They barb us with their wit and beguile us with their charms. They lead us by the nose ring and trip us when we show the least sloth. I ask you, Wakumassee? Is that any way to be treated? Are we men or mice?"

Waku felt he had to say something, so he said, "Men?"

"I gave up my claim when I discovered I

could do as I pleased only so long as it pleased my wife. No wonder I go through life so confused. How about you?"

At last something Waku understood. "I confused too." In fact, it was safe to say he had never been so confused in his life.

Mc-Nair smiled and clapped Waku's good shoulder. "That's the spirit! What say that once you're fit we tip a glass to the Bard and another to all the injustice in this female-afflicted world?"

Wakumassee began to wonder if maybe the white-haired white man, for all his friendliness, was not entirely sane.

CHAPTER SEVENTEEN

A rainbow of emotion had played over Evelyn King. First there was red-hot anger at being attacked, then black fury as she was bodily carried off. Both were eclipsed by the yellow blanch of fear at her impending fate. The fear, though, was fleeting, and was replaced by the pink flush of embarrassment. Then came the ruddy complexion of a volcano on the brink of eruption.

Evelyn struggled mightily at first, but with her arms pinned to her sides and her feet off the ground, she could do little more than wriggle like a worm on a hook. But where an ineffectual worm's ultimate end was foreordained, Evelyn's was not. She subsided, conserving her energy and biding her time for when her captors made the mistake of releasing her, as they assuredly would.

The hand over Evelyn's mouth was firm, but the fingers did not gouge deep, almost as if the warrior who carried her was making a conscious effort not to hurt her. With her back to his chest, Evelyn had not had a good look at his face. All she could tell was that he was tall and sinewy and possessed remarkable strength and stamina.

Evelyn had noticed, too, that his arm was clamped about her middle, not higher up or lower down. It held little significance to her until, at one point, when he was leaping a low log, his grip slipped and his arm slid up over her bosom. He instantly jerked it back down.

For an abductor he was being awfully considerate. Evelyn tried to twist to see him better, but he shook her, lightly, and growled words in a tongue with which she was unfamiliar.

From time to time during their flight, Evelyn glimpsed the others. One was a middle-aged warrior, another a woman of comparable age. Husband and wife, Evelyn suspected. The last of her green-clad attackers was a girl not much older than she was, who kept glancing at her with what Evelyn would swear were looks of sympathy.

Then came the point at which the older man and woman separated from the younger woman and the warrior holding Evelyn. By then Evelyn knew help was on the way. She had heard her mother shout her name, and as surely as the sun rose and set, her father and brother would not be far behind.

Evelyn almost felt sorry for her kidnappers. Her father and Uncle Shakespeare were two of the best trackers alive. Everyone said so. As for Zach, he might not be quite the tracker they were, but he once trailed Evelyn over a thousand miles to save her from an enemy. Nothing short of dying would stop her brother from rescuing her.

Now the warrior holding her stopped and turned. So did the girl. Distant hoofbeats had alarmed them. They briefly consulted, and the girl picked up a small boulder and fled in one direction while the warrior took another. When he leaped off a bank into a stream, water splashed Evelyn's face and dress. To her bewilderment, he eased her higher on his chest to spare her from becoming soaked.

What kind of Indians were these, anyhow? Evelyn wondered. Their green buckskins were unusual. The four were not Crows, not Cheyenne, not Blackfeet, Utes, Arapahos or any other tribe she had come across, that was for sure.

The warrior was moving as fast as her weight allowed, his legs kicking arcs of spray with every stride. His breathing became labored, a sign he was near the end of his endurance.

On the right side of the stream the bank fell away. High grass fringed somber woods. Her captor waded out of the stream, adjusted his hold on her, and wound in among stately spruce. His green moccasins squished for a while and then stopped. Shortly thereafter, he stopped and released her.

Evelyn had no warning. She fell on her side, on her elbow. Pain speared up her arm. Wincing, she twisted to gain her knees and run off but her captor upended her onto her back. She slammed down hard, taken aback by the violence. A sharp retort was on the tip of her tongue.

The warrior loomed over her. He relieved her of both pistols and her knife.

As Evelyn had surmised, he was tall and well-muscled. She had not guessed how young he was. A mane of raven hair fell to his shoulders. In every respect other than his green buckskins, he was just like warriors from every other tribe Evelyn had contact with, except that in all the years Evelyn had lived in the mountains, and among all the tribes she had met, she had never set eyes on anyone anywhere near as handsome.

Evelyn blinked in surprise, not at his features but at her reaction to them. She had no business admiring his good looks. She was his prisoner, for pity's sake. But his dark, piercing eyes, his fine eyebrows and small but perfect nose, his full cheeks and the set of his jaw, combined to paint a portrait of as attractive a young man as Evelyn ever beheld. She looked away, horrified by the feelings that rippled through her, feelings new and alien and more than a little frightening.

Apparently convinced she would not try to run off, the young warrior stepped back. He had a rifle slung across his back, an ammo pouch and powderhorn slanted crosswise across his chest.

"Consarn me." Coughing to clear her throat, Evelyn asked, "Who are you? Do you speak English?" He made a chopping motion with his hand, as if to signify he did not comprehend. She tried Shoshone. She tried the few words of Crow she knew. She confidently tried sign language.

The young warrior stood and stared.

"You don't know sign?" Evelyn was flabbergasted. "Where are you from? The moon?" For some reason that struck her as humorous and she laughed.

Degamawaku of the Nansusequa fought

down a wave of admiration. Here she was, unarmed and at his mercy, yet she showed no fear. Her eyes, those wonderful, special, lovely green eyes, were bottomless pools in which he felt himself sinking. With an inner wrench, he tore his gaze away.

"What's the matter with you?" Evelyn asked. "Are you sick?" He had gone unaccountably pale.

Dega sensed she thought something was wrong with him. He took another step back, his mind in a jumble. The effect she had on him was disquieting. "Are you a medicine woman?" he asked thickly.

Evelyn yearned to understand. If she could find a way to communicate, she could find out why the four of them had jumped her, and why he had carried her off. She made bold to sit up. When he did not object, she went to stand, but he thrust her own knife at her and she stayed where she was. *"Maiku,"* she said. *All right.* Why she spoke Shoshone, when she so rarely did so even to her own mother, was a mystery.

Dega was appalled. He had not meant to jab at her with the knife. His hand had moved on its own. Retreating a few paces, he squatted and set the knife and her pistols on the ground. "I am sorry," he said, knowing full well she could not understand. "I

347

do this for my father and not for me."

Evelyn placed her elbows on her knees and her chin in her hands. Since he was making no effort to harm her, she would patiently await her parents and her brother. The thought jarred her. Zach might shoot the young warrior dead on sight.

Dega saw her head come up and her eyes narrow. He glanced over his shoulder, thinking someone was sneaking up on him, but no one was there. Her green eyes were boring into him like twin lances. "What?" he asked.

Touching herself, Evelyn said her name. She repeated it twice, slowly.

"Ev-lyn," Dega said. No word in the Nansusequa tongue resembled it in any way. Her name was special, like her eyes. He touched his chest. "Dega," he said several times, then realized he had used his familiar name, the name only his family and loved ones were permitted to use. Everyone else must call him Degamawaku.

"Dega." Evelyn rolled the name on her tongue. She liked the sound of it. Encouraged by his readiness to share, she smiled, spread her arms wide as if to embrace him, and said warmly, "Friend. *Hainja*."

Shock rocked Dega. Among his people, when a man or woman looked the other in the eye and spread their arms as Ev-lyn had just done, it was a sign of the deepest, most abiding love. She had to have another reason. When she did it a second time, he studied her face, her posture, her whole bearing. He detected genuine warmth, which, in its way, was almost as astounding. How could she be so nice to him after how he had treated her?

"Friend," Evelyn said yet again. *"Hainja."* She smiled her broadest smile to accent her point.

Dega managed a thin smile in return. He did not know what she expected of him, and that troubled him. It could be she wanted him to let her go. But he intended to hold her there until dark, then take her to the clearing where his family was camped. That was the plan his father had come up with in case any of them were separated from the others.

His father. Dega had always been an obedient son. He was devoted to his parents, as custom called for. Among some tribes the old were left to fend for themselves but not among the People of the Forest. It was Nansusequa tradition that the aged and infirm were to be looked after by their children.

Dega diligently did all his parents asked of him. But this latest, the idea his father had of wiping out the valley's inhabitants so that their family could claim the valley as their own, was not the Nansusequa way. It was not Dega's way. He could never kill this gentle girl in front of him. He liked her too much.

Yet another bewilderment. How could he like her so much, Dega asked himself, when he hardly knew her? But he could not deny she did something to him. She stirred him, deep down, in a manner no one had ever stirred him before. Stirred him so greatly that he broke out in a sweat, which in itself was rare.

Dega started to raise a hand to his brow. Maybe he *was* sick. He did not feel hot but he might have a fever. He certainly felt warm. That would explain his erratic thoughts, his erratic emotions. He was not himself. He only thought he liked the girl. Then she smiled again, and those green eyes of her lit with a glow he could not fathom, and he knew as surely as he had ever known anything that he did indeed like her, and liked her a lot.

Evelyn was listening for hoofbeats or shouts. That she had not heard either in a while was mildly troubling, but she still expected her parents or her brother to eventually appear. *I will be patient,* she told herself. *I will show this warrior that I am the friendliest person who ever lived, and he will not want to hurt me.* To demonstrate her friendliness she began to point at things and say what they were, in Shoshone, not English.

Dega enjoyed the diversion. It took his mind off why the girl was there and what his father would want done to her. When she pointed at things and said their names, he would point at them, too, and say what they were in his tongue.

The shadows slowly lengthened. They sat and smiled and taught one another the languages they spoke, or, in Evelyn's case, one of the two languages she had learned as a child but infrequently used until today.

Neither realized how long they sat there. Time was suspended on the mutual buoyance of their interest. Their real interest, not their languages, which were a convenient means to an end.

Then Evelyn's stomach growled. They both heard it. She squirmed with embarrassment, and Dega was upset that he had let her go hungry for so long. As her captor, he was responsible for her needs.

Dega stood. He touched his own stomach and then his mouth and said, "I will find food for you. Come." He beckoned.

Evelyn understood and rose. He turned to lead her into the woods and she pointed at the grass at his feet. "What about those?"

The flintlocks and her knife. Dega had forgotten about them. He picked them up. He would rather have his hands free, but they were hers and he could not leave them there. She came up beside him and Dega tensed, thinking she would try to take them from him. But no, she merely walked at his side. Out of the corner of his eye he drank in the vision of her beauty. She was exquisite, this captive of his.

The stream was their first stop. Dega stood guard while Evelyn drank and washed her face and hands. When she was done, they bore west along the stream and had gone only a short distance when a perplexing sight brought him up short.

Something had crossed the stream. In the soft earth were its tracks. Tracks the likes of which beggared belief. They were small circles, with no pugs or claws. The thing had approached the water on the other side, forded, and come up the bank on the same side as Dega and Evelyn. Where it came out of the water were two furrows in the soft earth, in addition to the circles.

Evelyn remembered the circles near the cabin. "What *are* those?" she said out loud.

She hunkered to examine them.

Dega joined her. His shoulder brushed hers as he squatted, but she did not seem to mind. He ran a finger along a furrow and it came up slick with mud. The tracks were fresh. So fresh that whatever had made them must be nearby.

Straightening, Dega scanned the forest. He had not realized it before, but the birds and lesser animals had fallen silent. Unease crept over him but he shook it off. He was a man, not a boy, and men did not succumb to nerves.

Evelyn was peering into the thick tangle of vegetation, too. She had that feeling again, that feeling of being watched. Experience had taught her not to ignore it. She followed the tracks up the bank. At the top the furrows disappeared and circles led into the undergrowth.

Going back to the water's edge, Evelyn examined the furrows more closely. They were not tracks, as such, but more like drag marks. Each was about the width of one of her knees. She bent low to the ground. She found no claw marks or pads but she did find something: a few gray hairs. Delicately plucking one with her fingernails, she held it up in the sunlight. Her father or Shakespeare might be able to tell what kind of animal the hair came from, but she could not. To her, hair was hair. Gray could be anything from a wolf to a rabbit. She looked up. Dega was watching her. "Here," she said, and held the hair out to him.

Dega carefully took it. Their fingertips brushed, and a sharp tingle shot up his hand and half his arm. By the way Ev-lyn jumped, he knew she had felt it, too. He smiled self-consciously, then inspected the hair. Ev-lyn stared expectantly at him, apparently hoping he could identify it. He used one of the words she had taught him earlier. *"Gai."* No.

They had delayed long enough. The sun was low in the west and Dega wanted to reach the clearing before dark. He turned to lead the way, and his arm tingled again, although in a different manner, when Ev-lyn grasped his wrist. He regarded her quizzically. She motioned at the strange tracks, then at the woods, and said words he did not yet know.

Evelyn was trying to tell her handsome captor about her feeling of unease. "Danger," she said, and slid a finger across her neck as if she were slitting her throat.

Dega gazed into the dense woodland. So she felt it, too. He set off and she fell into step beside him, walking so close their arms rubbed now and again. It made it hard for him to concentrate. Which was silly. It was only an arm.

The horizon swallowed the sun. Soon twilight shrouded the mountains.

Dega came to the clearing, only to be knifed by disappointment. It was empty. The embers of the fire were cold. No one else had arrived yet. He sat on a log and pondered what to do. He was worried. His parents and Teni should have been there by now.

The dead fire and the log and other signs told Evelyn this was where Dega and the others had been camped. The charred coals were directly under the overspreading boughs of a pine so that when smoke rose it was dispelled by the branches and could not be seen from far off.

Evelyn did not sit down. Her unease had grown. Since finding the tracks by the stream, she'd had the impression, vague but persistent, that they were being followed. That they were being stalked. She touched Dega's shoulder and gestured at the dark wall of encircling vegetation, a wall that would soon be pitch black.

Just then, so clear they both heard it, a twig snapped.

Dega was erect in a twinkling. He moved toward the edge of the clearing. Twigs did not break by themselves. Something was out there. That was what the girl had been trying to tell him. It could be anything. Deer. An elk. A porcupine. Or it could be whatever had made the tracks by the stream.

Evelyn strained her eyes for a hint of movement. She rose onto the tips of her toes, she crouched, but nothing. She was starting to rise when she glimpsed — or thought she glimpsed — a pair of eyes reflecting the last of the fading light. They were almost as low to the ground as she was. Mere slits that somehow filled her with dread so potent, she froze. Then she tilted her head to try to see them better, and the slits were gone.

Dega was watching Ev-lyn as much as the woods. He liked watching her; her exquisite face, her unconscious grace, the vital sheen to her hair. He saw her start, and instantly squatted to try and see what she saw. *"Hagai?"* he whispered, which was the Shoshone word she had taught him for "what."

Evelyn forgot herself and answered in English. "Something. I don't know. An animal, I think."

Her tone, ripe with apprehension, affected Dega. Clasping her arm, he stepped back from the trees until they were in the middle of the clearing. Their eyes met yet again, and Dega came to the decision he had made when he first saw her but which he had denied ever since. He held out her knife and pistols.

Evelyn looked at them, then at him. "Thank you," she said softly, her cheeks unaccountably warm. She slid the knife into its sheath. She checked both pistols to verify they were loaded and ready, then slipped one under her belt. "Now let it come."

Dega unslung his rifle. Suddenly it did not seem adequate. He wished he had a bow and arrows. With a bow he was skilled. With the rifle he was like a child taking his first steps.

Another sharp *crack* came out of the woods. Only this one came from the opposite side.

Evelyn and Dega whirled. The *click* of Evelyn thumbing back the pistol's hammer was distinct.

Dega pressed his cheek to the rifle. The twigs had been snapped on purpose. Whatever was out there wanted them to know. An animal would never give itself away. "It is a man," he said aloud.

Night was descending with typical swiftness. Gray became black. Random shadows became an inky soup. Stars speckled the firmament but the moon was absent, and without the moon the dark was thrice compounded. The ink flowed out of the vegetation and enveloped the clearing.

Evelyn could barely see Dega. He was a silhouette, a profile. She sidled closer. So they could protect one another, she told herself.

A rustling sound came from their left. Again they spun. The thing was circling them. Evelyn had heard her father say bears would sometimes circle prey before attacking, but in her bones she knew this was no bear.

Suddenly there was a rush of movement. Something long and thin arced out of the brush. Dega fired. He did not expect to hit it but he did. He heard the *thwack* of the lead ball, and the long, thin thing fell to the ground almost at their feet.

Evelyn guessed what it was before she bent and picked it up: a tree limb. A limb that had been trimmed of shoots and leaves. It was straight enough and thick enough to serve as a spear but neither end had been sharpened. Throwing it at them seemed pointless. All it had accomplished was to make Dega waste lead.

Then another purpose occurred to her. The flash of Dega's rifle had shown exactly where they were. Evelyn stiffened and turned to warn him, but before she could open her mouth there came a *swish* and the fleshy *chock* of cold steel slicing into human flesh.

Agony exploded in Dega's right shoulder. With it came the moist sensation of blood on skin, his blood on his skin. He staggered but did not fall. His right arm became so numb, he could not hold the rifle. It clattered as it hit.

Despite her tender years, Evelyn had seen blood spilled on more than one occasion. She had witnessed whites battling red men, whites battling whites, red men battling red men. She had heard the heavy punch of lead balls when they struck the human body, and the sound a knife made when it sliced into flesh. She knew what had happened to Dega; she just did not know where the knife had hit him. Lunging, she wrapped her left arm around his waist and pulled him toward the woods on the other side.

Dega did not resist. He was growing weaker by the moment. He groped at the wound, tracing the contours of the knife with his fingertips. It was buried to the hilt. He gingerly tried to pull it out but only succeeded in worsening the flow of blood.

Evleyn did not take her gaze off the spot where the limb had come from. She was rewarded with a shaking of the brush, and a figure appeared, hunkered so that only his head and shoulders were visible, and then only in silhouette. Impulsively, she aimed and fired. The silhouette vanished, but she doubted she had hit it.

The undergrowth closed around them. Dega tottered to the south but Evelyn firmed her hold and led him to the east. In that direction lay the valley floor and help.

His teeth clenched so he would not cry out, Dega did his best not to hamper her. But he could not move as fast as they needed to move. His stomach was a pit of nausea, and waves of dizziness made focusing impossible.

Evelyn had jammed the spent pistol under her belt and drawn her spare. She was bearing most of Dega's weight, her cheek against his shirt, and she became alarmed when the shirt, and her cheek, grew wet with what could only be slowly spreading blood. Ducking under the low boughs of a spruce, she eased him down so his back was to the trunk. "Dega?" she whispered.

His name came to him as if down a deep hole. "Ev-lyn?" Dega breathed. Between the dizziness and the nausea he was close to passing out.

Lightly running her fingers up his chest to

the knife, Evelyn grimaced at the contact. She explored the hilt. Blood dampened her hand and trickled between her fingers. The blade had to come out, that much was certain, but would pulling it out help or make him worse? Should she or shouldn't she?

Dega decided the issue. "Take the knife out," he whispered in his own tongue, and weakly moved his left hand to show what he wanted done.

"Oh God." Evelyn put one hand flat on his chest and gripped the hilt with her other. "I hope I'm doing the right thing," she said, and yanked. The blade came out much more easily than she had anticipated. She tottered back, thrown off balance, then immediately bent over Dega. The blood flow did not appear to have increased.

Evelyn was smiling in relief when the feel of the knife hilt on her palm stirred a recollection of a knife that was exactly the same, from the texture of the antler hilt to how much it weighed to the general shape of the blade. Puzzled, she stepped from under the spruce and held the knife aloft so the starlight played over it.

Several seconds went by before the truth dawned.

Evelyn had seen this knife before, many

times. She had held it before, used it to skin deer and elk.

It was her mother's.

CHAPTER EIGHTEEN

Life throws moments at people, who never forget them for as long as they live. Moments of crushing clarity, moments of blinding beauty, moments of sublime peace, and, for Evelyn King, a moment of unrivaled terror that turned her world topsy-turvy and tore at her heartstrings with razor talons.

Evelyn stared at the knife she held over her head, trying to make sense of an impossible madness. If the knife was her mother's — and it was — then it had fallen into the hands of whoever was out there in the dark, and since her mother would never willingly part with the knife — it had been a gift from Evelyn's father — the inescapable conclusion was that it had been taken from Winona's cold, lifeless body.

Evelyn ducked under the spruce. She would think more on her mother later. Right now she had two lives to save, hers and the handsome young warrior she should hate for abducting her, but didn't. His chin was on his chest. Unconscious, she thought, but when she touched his arm, his head rose and he softly spoke her name.

"We have to get out of here," Evelyn said. "He'll find us if we don't."

Even though Dega only knew a dozen or so words of the white tongue, he understood her. They must keep moving. Whoever had thrown the knife at them would try again, and next time, he might try to kill the girl. The image of her lying on the ground in a scarlet pool galvanized Dega into standing without her help. "We must hurry," he said in Nansusequa, and lurched from under the spruce.

Evelyn followed, twisting at the waist so she could watch their back trail. She held on to her mother's knife.

The silence of the timber was nigh unnatural. Even the wind had stilled, so that every tree, every leaf, every blade of grass and every bush, had an unreal quality, as if the plant life had been carved from obsidian and was not living matter at all.

Evelyn bumped into Dega. He walked with a shuffling gait, as unsteady on his feet as a sailor on a storm-tossed deck. The loss of blood was to blame. Evelyn had seen wounded warriors so weak they could not lift their heads off the ground. She looked back, just in time to detect a spurt of movement as a squat shape flowed over the ground a score of feet back. Their attacker was closing in. Perhaps overconfidence had made him careless. Or maybe he wanted them to know he was there to further fray their nerves.

Evelyn considered yelling, in the hope her father would hear, but it might provoke their stalker into rushing them. In the shape Dega was in, he wouldn't last ten seconds. And, too, there was no guarantee her father would hear her.

Dega stumbled but plodded on. His legs were next to useless. At any moment he might collapse.

Devoting her attention between the stricken warrior and the forest, Evelyn almost missed another glimpse of the man out to kill them. Lightning quick, he scuttled from one tree to another. She could tell nothing about him other than that he appeared to be down on all fours.

A small log barred Dega's path. He willed his right leg to lift and nearly lost his balance. Furious at his weakness, he stumbled on into the night. The girl put a hand on his back, as if to reassure him, but it only fed his fury. She was in danger because of him. She would be safe in her cabin if he had not taken her. Yet, incredibly, here she was, protecting him, placing her own life at risk to preserve his. He could not permit that. He must do something.

A boulder-strewn slope spread before them. Dega started down. He went slowly in order to avoid obstacles he might trip over. Then a slender shoulder slipped under his arm, and a hand snaked around his waist.

"I'll help you," Evelyn said.

Dega had occasionally sat in on the long talks between his father and Reverend Still-joy. He struggled to remember, to find the right English. "Go me," he said, and fluttered his fingers to demonstrate.

"Don't worry. I won't leave you."

Dega tried again. He had to make her understand. He chose another word that might work. "Leave."

"What?" Evelyn studied his pale, sweaty face. "You want me to go on without you? Is that it?"

"*Haa,*" Dega said, the Shoshone word she had taught him for "yes."

"Not on your life," Evelyn told him. "Not with you ready to keel over. We're in this together."

Degas deduced all that meant 'no.'

"Please."

"Hush. Save your strength. It's only four or five miles to my family's cabin. We can make it." Evelyn was not being sincere. Their would-be slayer was bound to strike long before they reached the valley floor.

"Please," Dega pleaded.

"Enough of that," Evelyn said more harshly than she intended. She was watching the trees and could not afford to be distracted.

Crestfallen, Dega was nonetheless deeply stirred. She possessed courage, this girl, and a poise beyond her years. Abducting her had been a mistake, and he would tell his father that when next they met. *If* they met.

A low whizzing broke the stillness. Evelyn glanced sharply around and saw an object streak toward them. "Get down!" she yelled, and sought to pull Dega down beside her. A melon-sized boulder thwarted her, and, ironically, saved Dega's life. He tripped when she pulled, and sprawled forward, with the result that the whizzing object passed over his shoulder.

Evelyn tried to keep him on his feet but went down herself, banging her knees on the rocks. Swiveling, she spotted a quicksilver form at the top of the slope. She had no chance of hitting it but she fired anyway and had the satisfaction of seeing it dart back into the foliage.

Doubled over, Dega battled more dizziness. Never had he felt so weak, so helpless. He wanted to scream and beat his fists on the ground. The yearning jarred him. He was Degamawaku of the Nansusequa. The People of the Forest prided themselves on their self-control, on never permitting their emotions to rule their reason. Yet here he was, behaving like an infant. He must teach his emotions who was the master. He must show the white girl he was worthy of her noble sacrifice.

Evelyn was reloading. She uncapped her powderhorn and measured out the right amount in her palm by feel alone. "What was that he threw at us?" she whispered. It had been too small to be a knife.

Dega felt his wound. The bleeding had stopped.

"Maybe we should stay right where we are," Evelyn speculated aloud. "He can't get close without us seeing him." She wrapped a patch around the lead ball and tamped it down the barrel.

Dega did not know what she was saying. It did not matter. Time for him to show her he was not helpless. Girding his leg muscles, he pushed erect, steadied himself, and was off down the slope.

"Wait!" Evelyn was caught by surprise. Wondering what had gotten into him, she hastened to catch up. Worried that he would fall and hurt himself, she did not keep one eye cocked behind them. The whizzing sound registered too late. She tried to turn but she was only halfway around when something struck her high on the left shoulder. A sharp, stabbing pain caused her to cry out.

To her right a few yards was a waist-high boulder. Dashing behind it, Evelyn dropped to her knees. She reached over her shoulder but could not quite touch whatever was imbedded in her back. A burning sensation had taken hold and was spreading. She bent her spine into a bow but still could not grip it.

A form brushed hers.

Dega saw what she was trying to do and gently moved her groping fingers aside. The thing stuck in her back was much too small to be an arrow and much too thin to be a knife. He bent closer.

"What is it?" Evelyn asked in English. Then, in Shoshone, *"Hagai?"*

Dega did not answer. He could not speak the tongue she had been trying to teach him or the white man's tongue well enough to describe it. Since to pull it out slowly would only increase her pain, he took hold of the end and gave a quick wrench.

A gasp escaped Evelyn. But she was glad to have it out. The pain lessened a bit but the burning sensation had spread to her neck and down her left arm to her elbow.

Dega held the object out for her to take.

"I've never seen the like," Evelyn declared. What she now held was a dart. Six inches long and as thick as her father's middle finger, it had been whittled from an ash branch. The tip had been sharpened and fire-hardened so that it was as black as coal. Three raven feathers were attached to the other end, much like an arrow. The feathers had been cut midway and pine sap applied to the cut edge. Then the feather had been pressed to the dart. Once the sap dried, it worked as well as glue.

"This is all it was?" Evelyn asked in relief. The dart was too small to do grave harm unless it hit someone in the throat or the eye. She went to cast it aside. A whiff of the tip stayed her arm. Holding it under her nose, she sniffed. The odor reminded her of the stink of rotting flesh.

Suddenly the burning sensation took on a whole new significance. Some Indian tribes, Evelyn was aware, applied poison to the tips of their arrows. One tribe dipped their arrowheads in rattlesnake venom. Another was partial to tainting their tips in the bodies of dead skunks. The reek on the tip of the dart might be from a skunk or something else.

Dega did not understand why she sniffed the dart and recoiled. He took it from her and held the tip to his nose. The foul odor stirred a memory. The Nansusequa did not poison their arrows, but they had clashed with tribes that did. When he was a small boy, a raiding party had attacked their village. Several Nansusequa warriors had been wounded by poison arrows. Two of the three died hideous deaths, their bodies swollen and covered with vile sores.

Dega threw the dart away. He bent over Ev-lyn, nearly touching his nose to the hole the dart had made. The stink was there, as strong if not stronger than it had been on the tip of the dart. Most of the poison that had been smeared on the dart was now inside her body.

"I will die if I don't get help," Evelyn said.

Once again her inflection made clear to him what her words could not. Taking her elbow, Dega motioned at the valley floor, then wriggled two fingers to suggest a pair of running legs.

"Yes," Evelyn said. *"Haa."*

The boulders slowed them even though Dega went faster than he had since being wounded. The constant weaving did not help his dizziness.

To Evelyn's dismay, she discovered that the faster she ran, the faster the burning sensation spread. Half her chest was on fire before they were halfway to the bottom. Pain seared her lungs with every breath.

A clattering sound, as of a dislodged stone, brought them to a stop. It came from a cluster of boulders ahead and to the right.

Dega and Evelyn immediately dropped down, Dega in front of Evelyn so if more darts were thrown they would strike him and not her. He did it so casually that he did not think she would notice.

Evelyn did. She moved next to him so they were in equal danger. No other sound came from the boulders but they stayed where they were. Their attacker was out there somewhere, waiting for them to make a mistake.

Abruptly, unexpectedly, another stone clattered, this time to the left.

New worry spiked Evelyn. Until that moment, it had not occurred to her there might be more than one enemy. A war party could be surrounding them right at that moment. Plucking at Dega's shirt, she turned and crept back up the slope until she was sure the warriors below could not possibly see her, then she made to the south.

Dega stayed close. She had helped him when he was weak. He could do no less for her.

The boulders thinned. A strip of mostly grass separated them from the forest. Twenty steps should do it. Twenty steps and they would gain good cover.

"I will go first," Evelyn whispered, and rose to do so.

But Dega was up and running before the words were out of her mouth. Weaving as much from weakness as his desire to make himself harder to hit, he ignored the throbbing in his chest. No war cries rang out. No more darts were thrown with inhuman accuracy. The instant the vegetation enfolded him in its verdant embrace, he turned and squatted and beckoned.

Evelyn saw his arm move, then could not see him at all for the gloom. He had made it. She could, too. Her left arm against her side, she bounded to join him. But after only a few steps a strange thing happened. Her legs tingled and slowed and then would not work at all. Like a statue stripped of its foundation, Evelyn tipped onto her side. Her left arm would not move no matter how hard she tried. Her right arm burned abominably but was not yet useless.

Evelyn waited, thinking Dega would come help her. She heard a whisper, and then what sounded like a blow, and silence. Fright clawed at Evelyn's insides like a badger in a frenzy. When she could no longer take the silence, she whispered, "Dega? Are you all right?"

The ensuing silence told Evelyn their attackers had him. She was on her own. She slid her right hand under her hip and levered herself up. Her entire body was burning, her chest worst of all. It could be that the poison would stop her heart, and that would be that.

Evelyn refused to stay there like a helpless lamb awaiting slaughter. She was a King and Kings *never* gave up. Since her legs would not respond, she hooked her right elbow under her and crawled. It was slow going. Half a foot at a time was the best she could manage.

An eternity of effort brought Evelyn to the trees. There was no sign of Dega. She kept crawling. Her arm grew leaden with fatigue but she kept crawling. The skin on her elbow scraped off but she kept crawling. She crawled until her right arm burned as agonizingly as the rest of her. She crawled until she could not crawl another inch.

Evelyn had done all she could. She thought of her mother and father, and how much she loved them. She thought of Zach, and the fun they had had growing up together. She thought of many pleasant memories and many pleasant times, and then she closed her eyes and composed herself, and waited to die.

The voice was soft but insistent. A young voice, the voice of a girl, speaking in an unknown tongue.

Through the painful haze of Winona's return to consciousness, she grasped at the voice like a person who was drowning would grasp at a rope. The voice pulled her out of herself. She blinked, floundering on the brink of the abyss that had claimed her, then opened her eyes and was back in the world of the living.

Or was she? Winona looked about her. The dark of the abyss was not much blacker than the darkness in which she found herself. She had the impression of being in an enclosed space. Her wrists were bound behind her. Her ankles were tightly lashed. The voice droned on, spurring her to swallow to relieve her dry mouth, and say, weakly, "Who is it? Who is there?"

The voice stopped, but only for a moment. An excited squeal brought a torrent of the unknown tongue.

"I do not understand what you are saying," Winona said in English and in Shoshone.

A new urgency came into the voice, as if the girl were trying to impart important information.

Winona's eyes were adjusting. She distinguished a small figure lying on its side. "Hold on. I will come to you." Which proved to be wishful thinking. No sooner did she start to wriggle toward the figure than she was brought to a stop by a tug from behind. Twisting her head, she saw why. The other end of the rope that secured her ankles was tied to a boulder too big and heavy for her to lift or slide.

Sounds heralded the arrival of someone else. Or was it some*thing* else? Winona wondered as she sought to make sense of a series of smacks and scrapes mixed with scritching and labored breathing.

Through an opening that had appeared to be nothing more than a shadow came the source. It moved with a strange swinging gait. In height it would come to about Winona's chest, or slightly less. It was almost as wide as it was tall. Behind it, crawling, came another something.

Winona tingled with fear. She heard the girl gasp.

The sounds, and the things, came to the center of the enclosed space, then stopped. Other sounds suggested the striking of flint or quartz. Sparks flew. The short thing bent down and Winona heard it puff lightly. Kindling caught, and tiny flames licked into life. The man — it had to be a man — added broken branches from a pile collected for that purpose. The flames grew, became a fire that cast welcome light and warmth.

What the light revealed stunned Winona.

The man who had started the fire wore tattered buckskins. Girded around his powerful chest was a strip of buckskin, and wedged under the strip was a crude knife and a thick club. But it was the man's face, and his legs, that interested Winona more, interested and horrified her. The face was hideously scarred. Not the random scars of some terrible accident, but deliberate scarring, whorls and circles and other shapes, that must hold special meaning.

The man had suffered an accident. His legs were gone from just above the knees, the stumps swathed thick in buckskin. He had cleverly improvised a pair of crutches to get about, and had wrapped rabbit hide around them. A rope latticed his powerful chest, an ingenious harness he to used to drag things, freeing his hands for the crutches.

The thing behind him turned out to be a young warrior he had been dragging. The warrior wore green buckskins, and was unconscious. A gash in his temple explained why.

An excited cry burst from the girl. She wore a green doeskin dress, and had been tied, wrists and ankles, exactly like Winona. "Dega!" she wailed, tears brimming. "Dega! Dega! Dega!" She tried to crawl toward the young warrior but was brought to a stop by her ankle rope, which, like Winona's, was tied to a boulder.

The scarred man was shrugging out of the harness. With remarkable speed and agility, he darted in close to the girl and swung his club with cruel effect. She slumped, insensate.

"There was no need to do that," Winona said.

Whipping around, the scarred man coldly regarded her. He slapped his club against his palm a few times as if debating whether to use it on her. Apparently he decided not to. He slid the club under the band on his chest and turned to his new captive. His ability to move about was uncanny. It was as if the crutches were extensions of his arms and hands. He dragged the young warrior to another of the dozen or so boulders that dotted the enclosure and bound him tightly in the same manner as Winona and the girl. Only then did he turn and hobble toward her, although "hobble" was a poor description of the fluid ease with which he moved. He could get about on those crutches as rapidly as most people could on two legs. Just beyond the reach of her ankle rope, he stopped and studied her through hate-filled eyes.

Winona met his gaze unflinchingly.

The scarred warrior raised his hands. He made the sign for "rope," and motioned for her to turn around.

Obeying, Winona felt him pry at the knots at her wrists. Soon her hands were free. Rubbing them to restore circulation, she shifted, and froze.

The scarred warrior had drawn his knife and was eyeing her as if he dearly desired to slit her throat. But after a few moments he slid it under the band, and moved back so she could not reach him. Again he employed sign, "Question. You know me?"

Winona wriggled her stiff fingers, then signed, "You be Drinks Blood."

A cruel grin slashed his scarred face. He was pleased she knew who he was. "Question. Husband talk Drinks Blood?"

"Yes," Winona signed. Nate had told her all about his harrowing experience at the pass. "You be Heart Eater tribe."

At the mention of his people, Drinks Blood scowled and placed his hand on his knife.

"Question," Winona signed. "Why you do bad?" She indicated her bound ankles and the girl and the unconscious young warrior. "Why you mean?"

In answer, Drinks Blood angrily smacked his twin stumps.

"Me no understand," Winona signed.

Fury and hate twisting his scars, Drinks Blood signed at great length, his fingers flying. "I do break husband. I hate husband. I be mountain when husband make thunder. I try run. Many big rocks fall. Big rock fall me. Fall my legs." Drinks Blood made a cutting motion. "Legs no have . . ."

Winona remembered Nate saying that there had been no sign of life in the pass after the explosion. Evidently Drinks Blood had been partly buried and dug himself out, crushed legs and all.

"I stop blood. I crawl forest. Take three sleeps but I crawl. I weak. I hungry. I kill squirrel with teeth. I kill bird with teeth. I eat. I live."

"Mountain thunder moons ago," Winona signed. "You be here all time?"

Drinks Blood seemed to not see her fingers move. "I make wood legs." He patted the crutches. "I walk much. I be good with wood legs. I go mountain but many rocks. No make through. No go people. No go Heart Eaters." He leaned toward her. "I think count coup husband. I think kill husband slow. Make husband afraid. Make husband hurt."

Winona did not respond. There was no reasoning with him. He hated them with every fiber of his being.

"I watch you. I watch family. I watch white-hair. I watch white-hair woman. I watch your son. I watch his woman. I think. I wait. I find here," Drinks Blood gestured.

The enclosure was not really an enclosure at all. It was a bowl-shaped cliff, the open end ten feet across and choked with firs and a thicket.

"I see green people come. I take green girl. I give your axe. They think you take green girl."

"That must be why they abducted Evelyn," Winona said to herself.

Sinister delight animated Drinks Blood. "I

have surprise, woman. I rope you. I bring surprise here."

To resist invited a clubbing. Winona turned so he could bind her wrists again, then watched him take the rope harness and move to the opening. He looked back. "Your husband take my legs. I take his family." A cold, sadistic laugh followed the scarred warrior out.

Winona King shivered.

CHAPTER NINETEEN

Nate King was surprised to hear so many voices coming from his cabin. He was especially surprised that they sounded cheerful. Because Nate himself was in the grip of a deep depression, feeling as joyless and glum as it was possible to feel. The happy voices made him mad.

Swinging down from the tired bay, Nate marched to the cabin door and went to fling it open. It was bolted from within. Balling his right fist, he pounded on the panel fit to bust the wood. "Open up!" he roared.

"By my troth!" responded a familiar voice. The door swung in, framing Shakespeare in a blaze of warm light. "How now, Horatio? What portends this foul manner?"

"They better be here," Nate said, shouldering past. He was hoping to see his wife, daughter and son. Instead, two strangers in green rose nervously from chairs at the table. The man took the woman's hand and she moved close to him as if for protection.

Blue Water Woman was at the counter and smiled in greeting.

Louisa was in the rocking chair by the fireplace. Jumping up, she ran over and gave Nate a hug. "I'm so glad you're back! Did you find them?" She glanced at the doorway and said in mild disappointment and surprise, "Oh!"

Teni had come in. She was shocked to see her parents. Sidling past the white-haired white man, she stepped into their waiting arms. "What has happened? Why are you here?" She noticed a bulge under her father's shirt. "Is that a bandage? Have you been hurt?"

"Save your questions, daughter," Wakumassee said. "We must talk with the man who brought you."

"There has been a misunderstanding," Tihikanima added. "We have wronged these people greatly."

Nate had not made hide nor hair out of their words. He turned to McNair. "What is this? Who are they? My family is in danger and I come back to find you celebrating?"

Shakespeare jerked his head as if he had been slapped. "That's about the cruelest thing you have ever said to me, son. You should damn well know better. I'm as worried about Winona, Evelyn and Zach as you are."

"Sorry," Nate muttered, although it still bothered him that he had heard them laughing and having such a grand time. "Who are they, then? And what in God's name do they have to do with this?"

"I suspect they have been duped, as we have been," Shakespeare said. "More on that in a bit. First, permit me to introduce Mr. and Mrs. Waku." He bobbed his white beard at the man and woman. "They call themselves the People of the Forest. Or the Nansusequa. As near as I can figure from what they have told me, they come from the deep woods along the Indiana-Kentucky border. Their people were massacred. They are the only ones left."

"Massacred?" Nate repeated.

Shakespeare grimly nodded. "By the local whites. They fled west and came to the mountains, looking for a new home. They ended up here."

"And took my daughter?" Nate growled. He glared at the trio and the woman and the girl gripped the man's arms.

"Try not to scare them to death if you can help it," Shakespeare said. "I'll get to Evelyn shortly. The mother, there, has told me something that will interest you greatly." He stepped over to the table and beckoned for Nate to join them. "Don't just stand there like a bump on a log. Pretend you have manners."

Reluctantly, Nate walked over.

"The gent here is Wakumassee. He speaks some English. His wife is Tihikanima. The daughter is Tenikawaku. They have an older son, Degamawaku, and a younger girl, Mikikawaku." Shakespeare paused. "Notice anything?"

"They all wear green?"

"Besides that," Shakespeare said. "Green to them has great medicine. But I was referring to their names."

"You've lost me," Nate said.

"Listen closely. Wakumassee. Degamawaku. Tenikawaku. Their names are actually three words in one. The children always take the first part of the father's name as the last part of their own. In the middle they stick a 'ma' for 'son of' or a 'ka' for 'daughter of.' So Degamawaku breaks down to Dega, son of Waku. Tenikawaku is Teni, daughter of Waku." Shakespeare chuckled. "I like how they do that. Too bad we don't do the same."

Nate did not share his mentor's enthusiasm. "My family is missing and we stand here talking about how wonderful their names are?"

Shakespeare's smile evaporated. "I think it fair to point out that their daughter and son are missing, too. In fact, this business started when their daughter disappeared. They thought we took her, so they took Evelyn. Their plan was to persuade us to swap Evelyn for Miki."

"Wait. Are you saying their daughter was abducted? And they blamed us? Why in God's name did they think we were to blame?"

"Because they found your axe near where their daughter was taken," Shakespeare explained.

"What?" Nate practically exploded.

"I've made it clear to them that we had nothing to do with their girl going missing," Shakespeare said. "They say they are sorry for taking Evelyn. That if the mother had known it was not a dream, things would be different."

Impatience bubbled in Nate like boiling water. "Damn it. How does a dream figure in?"

"Since we didn't take Miki, there has to be a third party involved. I asked them if they had seen sign of any others in the valley. Or if anything unusual had happened. Something did." Shakespeare flicked a finger at Tihi. "About a week ago, the mother, there, was taking her turn sitting by the fire late at night and keeping watch. The rest were asleep. She couldn't keep her eyes open and kept dozing off."

"And she had a dream?"

"She saw a face. It seemed to float in the air at the edge of the firelight. It was staring at her, and it scared her. When she sat up, it vanished, and she assumed it had been a dream."

"Maybe it was," Nate said sourly. A dream that had no bearing on his family's plight.

"You haven't heard the rest," Shakespeare said. "The reason the face scared her so much is because it wasn't normal. She thought it might be the face of a ghost. Or an evil spirt."

"That's ridiculous."

"Is it, Horatio? I will use her own words as her husband translated them to me. The face Tihi saw 'was covered with scars, terrible, terrible scars, scars that made the face look less than human.' "

Icy fingers closed around Nate's heart. "It can't be! I sealed off the pass."

"The Heart Eaters must know of another way," Shakespeare said. "Tihi only saw the one but there might be an entire war party."

Nate turned toward the door. He was all

for barging out into the night and scouring the valley from end to end. A firm hand on his arm restrained him.

"We can't do much good in the dark," Shakespeare advised. "We'll wait for daylight. Waku has offered to help. He's sorry for what he's done, son. Truly and sincerely sorry."

Waku nodded when the great bear of a white man with the black beard looked at him. "Very sorry," he stressed. "Me think bad in head. Me do bad."

"You were tricked," Shakespeare said.

"Yes," Waku said. But that was only part of it. He had been so consumed by hate, he had not been himself.

Nate suddenly thrust his big hand at Waku for Waku to shake. "No hard feelings, then. We've all been deceived. Now that we know, we can take the fight to them. If they have harmed your children or mine, we will track them down and kill every last one of the sons of bitches."

Waves of pain crashed over Dega like waves crashing onto a rocky shore. He blinked and opened his eyes, and promptly wished he hadn't. The pain worsened to where he had to squint against the glare of a nearby fire. Inadvertently, he groaned.

"Dega! Oh, Dega! I am so happy to see you!"

Jarred out of lethargy, Dega turned, or tried to, and broke out in a broad smile. The pain, and the blow to the head that had felled him, were temporarily forgotten. "Miki! We feared you were dead, little sister."

"We both may soon be," Miki responded, and gazed anxiously past him. "Maybe I should not be so happy you are here. I do not want you to die."

Dega looked around, taking in the cliff and the opening and the pink flush of dawn in the sky, and the wife of the white man with the black beard, the mother of the girl who stirred him in a manner no girl ever had. His meager grasp of the white tongue limited his greeting. Then he remembered the first words her daughter had spoken to him. He said them as best he was able. "Consarn me."

Winona had been fervently hoping the young warrior would revive before Drinks Blood came back. Now she beamed and declared, "You speak English! Wonderful! We are prisoners of a warrior out to kill us. He is gone now, but he will be back. We must work together to free ourselves."

Dega squirmed uncomfortably. Whatever

she said might be important. She was looking at him as if she expected an answer.
"Consarn me," he declared again, and
smiled.

"Oh," Winona said, comprehending. "Do
you know any *Sosoni?*" she asked in her
language.

Remembering the words Ev-lyn had
taught him, Dega brightened. *Sosoni* had
been one of them. "Haa!" he replied.

"You do?" Winona could not believe her
luck, and in Shoshone repeated, "We are
prisoners of a warrior who will soon kill us.
We must work together to free ourselves.
Do you understand?"

"Haa," Dega said.

"Good. Crawl toward me and I will crawl
toward you and see if we can untie one
another."

The young warrior did not move.

"Did you hear me?" Winona asked.

"Haa," Dega said.

"Buffaloes have wings."

"Haa."

Crestfallen, Winona said more to herself
than to him, "You do not understand *Sosoni*
any better than you do English, do you?"

"Haa."

"Say that one more time and I swear I will
scream."

"Haa."

"Damn." Winona reverted to English. She wriggled toward him as far as the rope would allow, then wagged her head to indicate he should do the same.

Dega caught on right away. Clenching his teeth against the throbbing in his head and shoulder, he copied her movements and discovered they were still an arm's length apart.

"If it weren't for bad luck I wouldn't have any luck at all," Winona said forlornly. Then her gaze fell on the fire. It had burned low, but it was not yet out.

Of the three of them, Winona was the nearest. At first glance it appeared to be well out of her reach. But she wondered. Crawling as far as the rope permitted, she extended her legs to their fullest. Her moccasins fell only an inch or two short.

Encouraged, Winona swung her legs from side to side, seeking to gain those extra couple of inches. The boulder her feet were linked to did not move. She swung harder and faster. The strain on her legs was almost unbearable, but she refused to give up. She put more of her body into each swing.

Suddenly, perceptibly, the boulder shifted. Not by much, but it definitely moved. Winona swung with renewed eagerness, her entire body swinging like a land-bound pendulum. Again the boulder moved a fraction.

Dega and Miki were riveted in fascination.

Winona nearly wrenched her hips out of joint with her next swing. But once again the boulder moved. Quickly, she flung her legs straight out, at the fire. Searing heat licked at her moccasins. Her feet grew blistering hot and her moccasins began to give off streams of smoke.

"You are burning!" Miki cried.

Flames were eating at the rope but not fast enough. Winona smelled charred hemp, then charred flesh. She did not know how much more she could take. She started to raise her feet out of the fire but shoved them back in again. A few blisters were preferable to being dead.

The streams became thick coils. Winona was sure her feet were being roasted to ruin. The pain was worse than any pain she ever felt, and that took some doing. She had known the pain of childbirth, the pain of bullet and knife wounds, the pain of animal bites, the pain of sickness. This was worse than all of them.

Finally, Winona could not bear it any longer. She jerked her feet clear and rolled, and kept on rolling. The rope that held her to the boulder had burned clean through. So had several of the loops about her ankles. She kicked, and her legs were free.

Flames still sprinkled her moccasins. Acting quickly, Winona rubbed them in the dirt, back and forth and side to side. Within moments the flames were extinguished. But the pain persisted.

Spent from her exertion, Winona lay still, gathering her strength. Her moccasins were black in spots. She refused to take them off and inspect the harm she had done to herself. That could wait.

Dimly, Winona became aware the girl and the young warrior were both whispering urgently. She roused and rose on an elbow. Belatedly, she heard what they already had, smacks and scrapes and scritching, as of crutches striking the ground. The sounds grew steadily closer.

Drinks Blood was returning.

"Everyone ready?" Nate King asked. The eastern horizon was bright with the promise of the new day although the sun had not yet risen. He was on his bay, Shakespeare on the white mare, Lou on a roan, Blue Water Woman on a dun she was fond of.

Shakespeare raised a hand toward the

heavens and recited, "To be or not to be, that is the question. Whether 'tis nobler in the mind to suffer the slings and arrows of outrageous fortune, or to take arms against a sea of troubles, and by opposing, end them!"

"Was that yes?" Nate asked.

"Most assuredly, Horatio. I have girded my loins for battle, and am all of one cloth."

Nate shifted in the saddle toward the three Nansusequa, who stood at the corner of his cabin. He had offered to let them have their pick of his extra horses, but they had declined. Their reason astounded him; they had never ridden horses before. They would search on foot.

"Remember," Nate said. "Three shots in a row means one of us has found something. Come on the run."

Wakumassee fingered the flintlock Nate had given him. "Three," he said. They had practiced loading the pistol until Waku was fairly certain he could do it.

"I hope there are enough of us," Louisa commented. "From what you've said, these scarred devils are worse than the Blackfeet."

"What stronger breastplate than a heart untainted?" Shakespeare quoted. "Thrice is he armed that hath his quarrel just, and he but naked, though locked up in steel, whose conscience with injustice is corrupted."

"What did you say?" Lou asked.

Blue Water Woman reined her dun close to the sorrel. "See what I must put up with day in and day out?"

Nate was in no mood for banter. "Let's ride!" he barked, and assumed the lead, bringing the bay to a trot as they crossed the clearing and plunged into the woods. He had barely slept a wink all night. Then, as now, worry twisted his gut like a blade. He could not shake the feeling that something awful had happened, or was about to happen.

Blue Water Woman proposed that she and Louisa search the timber lining the valley floor while Nate and Shakespeare climb higher, but Nate and Shakespeare were against the idea.

"Eight eyes are sharper than four eyes," was how McNair summed up his objection.

Nate had them spread out. He insisted they stay within sight of one another at all times. They must take every precaution. The Heart Eaters would be out for blood, and there was no telling how large a war party they were up against.

That the Heart Eaters were back upset Nate to no end. He did not want a repeat of what he had gone through with the Utes.

For years the Utes had tried to drive him and his family from their previous home because it was at the fringe of Ute territory. They constantly had to be on their guard. He had hoped that things would be different here, that he had discovered a sanctuary safe from all hostiles. He should have known better. In the wilderness, nowhere was ever truly safe.

It was the price Nate had to pay for that which he valued more than anything else, namely, his right to live free. Not the false freedom civilization offered but the freedom to do as he pleased without being accountable to anyone or anything other than his own conscience.

All those years Nate spent growing up in New York, he never gave much thought to the fact that he had to abide by laws and rules imposed by others. Everyone else did, and he was just one of the many. If asked back then, he would have said that the laws were necessary, that without them, society would break down. Laws kept the lawless in line.

It never occurred to Nate that he was, in effect, confined in an invisible cage of insidious devising. He must abide by the dictates of politicians and others in high authority to whom laws were a means of controlling those under them. Since the control was so subtle, and supposedly exercised for the common good, the vast majority of people accepted it as inevitable.

Only later, after Nate had come to the Rockies with his uncle and experienced his first taste of true freedom, did Nate awaken to the difference. Laws were a leash, and having the leash removed opened his eyes. He came to believe that no one should have the right to lord it over anyone else.

It was a belief shared by the Shoshones, among others. Nate saw a degree of irony in the fact that most Indians lived more freely than the whites back in the States who regarded them as inferior.

A whinny from the bay brought Nate's musing to an end. Chiding himself for being careless, he rested the Hawken across his thighs. They were climbing a wooded slope, Shakespeare to his right, the women to his left. Their eyes ceaselessly in motion, they searched for any clue to the whereabouts of the missing.

An hour went by. Two hours.

Nate headed in the general direction of the stream where he had lost the tracks the previous day. When they reached it, he stayed on the south side with Lou while Shakespeare and Blue Water Woman crossed over. They had paralleled the ribbon of water a short distance when Blue Water Woman called out and pointed.

Nate and Louisa crossed. They had found where Evelyn's abductor, Waku's son Dega, had left the stream. The trail led into spruce. There, Dega had set Evelyn down. Nate breathed a sigh of relief when he saw his daughter's tracks. She had been alive and well up to that point.

Nate and his companions rode faster. Evelyn and Dega had made no attempt to hide their tracks. They had angled back to the stream and headed west. Nate was in such a hurry to catch up that he nearly rode past the spot where the pair had stopped. Drawing rein, he leaned down. "Look at this."

Shakespeare had caught sight of them, too: more of those strange circles, like the ones they had found near their cabins. "Deucedly peculiar," he remarked.

"What are they?" Louisa wanted to know.

"Do you think they have anything to do with the Heart Eaters?" Blue Water Woman asked.

Nate had not considered that, but he could not see how. The only footprints were those of Evelyn and Dega. He climbed down. A pair of long furrows drew his interest. He ran his fingers along one, trying to figure out what made it. His best guess was that something had been dragged or pulled up the bank. At the top the furrows ended and the strange circles resumed.

Judging by the tracks, Evelyn and Dega had examined the circles and furrows at some length. But they had not followed them. Instead, the pair headed in a different direction.

"Maybe we should split up," Shakespeare suggested. "You take Lou and go after Evelyn. Blue Water Woman and I will follow those circles. I'm mighty curious to find out what makes them."

"We stick together," Nate said.

"Need I point out there has been no sign of the Heart Eaters?"

"Need I point out what we went through up at the pass?" Nate countered. "We stick together," he repeated.

Shakespeare chuckled. "You make a most excellent grump."

As Nate expected, Evelyn's and Dega's tracks eventually brought them to the clearing Waku had described. It lay bright and stark under the midday sun. They dismounted to give the ground a close scrutiny.

Suddenly Louisa gasped. "Over here! Is this what I think it is?"

Red drops speckled the grass.

"Dry blood," Nate said, his gut churning. He found more, a lot more, enough to convince him that either Evelyn or Dega had been badly wounded. His heart in his throat, he found where they had fled the clearing. The tracks clearly showed his daughter had been supporting the young Nansusequa.

"Who attacked them?" Lou wondered.

"Here's a clue," Shakespeare said grimly. He was staring at patch of bare earth near his feet.

Nate went over. "More of those damn circles." He swore luridly, a reaction to the dread that seized him.

"How long ago were they here?" Louisa asked. She was nowhere near the tracker the men were.

"Some time before midnight would be my guess," Shakespeare answered.

"That long ago?" Lou said, aghast. "Then we might be too late."

Nate was thinking that very thing.

CHAPTER TWENTY

Winona had no time to free her hands. Nor, with Drinks Blood almost to the opening, did she dare try to bolt. With two options denied her, her agile brain settled on a third. Hurriedly, she kicked the burnt shards of rope behind the boulder she had been tied to. Then she quickly lay on her side, her legs bent behind her to give the impression her ankles were still bound and she was still secured to the boulder.

Seconds later the scarred warrior emerged from the vegetation, his visage as hideous as ever. The rope harness was snug on his powerful chest. Once again he was dragging someone.

Winona looked, and the blood in her veins congealed to ice. Horror was to blame, a horror so profound and so overwhelming it paralyzed every nerve in her body. Horror such as only a parent could feel on seeing one of her children at death's threshold.

One glance at the person being dragged was enough to conform that, if she was not already dead, she was close to it.

Evelyn lay as still as a corpse. Her hair was disheveled, her dress streaked with dirt and grass stains — and blood. Her eyes were closed, her mouth parted. There was no sign she was breathing. As if that were not heart-wrenching enough, Evelyn's skin was a ghastly yellow color, as if she had rubbed herself with dandelions — or been the victim of a potent poison.

Winona remembered a Shoshone warrior who had turned yellow. He had taken an arrow in the ribs, and the barbed tip had turned out to have been dipped in a dead animal. Despite the best efforts of Shoshone healers, the warrior had died an agonizing, lingering death.

Without thinking, Winona blurted, "Blue Flower!"

Drinks Blood was removing the rope harness. Sneering, he threw it down, tucked his crutches under his arms, and came over. But he was careful not to get too close. His fingers flowed in sign language. "Question. Happy see daughter?"

Nearly losing control, Winona shrieked, "What have you done to her? Why does she look that way?"

Drinks Blood laughed. He had not understood but he was enjoying her distress. "Question. You want hold?"

"Of course, damn you!" Winona fumed. "I want to know what you have done to her."

Grinning, Drinks Blood signed, "Watch daughter die. Watch me cut." He made a chopping motion. "Make many little parts."

Winona rarely lost her temper. Among her family and friends and fellow Shoshones she was admired for her calm bearing. It was said, and rightfully so, that when all others around her were losing their heads, she always kept hers. Her son and daughter could count on one hand the number of times she had yelled at them. Her husband could count on one finger the number of times she had cried.

But Winona became emotional now. She more than lost her temper. A searing blaze of white-hot rage seized her. All she could think of was Evelyn, her sweet, precious Evelyn, dead or dying, slain by the abomination in front of her. Consequently, she did what any mother would do, which, in her case, made it all the more remarkable. Screeching like a bobcat, she whipped her body around and slammed her legs against Drinks Blood.

Her attack caught the Heart Eater unaware. The force of her blow sent him tumbling in an ungainly somersault that ended with Drinks Blood thudding onto his belly in the dust. He lost both crutches. But such was his iron resilience that he did not stay down long. In the time it took Winona to scramble to her feet, Drinks Blood shook his swarthy head to clear it and heaved onto his stumps.

For tense moments they glared their mutual hate: Drinks Blood's the hate of one who regarded those not his kind as his natural enemies to be slain at will, Winona's the hate of a mother whose most cherished treasure had been desecrated.

Winona's hands were still bound, but that did not stop her. She threw herself forward, lashing out with a well-aimed kick.

Even without his crutches, Drinks Blood was far from helpless. He had lost the lower half of his legs but not his natural agility or his exceptional strength. As her foot darted at his throat, he scampered aside, using his hands and stumps for leverage, in a display that would have dazzled a white acrobat or wrestler. Her kick missed, and at its apex, when it was still in midair, Drinks Blood flicked a steely hand, seized her ankle, and gave a brutal twist.

Pain exploded in Winona's leg. She felt

herself being upended and was helpless to prevent it. Down she went, dumped on her back, but none the worse for the upset. Instantly, she rolled onto her side to regain her feet. It was her one advantage over her adversary. But she was only to her knees when a stunted cyclone ripped into her with battering force.

A hand clamped onto Winona's throat. A fist smashed into her eyebrow, into her jaw. She spun the upper half of her body around in an effort to dislodge him, but the Heart Eater grabbed hold of her black tresses and clung.

Winona tried to butt Drinks Blood in the face, but he jerked his scarred visage aside. The fingers in her throat dug deeper and she abruptly found her breath choked off. Sputtering and gasping, she pushed erect, then almost tumbled when his shifting weight threw her off balance.

Drinks Blood was aglow with bloodlust. He pummeled her face and neck, seeking to pound her into submission. He did not resort to his knife or his club, which suggested he wanted her alive to sate his perverse pleasures.

Blood was in Winona's eyes. Her chest was on the verge of bursting. Unless she shook him off or dislodged him, Drinks Blood would subdue her and bind her legs and she would be back where she had been. That must not happen. Evelyn's life was at stake. Desperate to break free, Winona glanced anxiously about. The high wall of the bowl-shaped cliff gave her an idea. A wild idea, an insane idea, but it held a glimmer of hope, and Winona would grasp at anything, however thin the straw. She launched herself at the rock wall, her head low, her shoulders hunched for what was to come.

Drinks Blood still had his five-fingered vise on her throat and his stumps clamped to her chest. Smirking sadistically, he glanced over his shoulder, guessed her intent, and sought to push clear.

Winona was expecting just that. Sucking precious air deep into her lungs, she bit down on his wrist, shearing her teeth through skin and flesh. Clear down to the bone she bit, and locked her jaws tight.

Drinks Blood howled, more from rage than pain. Swearing vehemently, he tugged and pushed and did all in his power to break her grip. He failed.

A blur in the morning shadows, Winona slammed into the cliff. She had the fleeting impression that every bone in her body had been shattered, every organ ruptured. Then she was on her back in the dirt, her ribs on fire, her body a welter of torment, while beside her flopped and flapped that which did not seem entirely human.

Caught between her and the cliff, Drinks Blood had impressions of his own; blinding, excruciating pain, his body crushed worse than when the pass had fallen on him, his lungs spurting blood. He thrashed and flailed, unable to stop himself. Then the pain began to subside, if only a little, and he discovered that he was not crushed at all, but only severely bruised, and that the blood dampening his nose and mouth was not from burst lungs but from his bleeding nose.

Winona started to rise. A callused hand snatched at her dress and she backpedaled. Whirling, she ran for the opening. If she could escape, she could free her hands and come back. But she had taken only a few steps when forearms banded with muscle looped around her ankles. She stumbled, recovered, and had her legs pulled from under her.

The fall was painless compared to slamming into the cliff. Winona rolled, or tried to, in order to get back on her feet. She felt Drinks Blood's grip loosen and she smiled to herself, thinking that in another few moments she would be in the woods where he could never catch her. Then she felt something else: hands digging into her flesh, using her body as a ladder.

Drinks Blood was climbing up her back.

Winona threw herself down on top of him. He grunted but held on. She whipped to the right and then the left but could not throw him off. Suddenly an arm was around her throat. Panicked, she scrambled to her knees and slammed back down, but he planted his stumps, and she could not fall on him a second time. Meanwhile, the arm around her throat constricted.

To be so close and be thwarted drove Winona into a frenzy. She flung herself from side to side, she spun, she kicked, she tried to butt him with the back of her head. She did all that and more, but she could not stop her chest from heaving and the world from fading. She had the sensation of pitching into a dark well, and as she plummeted, she cried out in the depths of her being, "I am sorry, daughter! I have failed you!"

The first surprise: She was still alive.

The second surprise: Her hands were untied.

In her befuddled state, Winona groggily assumed something had happened, that someone had come to rescue them, and she sat up, blinking in the bright glare of the sun and wishing she had not been so hasty. She was solid pain. Bruises and welts covered her body. Even her scalp hurt from where he had pulled her hair. She licked her swollen lips, swallowed thickly, and took stock. Her hands were free, yes, but her feet were bound with more rope than last time, and the end of the rope was once again secured to the boulder. Dega and Miki were as she had last seen them, watching her, Miki with sadness in her eyes, Dega with an expression she could not assess. "What?" she croaked.

Degamawaku wanted to tell Ev-lyn's mother many things. He wanted to tell her that in all his life he had never witnessed anything like her struggle against their captor. He wanted to tell her she was different from any woman he ever knew, that she was incredible. He yearned to let her know that she had his highest respect and always would, but all he could do was smile encouragement and say, *"Haa."*

"Wonderful," Winona said, and wearily bowed her head. A scraping noise made her snap it up again.

Drinks Blood was only a few feet away, braced on his crutches, regarding her, if it were possible, with more hate than ever. His

410

body bore as many bruises and welts as hers, and his buckskins were covered with dirt and dust.

Winona had the impression he was waiting for her to sign something so she did. "Question. I alive?"

Twin fires blazed in those pits he called eyes. "You not die quick. You die slow. Cry much."

Winona suppressed a shudder. So that was it. He wanted her alive so he could kill her slowly. So he could torture her. "As my husband would say," she said in English, "you are one sadistic bastard." The mention of Nate reminded her of Evelyn and Zach, and she turned toward where her daughter had been lying.

Evelyn was gone.

A groan tore from Winona and she glanced madly about. The moan became a wail that she choked off. A frail, crumpled figure lay over by the cliff, the yellow of her skin sickeningly vivid. "Question. Why there?"

Drinks Blood did not answer right away. Smiling, he leaned back on his crutches and folded his fingers on his chest.

"Why?" Winona signed again, and when he would not respond, she forgot herself and shrieked, *Why, damn you?*

Drinks Blood lowered his hands. His smile

widened. He signed two words. Just two words. "She dead."

A great thunder filled Winona's ears. Her mind twisted and spun. She was not aware that she passed out but the next she knew, her chin was on the ground and she was breathing dust. She sat up, the signal for a deluge. Tears streamed down her cheeks, but she did not care.

Drinks Blood had not moved. Fingers laced, his flat eyes glittered with pleasure at her loss.

Winona gave voice to uncontrollable sobs. She knew it would delight him, and the last thing she wanted to do was that, but she could not help herself. Evelyn was gone! The sweetest daughter any woman ever had. *Her* daughter. Her child. The girl she had raised so lovingly, so devotedly. Dead. Gone. Slain by the inhuman monster leering at her.

Winona averted her face. She refused to look at him, refused to let him look at her. Through her anguish and her tears she noticed that Miki and Dega were not staring at her but had turned away out of sympathy. Their kindness touched her. Then she saw their faces, saw their wide eyes and their wide mouths, and she looked in the direction they were looking, toward the opening. All of a sudden, her tears stopped. Lightning seared her, and she could scarcely breathe. Her own eyes went wide and her mouth parted. "Zach!"

Zachary King had been searching for his mother since the day before. When darkness fell, he had stopped and waited to strike out again at first light. He had found where she had been attacked, and he stuck to the sign like a wolverine that had caught the scent of blood. Then the cliff loomed ahead. He had dismounted and was warily approaching on foot when his mother's shriek brought him on the run.

Now Zach stood in the opening, his Hawken leveled at the apparition on crutches. He was all set to shoot it in the back, but the shock of seeing his mother so bloodied, battered and bent stayed his hand.

It was then that Drinks Blood whipped around, adroitly handling his crutches, swinging his stumps under him. He grabbed his knife and froze with his hand on the hilt, staring into the Hawken's muzzle.

Winona did not understand why her son was just standing there. "Shoot him, Zach! What are you waiting for?"

Zach curled his finger around the trigger, but he did not squeeze. Molten lava was oozing up out of his core, out of the secret vault in which he contained it except when, at moments like this, his feelings threatened to run away with him. Shooting would be too quick, too easy. Too painless. The scarred warrior deserved worse. Much worse.

"Kill him!" Winona cried. She had seen that look on her son before and knew what it portended. "Please!"

Her appeal dispelled some of the red haze before Zach's eyes. He blinked, grinned at the warrior, and said, "You heard my ma. Quick it is, then." He went to sight down the barrel, then noticed the other two captives, the young warrior and the girl in green. The young warrior was tugging against his bounds and bobbing his head and saying the same word over and over again.

"Do it now!" Winona yelled.

Zach was trying to make sense of the word the young warrior was saying. Then it hit him. "Ev-lyn." He glanced at the young warrior. "Evelyn?" he repeated. "My sister? How do you know her?"

The young warrior kept bobbing his head, as if he wanted Zach to turn toward the cliff.

Zach did.

A groan slipped from Winona. "Don't

look, son," she begged. "You know what it will do to you. Please don't look. Turn away. Look at me instead." She said it in a rush while crawling toward him.

"Sis?" Zach took a step toward the still, sprawled form. He felt as if all the blood were draining from his body. He was light-headed, and there was a peculiar buzzing in his ears. "Evelyn?" He looked at Winona. "What happened?" He looked at the scarred warrior with the crutches. "What did you do to her?"

Drinks Blood saw the muzzle of the rifle dip. He savored the shock and the hurt he had caused. "She dead!" he signed. "I kill!" he gloated. Then he did what to him seemed a perfectly natural thing to do. He threw back his head and laughed.

Zach King swayed. The Hawken drooped to his side. It was the single most awful moment of his life. He might have stood there indefinitely had the scarred warrior not started to draw his knife. Instantly, Zach leveled the Hawken and the warrior stopped.

"It's Drinks Blood, Zach," Winona said. "The one your father told us about. Shoot him, son. Shoot him now."

Straightening, Zach took deliberate aim.

Drinks Blood read his death in the other's

posture but he did not cower in fear. He thrust out his powerful chest and jutted his jaw in defiance.

"No," Zach said, and lowered his rifle.

Winona rose on her elbows. "What are you doing?"

"He killed Evelyn." Zach sidled to one side and leaned the Hawken against the cliff. He drew both pistols.

"That's it!" Winona cried. "Shoot him with them! Just so you shoot him!"

Zach set the flintlocks next to the Hawken.

"Oh, God," Winona gasped. "You're not going to do what I think you are going to do? Please, son. Shoot the Heart Eater." But Zach was not listening. *"Kill him!"* she screeched, terrified by the thought of losing both her children.

Drinks Blood glanced from the son to the mother and back again. His scarred brow knit in puzzlement.

The inner gate in Zach that held back the molten lava was open. The lava boiled and frothed in a seething torrent. The red haze returned, redder than before, redder than it had ever been. Zach stepped away from his guns. His feet, his legs, his entire body felt incredibly light. He became aware of his body in ways he ordinarily was not. Once, years ago, he had tried to describe the feeling to his father. The best he could do was that he *became* his body, if that made sense.

Winona's next cry died in her throat. It would do no good. It was too late. All she could do now was pray.

Zach stepped to within six feet of his sister's killer, and stopped. He slowly drew his Bowie and then his tomahawk.

Drinks Blood could not hide his surprise. Or his delight. He drew his knife and war club. Gripping his crutches with his upper arms, he hunched forward, braced for the younger man's onslaught.

But Zach did not attack. He hefted the Bowie and the tomahawk. He smiled, a thin, cold, almost cruel smile. Then he sank to his knees.

"Please, no," Winona said.

Before, Drinks Blood had been surprised. Now he was astounded. He stared at the young breed, unable to believe his eyes. Then he laughed. He laughed long and hard, but not in scorn, not in derision. He laughed because here was a warrior he could admire. Here was a warrior he could respect. When he was done laughing, he shrugged the crutches from himself and rose on his stumps. With the tip of his knife he described three circles in the air, each larger than the other.

Zach tucked at the waist and held the Bowie and tomahawk in front of him. He crouched there, a statue.

Drinks Blood waited. His brow knit again, and he cocked his head. He feinted with his war club, but the one called Zach did not move. He flicked his knife, but still provoked no response.

To Degamawaku, the series of developments brought no end of wonderment. First the daughter, then the mother, and now the son. He had never known a family like this. He waited breathlessly for the son to close on the other, but nothing happened. Dega did not understand. Fear was certainly not to blame. The family did not seem to know they were ever supposed to be afraid.

To little Miki, who had known only terror since Drinks Blood abducted her, this was the moment she had yearned for. The moment when the terrible man who had slapped and punched and abused her paid for his slaps and punches and abuses. To see him waiting there, not doing anything, made her think he did not really want to fight. He must be afraid. The terrible man was scared. That struck her as funny. She laughed, a mocking titter, and said in Nansusequa, "You are a coward."

Drinks Blood did not understand what

the girl said. But he understood her laugh. He understood that quite well. His ears burned, and his pulse quickened with anger, and he did what he otherwise might not have done. He uttered a lusty war whoop and flung himself forward.

Zach was ready. He had been ready. He had been in combat many times and he knew the victor was not always the first to strike but the one who struck the surest. Rearing on his knees, he met the rush head-on.

Drinks Blood swung his war club. Zach countered with the tomahawk. Drinks Blood thrust his knife. Zach parried with the Bowie. Twisting, Drinks Blood aimed a vicious stab at Zach's groin, but Zach shifted, the blade missed, and Zach arced his Bowie out and up. A trail of scarlet rose in the big blade's wake. The sharp sting of being cut caused Drinks Blood to retreat a step, but Zach was on him before he could set himself, the tomahawk sweeping at the crown of his head. Barely in time, Drinks Blood swept his war club up to block the blow. In that span of perhaps half a heartbeat, the Bowie was a nigh-invisible streak. Drinks Blood felt it bite into his chest, felt skin and flesh part. He staggered on his stumps and looked down. Blood flowed from a gash as long as his forearm.

Zach had drawn back a step. He was not breathing heavily. The Bowie and tomahawk were low in front of him.

Drinks Blood looked up. He sensed it then, although he denied it. He swallowed, braced his stumps, and attacked. This time in silence, this time grimly and soberly and with one intent and one intent only. Not to wound, not to maim, but to kill.

Zach moved to meet him. Drinks Blood sheared his knife at Zach's jugular, only to have his blade ring on the Bowie. Snarling, Drinks Blood whipped halfway around and drove his war club at Zach's head. It was a move that never failed. It failed now. The tomahawk materialized between them. The club was swatted aside. Drinks Blood tried to draw back, but in a stroke too swift for the eye to follow, Zach buried the tomahawk in his shoulder.

Drinks Blood staggered. His arm numbed and the war club fell. His shoulder was bleeding badly. He stared at Zach, incredulous. That which he had sensed, he now knew to be certain. Drinks Blood could not beat him. There was only one thing to do. He switched the knife from his good hand to his numb hand so he could drop his good hand to the pouch at his waist. The pouch that contained the last of his poisoned darts.

Winona saw, and screamed a warning.

Drinks Blood was smiling. He raised his arm to throw the dart. Suddenly steel gleamed, and his hand did a strange thing. It separated from his wrist. Warm crimson spattered his face. He looked up and saw the tomahawk on a downward sweep.

Zach stood over the body and swung his tomahawk, again and again and again. He swung until his arm hung limp from exhaustion, until there was nothing left of the scarred face but bits and pieces. Straightening, he gazed at his handiwork, then slowly turned and walked to the limp body by the wall.

Winona did not experience the elation she thought she would. She wanted Drinks Blood dead, wanted him to die horribly, and she got her wish. But she felt nothing, nothing at all. Then came the words Winona would remember and cherish for as long as she lived, the words that meant the difference between a whole heart and a shattered heart, the words that meant everything.

"Ma! She's alive!"

EPILOGUE

She opened her eyes. She was in her room, in her bed, deliciously warm and snug under her quilt. The door was open and sounds came from the front room, the clank of a pot, and low voices. Everything was as it should be. "It must have been a dream," she said aloud. Or more like a nightmare. She remembered it so vividly: the handsome young warrior, the chase, the dart.

"It was no dream, little one."

Evelyn King started and glanced at the person seated in the chair next to her bed. It was the last person she expected to find in her room. "Blue Water Woman?"

Shakespeare's wife smiled. "We have been taking turns keeping watch over you. You had us very worried. It has been three weeks."

Evelyn grasped her meaning, and was dumfounded.

"Your fever broke a few days ago. Only

then did we know you would live." Blue Water Woman leaned over the bed and placed her palm on Evelyn's forehead. "Yes. You are on the mend."

"It was that dart, wasn't it?" Evelyn asked.

Blue Water Woman nodded. "The poison nearly killed you. It was your brother who discovered you still had a pulse. Your mother grabbed you and took his horse and rode like a madwoman to get you here. She refused to sleep, stayed with you day and night until she collapsed. After that, your father made her take turns with the rest of us."

"Oh my," Evelyn said. She went to sit up and was surprised at how weak she felt. Lifting the quilt, she looked down at her nightshirt and could tell by how it clung to her body that she had lost weight. "The one who hurt me with the dart?"

"Your brother dealt with him."

Evelyn's throat tightened, and she had to cough. "Is everyone else all right? There was someone I met, a warrior who wore green buckskins." She did not finish what she intended to say.

"He was a laid up for a week. He and his family are not here now."

"Oh." Evelyn closed her eyes. "That's too bad. I wanted to thank him. He was nice to me."

"He took you against your will."

"But he did it nicely," Evelyn insisted. She did not care to talk about him anymore so she changed the subject. "Would you tell my folks I would like to see them?"

"Of course."

Evelyn supposed she should be giddily happy that she was alive and well, but she felt strangely sad. She heard a commotion, and when she opened her eyes, her bed was surrounded by those she loved most in the world.

Winona's cheeks were wet with tears of joy. "At last," she said. "At long last." She cradled Evelyn in her arms. "You have no idea how worried I have been, daughter."

"That makes two of us." Nate sounded as if he had a cold. He added his long arms to his wife's.

"Welcome back to the land of the living," Louisa said.

Zach stood at the food of the bed, his thumbs hooked in his wide leather belt, next to his Bowie and tomahawk. He smirked when Evelyn looked at him over their mother's shoulder. "Do you suppose you can try to go a year without being kidnapped? It would make all our lives a lot easier."

"Thank you," Evelyn said softly.

"It's what brothers do," Zach said gruffly, and wheeling, stalked out.

That left the last of them, standing next to Blue Water Woman. Raising his booming voice to the rafters, he quoted, "Sweet Moon, I thank thee for thy sunny beams. I thank thee, Moon, for shining now so bright. For, by thy gracious, golden, glittering gleams, I trust to take of truest Thisby sight."

Evelyn grinned. "Uncle Shakespeare."

"Sweet melody to my ears, those words," Shakespeare said. Apparently, he had caught the same cold as Nate.

The next several days were some of the best of Evelyn's life. She had never felt so loved. She was fed and pampered and treated as if she were made of fragile china. On the fourth day her mother announced she needed to get some air. Evelyn was helped into a dress and taken outdoors for the first time since she was stricken. The sun was almost too bright to bear.

Everyone was on horseback, waiting, which surprised Evelyn, although not nearly as much as the travois attached to her mother's horse. "What's that for?"

"What do you think?" Winona rebutted, and took her hand. "Lie down and I will cover you. We must keep you warm."

"This should be fun." Evelyn had not ridden on a travois since she was a little girl. She remembered the feel of the furs and the poles that formed the frame.

"Are you comfortable?" Winona asked.

"Just don't ride over any rough spots," Evelyn teased. She pulled the bear hide to her chin and gazed at fluffy clouds sailing high over the lake. The world had never been so beautiful.

They started off, riding east at a walk. Zach rode ahead, as he usually did, Lou at his side. Shakespeare and Blue Water Woman started arguing over whether men or women had sweeter dispositions, and Shakespeare roared, "Thou are the Mars of Malcontents!"

Evelyn giggled. Everything was back to normal. A shadow fell across her, and her father loomed large against the sky.

"You will be back on your feet in no time."

"I hope so."

Nate had something else on his mind, something that had been weighing heavily. "I want you to know I'm sorry, as sorry as I've ever been about anything."

"What on earth do you have to be sorry about?" Evelyn asked.

"For Drinks Blood. I should have made

sure up at the pass. I'm partly to blame for all we went through."

"That's nonsense. The man I admire most in the world once told me that we shouldn't put on airs like we are the Almighty."

Nate chuckled. "Did he now?"

They went farther than Evelyn thought they would go, past the McNair cabin and on around to the end of the lake. She figured they would stop but they rode into the forest. "Where are you taking me, anyhow? St. Louis?"

"This is far enough," Winona said, reining her horse so the travois slid in a half circle.

For the second time that day Evelyn was dumb-founded.

A structure had seemingly sprouted out of the soil. As long and wide as two cabins, it was constructed of logs, with a roof of intertwined tree limbs. Five figures in green stood beside it, smiling in greeting.

"I would like you to meet our new neighbors," Winona said.

Evelyn found her voice. "What?" She could not take her eyes off one of them.

Nate brought his bay up next to the travois. "It's a big valley. I reckon we don't need it all to ourselves."

"What?"

"They lost their home, Evelyn. They lost

their people," Nate said. "They need a new place to start over, and I offered to let them stay here if they wanted."

"What?"

Zach came up on the other side of her and snickered. "You must forgive my sister," he said to the five in green. "She is just learning to talk. Next we hope to break her of diapers."

Nate leaned from the saddle to rest his big hand on the travois. "I know this comes as a shock. We couldn't talk it over with you. We had to decide quickly so we could help them build before the cold weather hits. I hope you don't mind."

"Mind?" Evelyn King beamed. "I don't mind at all."

The employees of Thorndike Press hope you have enjoyed this Large Print book. All our Thorndike and Wheeler Large Print titles are designed for easy reading, and all our books are made to last. Other Thorndike Press Large Print books are available at your library, through selected bookstores, or directly from us.

For information about titles, please call:
(800) 223-1244

or visit our Web site at:
www.gale.com/thorndike
www.gale.com/wheeler

To share your comments, please write:
Publisher
Thorndike Press
295 Kennedy Memorial Drive
Waterville, ME 04901